THE BOOK
OF SEILA

THE BOOK OF SEILA

A Dystopian Novel

Wilda Hughes

Independent Publisher
Flowery Branch, Georgia

Publisher's Note: This is a work of fiction. Names, characters, places, and incidents are a product of the author's imagination. Locales and public names are sometimes used for atmospheric purposes. Any resemblance to actual people, living or dead, or to businesses, companies, events, institutions, or locales is completely coincidental.

Book Cover Layout ©2025 James, GoOnWrite.com

Scripture passages quoted in this book are taken from the KING JAMES VERSION (KJV): KING JAMES VERSION, public domain.

The Book of Seila/ Wilda Hughes. -- First Edition
ISBN: 979-8-218-55913-7 Paperback
ISBN 979-8-9988033-0-7 Ebook

For my beloved children and grandchildren who I pray will never have to walk the dark future that I envisioned in this book.

With special thanks to my dear daughter, Laura, for her creative advice and endless alpha and beta reads in support of this novel.

And in memory of Jephthah's daughter and all the nameless daughters of Eve.

Contents

1 Escaping North 1

2 South to Wendell 15

3 Marriageable 33

4 Wendell Prison 51

5 Bible Study 63

6 Secrets 81

7 Jephthah's Daughter 98

8 Where Is Your Sister? 110

9 Temptations 118

10 Conviction 124

11 Gossip 134

12 Accusations 144

13 Cellmate 163

14 False Tales 170

15 No Medals 181

16 Family Ties 191

17 False Memories 205

18 Breakdown 217

19 Coaxing Confessions 230

20 Scaring Sister Mary 242

21 Visitation 252

22 Execution Day 272

23 Aftermath 285

{1}

Escaping North

IN THE HEAT of a Southern summer, two young women bounced around the narrow backseat of a white Ford truck, driven by a young man known as Johnny Mac. Johnny was taciturn, and if he had any affect, it was hidden under a bushy brown beard and a ball cap. Nothing appeared to distinguish him from most of the other men of the new Covenant States, except for the fact that he was helping them. The sisters were running, working their way north from Jacksonville, Florida, to escape the Covenant States.

The older sister, Seila, said, "Johnny, I don't know how we could ever thank you enough for doing this."

Johnny grumbled over the creaking of the truck, "Just remember, if you're caught, you don't know me."

The younger sister, Jim, said, "Oh don't worry about Johnny, Seila. He's a pussycat."

"Jim? Aren't cats the serial killers of the animal kingdom?"

They all laughed, even Johnny, but Seila's laugh seemed a little strained to Jim.

Jim's real name was Ruby, but their dad used to call her, "my little gem." At three years old, little Seila parroted back, "Jim," and the name stuck while they were growing up.

Although Jim was the younger sister, she had lived on the run for five years since escaping a Redeemer conversion camp. But this was all new to Seila, and Jim worried about her. Seila used to have what some might think of as a generous, friendly face, with an easy smile and dimples, but her smile had been gone for some time now.

The sisters grew quiet, chewing fingernails or twirling loose curls around anxious fingers while the truck creaked over uneven roads and backlots. Jim had helped Seila dye her hair blonde before they left Jacksonville, but Jim's hair was still dark. She had it tied with a blue kerchief that she took off periodically to soak with her water bottle and wipe her face and neck. The truck had no air conditioning, and sweat rolled infrequently into her irritated eyes.

Jim sat up straighter and peered down the red, dirt road. She said, "This must be the road Flannery O'Connor was thinking about in *A Good Man Is Hard to Find*."

Seila said, "Okay, I'm not scared now."

Johnny smiled and said, "Keep talking like that, girl, and I'm going to put you out of my truck."

"As well you should. Sorry. It's not creepy at all."

The sun went down as Johnny drove them down a forest service road about 15 miles south of Wendell, Georgia. They watched the sides of the road intently, until they saw silhouettes of men spring into full color and step into the beam of Johnny's headlights.

The men leveled assault rifles at the truck as Johnny slowed to a stop and rolled down the window. The men told him to get out of the truck. As Johnny climbed down, he asked, "Hey y'all, is that you, Derek?"

"Johnny Mac, good to see you man. What are you doing all the way up here? Didn't you move to Jacksonville?"

"Come to see my mama. She alright?"

"She's alright. Who you got in the truck?"

They walked away from the truck, and it became harder for Jim and Seila to hear them.

In the backseat, Jim and Seila could do nothing except wait in silence and listen. Jim put a hand on Seila's shoulder briefly, then whispered for her to put her hands behind her back as if handcuffed. The conversation outside the truck was muffled and might as well have been a foreign language. Mosquitoes whined through the truck window and alighted on them, but they didn't dare move or call more attention to themselves.

Then Johnny walked back to the truck and eased into the driver's seat, turned, and nodded his head. They both remembered to breathe. He drove the truck forward slowly on the bumpy road.

Jim said, "You knew those guys?"

"Cousins."

"Thank God."

"God ain't got nothing to do with it. Those old boys; they're believers. They'd kill you dead if they knew who you were, and they'd probably break a few of my ribs. Blood only goes so far these days." He took a deep breath and exhaled, "Fortunately for us, they're on the trail of a mother and her teenage daughter right now. But it's not so fortunate for the mom and her kid. Someone's put out a big bounty for them."

Jim asked, "How many miles will we get between them and us?"

"About seven more miles before we get to your trail. They might still come after us if they get to thinking too much about the bounty you two might bring. I told them I found you on the road back there and was going to take you in after I saw Ma. If I go back the way I come, without you, I'm screwed."

Jim asked, "What are you going to do?"

"I know another way. I don't know. Hell, maybe I'll come with you."

Jim smiled wryly and said, "Yeah, it's a free country."

Johnny laughed in derision and then said, "No, I guess I can't leave Mama."

Jim looked back, craning her neck at the darkness behind them, and then faced front to the darkness ahead. It was a long, seven miles before Johnny pulled over on a dirt track, barely visible in the dark.

Johnny asked, "You know where you're going?"

Jim swept her flashlight over the dark weeds, "Yep, I see it." She'd run this trail before.

Jim and Seila got out of the truck and lifted their backpacks from the truck bed. They carried bare essentials of food, clothing, lighters, a compass, maps, water filter bottles, knives, sleeping bags, and precious water. They did not pack tents, because they would have to break camp quickly and with little notice. It was going to be a long, hard slog getting to their first safe house in the resurrected underground railroad that Jim and Johnny helped set up. In fact, the first safe house was on an old horse farm managed by a long-time friend of Johnny's.

Jim and Seila's biggest challenge would be making it past the town of Wendell. Wendell was rumored as one of the worst places in the South for women. It was said that the water at Wendell prison often ran black, and women were so crowded in cells that only some of the women could lie down and sleep at a time, while others sat up in the tight spaces. Dysentery was rife and toilets were backed up almost by design. Worst of all, Wendell's Redeemers had a reputation for torture that called to mind witch trials or the inquisition.

Jim thought that for women, history indeed repeats.

Johnny stayed in the truck while they got their gear, and then Jim stopped by the driver side window. Johnny reached out his hand and took her hand in his. He said, "Stay safe."

She squeezed his hand and said, "You, too."

Then he creaked his truck back down the road as they watched him go.

When he was gone, Seila asked, "How do you know Johnny Mac?"

"Johnny's brother, Bobby, was a good friend of mine. Redeemers killed him."

Seila's forehead furrowed and she said, "I'm so sorry," because she had heard what happened to Bobby on the night that Jim was taken to the Redeemer camp.

Jim and Bobby were nineteen years old when the Redeemers streamed in both doors of their neighborhood bar, back when you could still go to a bar. The Redeemers were dressed in black, with black balaclavas and carrying assault rifles. Jim was perched on a bar stool, confused. Then she noticed the red cross shaped like a dagger on their police vests, turned to the bartender and said, "I'd like another beer." The frivolity ended there as she and her friends were forced outside and to their knees on the hot tar pavement. The Redeemers called them abominations before dragging Bobby away from the others and stomped him to death. She and her friends were forced to watch as they recoiled from every blow, and Jim doubled over, making strange grunting sounds as she tried to breathe. Afterwards, Redeemers dragged her and the other women from the pavement, and Jim barely felt it when the skin on her knees peeled away from the tar. That was her first clash with the Redeemers.

The hike for the sisters was slow-going as they picked their way over the old service roads, faint hiking trails, and abandoned highways overgrown with weeds clinging to the dirt that settled between chunks of broken pavement.

In some cases, trees were flattened by previous hurricanes or tornadoes, and the sisters hurried over them lest they be caught in the open.

It was late Summer and still hot. The air was thick and wet. Flies buzzed around their heads and mosquitoes whined around them in the dark shady places.

Between the two sisters, exhaustion and loss was so complete, they spoke little. Even if they could talk, it was best to keep moving quietly.

At night, the sisters lay down, with cramped and aching muscles, and in the morning, they revived enough to swallow aspirin and keep going, one weary step at a time. And water was a constant challenge. They stopped frequently for sips of water and to pour a little water on their faces. They pumped and filtered water from creeks, and at times, the barest of trickles.

One day Seila said, "If there are any birds out here, they've stopped singing."

Jim noticed it, too. The quietness of the woods was as unnerving as snapping twigs. Jim said, "They either died or got the hell out of this godforsaken place."

After a while, Jim said, "You know when birds are singing, they're really just gossiping and griping at each other?"

"Humph."

After another muggy day in the piney woods, they made it ten miles or so north of Wendell, Georgia, and reached the charred edge of a past wildfire. The safe house was a day's walk ahead, but wildfires had ravaged the path in front of them for quite a distance and they would be exposed for at least a mile. Jim said, "We have to walk by moonlight now. We have a few hours before we'll have enough light, so we should try to get some rest."

They both dropped their packs and slumped to the ground, neither woman feeling strong enough to unroll sleeping bags. They drank from their water bottles, and sweated in the hot damp air, like syrup, that didn't move.

Jim scratched the back of her damp neck and said, "At least we made it a fair distance past Wendell."

They balled up shirts to use as pillows, and lay down.

"Jim?"

"Yeah."

"Whatever happens, I want you know that I love you, no matter what."

"I know you do. Same here."

"You know this is not your fault, right?" Seila asked. She was referring to Seila's husband, Charlie, who was dead now and the reason Seila had to escape.

Jim sighed, "I know. The Redeemers killed Charlie, but I can't stop thinking that if I hadn't been out past curfew, and if he hadn't come to my defense, he'd be alive now."

Seila said. "Curfew or no curfew, it was Charlie's choice and he did the right thing."

After a few minutes of silence, Jim said, "He was a good man, Seila."

Jim heard Seila stifle a sob and put out her hand to touch Seila's shoulder.

"I'm okay," Seila said and turned over, away from Jim.

Jim knew that, despite the civil wars, Seila had lived in material comfort until Charlie was killed. He'd protected her from the worst of the Redeemer abuses, and now she had to face the harsh realities of the Covenant government while she was still grieving his loss. In new Covenant times, women needed male relatives or husbands for protection. Since Jim and Seila had neither, they were thrown on the mercy of the pastors, deacons and Redeemers of the new Covenant States. Occasionally, women were given a special dispensation to live together under supervision, but Jim was already a wanted woman and now Seila was, too. It just wasn't possible for them.

In a little while, Seila turned back towards Jim and asked, "You could be in Vermont already. Why did you stay?"

Jim smiled, and rolled to face Seila. "I don't know. I had this really annoying sister to rescue."

"It was my job to rescue you."

"You did. Five years ago. Now sleep. Time is short."

They tried to sleep as the moon slowly rose. Their sleep was shallow because one part of them stayed alert to the rustle of the dark woods.

When the moon was up, Jim woke and sat against a fallen log, looking up occasionally at the clouds obscuring the moon. Terrifying storms could arise suddenly these days, but she wouldn't worry Seila with that.

Seila sat up and said, "I miss my bed and a long soak in a tub."

Jim said, "I was just thinking of a commode. I'd trade a bed and a long soak for a commode."

As they waited, they listened for any sound in the woods behind them or signs that they were discovered. Occasionally twigs snapped from a foraging animal, which startled both women. Bear, wild boar or man could be deadly.

Seila pulled her pony tail free from her sweaty neck and whispered, "Jim. Do you think it's a deer?" She peered into the woods and tried to discern if any dark shapes moved.

Jim was wet from the heat and from tension. She said, "I don't hear anything."

They took deep breaths and waited. Jim scratched a mosquito bite on her arm, which was in danger of infection.

Just then a slight breeze rose up and rustled the woods, and clouds parted to reveal the moon, prickling their skin. The woods were various shades of blue in the moonlit night. In another time, it would be transcendent. Now the light from the full moon was too bright, too revealing. Yet they needed that light if they were to cross the charred ground ahead.

When a cloud crossed in front of the moon again, the woods darkened.

Jim knew that Seila's feet were blistered from weeks of hard walking over uneven ground. She opened her pack and found the first aid pouch, passed it over to Seila, and spoke low, "You'll want to tend to your blisters before we get going."

"I don't know if I can make it another day."

"We'll make it. Together, right?"

"Yeah, we're doing this."

Jim pulled two granola bars from her pocket and held one out. "Here, I've been saving this for you."

Seila snatched it from her hand and sat up straighter. "Oh my gosh!"

"Ssssshhhhh."

The smell of apple and cinnamon hung on the still air as they tore off the paper. They ate in small bits, savoring the sweetness and spice. After they ate, they waited for the clouds to clear again. Jim thought she heard Seila weeping, or was it someone else? Then she knew, it wasn't Seila. She listened to the sounds of the woods. Twigs snapped, very close now. She and Seila sat up straighter, as rigid as concrete statues, staring hard into the dark. They didn't speak or breathe. Something was taking shape, something dark. But then the clouds above drifted enough to allow brief moonlight in, and they found themselves staring at a woman clutching a teenage child just beyond the trees.

They stared at each other with hearts beating, and a slick curtain of fear hung between them all. "It's okay" the mother said, "we don't mean any harm. It's just me and my daughter. My name's Juanita and..."

Jim interrupted her, "Where did you come from?"

Juanita and her daughter's eyes were large, dark pools of worry. She said, "We....we need help. We're from Wendell. My daughter. We have to save her."

"What's wrong with her?" asked Jim.

"She's supposed to get married. She's too young. Please. We have food and water. We can share." Their eyes pleaded and kept looking back from where they came.

And that's when the sound of more crashing in the woods split the night. They ran in different directions. Jim didn't make it 20 feet before she fell into a ravine, hitting the ground with a painful grunt. Jim scrambled under a rusted refrigerator propped against the bank with enough of a crevasse under it to slide into. She lay still as she listened to women shrieking and men yelling. Jim trembled violently and fought against the impulse to come out of hiding to help Seila. She put her hand over her mouth and held still.

Jim heard a man shouting, "Is this all? IS THIS ALL?"

"Yes, yes," Seila cried.

Someone told the others to spread out and look for other escapees, and Jim heard them trampling the woods. A flashlight scraped the ravine.

Another man asked "What are you doing here?"

Jim couldn't hear the response but she heard a man say, "She's fourteen. It's her time to prepare. You should have let her go."

Then Jim heard him ask, "Who are you and what are you doing out here?" but again Jim couldn't hear the answer. "What's this? Poison? Contraceptives? You see this, men? What's this?"

Jim could just barely hear Seila's shaky voice saying, "It's first aid, moleskin for my feet. Not poison."

The man with the commanding voice said, "Zip tie them, then take her and her."

Juanita cried out, "Not my daughter! Please! She's innocent! I made her come! It's not her fault."

"Go!" he ordered the men. "I'll talk to this one alone."

After a long pause with only the sound of Juanita wailing for her child, the crying suddenly stopped and Jim heard Juanita exclaim, "Dr Speers! Oh, thank heaven it's you!"

From under the rusted refrigerator, Jim sweated in her hiding place and listened. An insect bit her arm so sharp that her eyes watered as she held still.

The man said, "Don't worry about your daughter. No harm will come to her. I'll take care of her myself, but we can't have you corrupting her, for her sake. I'm saving your daughter. Do you understand that?"

The woman said, "I trust you, Dr. Speers. You're a godly man. It's them others, I don't trust."

Then the woman screamed and her scream was cut short.

Jim heard the man leave as his footsteps crunched over the hard ground and dry twigs. Jim felt sick, thinking about what they would do to Seila, and she felt like she was choking as she fought to breathe.

In a few hours, she crawled up the ravine. It was still and quiet again. Clouds had cleared and she could see the crumpled body of Juanita in stark relief under the blue moonlight. The Redeemers had taken the packs, but she found a dropped knife, a necklace with a gold cross glinting on the ground, and a water bottle half buried in a pile of leaves.

She had no means to bury Juanita, so she opened the knife and scratched a message on a piece of wood to leave by the body—Murdered by Dr. Speers.

She took a deep shuddering breath and looked in all directions, and then set off across the burned field, north.

{2}

South to Wendell

INSTEAD OF GOING north or west to safety, George and Janet Moore were heading deeper south, from Atlanta to Wendell, Georgia. It was safe enough for George, but Janet was only safe under George's protection.

Janet threaded her fingers through her dark chin length hair, pulling her hair back. She used to wear her hair in a ponytail, but it wasn't long enough now. Janet was slim and short, which George liked, and she was wearing a yellow silk blouse and a full turquoise skirt. She was forty years younger than George, which was appropriate for George's political and economic class.

George was 65 years old and sometimes Janet had trouble looking at his fleshy face and large, thick nose. When Janet looked down or away from him, George mistook her revulsion for modesty, which he admired in a wife. Fortunately for Janet, George was not an observant man.

They were going to Wendell, a prison town in middle Georgia, where George had been raised. It wasn't far from where he used to run about the piney woods with other young men in one of the Georgia militia groups, before the Redeemer's war to make America Christian. George was enjoying the spoils of that war, of which he took part. Janet was trying to survive its aftermath.

The air in Atlanta was acrid and the sky was dull, not from cars anymore but from manufacturing. It had an oily chemical smell and some areas warned drivers to keep their windows closed.

Janet was terrified of Wendell, but still she went. And she dreamed of Vermont. Someday she would go to Vermont. But the duplicitous don't flee, because to flee is to reveal your hiding place, to encourage the chase, like most of her friends did, long dead now. No, you stayed and you froze. Janet focused on the sounds of the road. Babump, babump, babump.

On the drive though Atlanta, the couple listened to a talk radio host discuss the Seila Lee Campbell case. Seila was the number one suspect in the deaths of three people in a terror attack in downtown Jacksonville, Florida, one of whom was her husband, Charles Carson Campbell. No one had seen her face yet, but everyone felt certain that she was guilty. New laws had made guilt or innocence rather irrelevant. It was the show that counted; it was the messaging and the ratings. Talking heads said, "Jehu didn't waste money on a trial when he had Jezebel thrown to the dogs."

George reached over and clicked off the radio.

"It doesn't make sense," Janet said.

"Your obsession with this woman is dangerous. The Devil's in it."

Janet watched a crowd of marchers outside the car window. Little girls wore dresses that displayed the Covenant government's black flag with a red cross shaped like a dagger down the center. The cross was encircled by twenty-one red stars to signify the twenty-one Covenant states. Adolescent girls wore long camo skirts, and boys wore green-camo pants. Marching bands thumped out the Believer's Victory song as God's fighting battalions marched to waiting buses that would transport them to military installations on the borders of the Southern Covenant States. Janet could tell from the glum expressions on faces in the crowd that not everyone was moved by the pageantry. Were we that easy to locate in a crowd? Some had forgotten to smile.

A small group trooped together down the sidewalk, "Hey hey, ho ho, anti-Christs have got to go. Hey hey, ho, ho…" Weaving between the cars, another group of swaggering men sang out, "What do we want?" "Jesus!" "When do we want him?" Now!"

George took a wrong turn into the Empty Quarter, which was not empty at all. Clusters of thirsty and emaciated people stumbled through its streets, squares, and lots, people whose eyes seemed like black holes, some dull and listless and others fierce. They won't, Janet thought, but she wouldn't have blamed them if they had dared to drag her and George from the car. George put his car in reverse and backed away while some men approached the car slowly.

"The eyes of God, George. They won't touch us."

The eyes of God were robodogs with automatic ballistics mounted on their backs that roamed the perimeters of the modern-day ghettos, and the eyes of God were cameras mounted on posts, and drones, so many drones. Drones might be in flight or they might scuttle across the road like cockroaches. The men scattered and ran, and the eyes of God turned their faceless lens to George and Janet as they backed out of the road.

People were dying of disease, hunger, thirst and despair while private investment companies held monopolies on the most basic needs. In a marriage of religion and capital, the Redeemers kept the peace in the name of Jesus. And still, they called for women to have more babies that they could not feed. Most people lived in fear that the black-booted Redeemers would arrest them for anything from heresy or political affiliation to their inability to pay off debts. Others no longer cared. In plain sight of the eyes of God, they shook their fists until a quick burst of retribution finally ended their dismal lives. They were lucky they weren't in Wendell though. It has been known since the beginning of man that there are worse things than death.

As George pulled onto the entrance ramp for I-75 South, they were halted at one of the many military checkpoints. Few people were allowed to travel to and from the locked-down cities and towns, and a license to drive was no longer universal.

Janet fastened her eyes on George as he presented his palm to the officer for the scan, but she was acutely conscious of the pistol butt at the officer's belt and his partner standing behind him with an assault rifle. The officer gave Janet a cursory glance, then he waved them on.

Scraps of paper and plastic blew across the pavement like tumbleweeds, and the grass grew from cracks in the outside lanes. Potholes dotted the roadways. Occasionally, military vehicles and buses passed them on the interstate.

As they slipped out of Atlanta, Janet felt the thick gray pall hanging over the city, a collective despair interwoven with the acrid air, and she thought about the other checkpoints they would drive through. The next checkpoint would be Forsyth, and they would have to pay a bribe for the checkpoint there, and then Macon, both in and out of the city.

On this drive, Janet felt like she was in free fall. She thought about a plunge she had made into the Ohio river when she was fourteen years old. She was visiting her cousins in West Virginia who dared her to swim from the bank of the Ohio river to a pier that workers tied coal barges to. The piers were tall cylindrical metal and cement posts. As her cousin swam out over the mud-colored Ohio current, she followed. And she followed him up the straight steel ladder, slick from his watery feet above her. It was a strenuous climb and the ladder was narrow. Halfway up, she looked down and thought that this was higher than it looked from the bank, and she was scared of heights. She considered backing down the ladder, but she would be the first girl to jump from a pier. She was going for it and kept climbing.

Finally, she stood on the cement top and peeked over the side. It was so much higher than she expected. She thought again about crawling backwards down the slippery ladder, but that now seemed more dangerous than jumping. Her cousin jumped and swam free while she stood and considered. People began to gather on the bank, and kids yelled, "Jump, jump, jump…"

She hesitated.

They say pride goeth before a fall, and so she took the easiest path. She jumped.

The first thing that surprised her on the way down was how long it took to fall. She had time for fear and regret and a slippery exhilaration. She screamed. And then she plunged, and that was the second surprise. She never expected to plunge so deep in the murky brown water. She kicked and swam up and up until she finally broke the surface and drew a deep breath. Her uncle met them at the bank, furious because this was not what girls do. It was dangerous! Anything could have been in that water.

The other kids thought she was brave, but the jump made her see that, for her, it wasn't bravery. It was just gravity. Drumming up a split second of courage can set you on a path from which you can't escape. Like marrying the wealthy widower, George, and moving with him to Wendell. She was in free fall. She was scared. But a force beyond her propelled her forward now, and maybe she would survive the plunge.

By late afternoon, they made it through the last checkpoint, and not once did anyone request a scan from Janet. It was worth noting. She was simply George's wife.

~

In Wendell, you could see a trace of blue in the sky, something Janet hadn't seen since before the war. And Wendell had trees. Most trees in the cities and towns had been cut down for fuel or lost to the pine bark beetle. But in Wendell, grand, spreading oaks draped in gray Spanish moss still bent over shady side streets moistened by a brief November rain. It was strange, magical. In the past, Janet might have felt something, but she knew that behind the tree-lined façade of Wendell, Georgia, was Wendell Prison Incorporated, a PrisonCorp subsidiary, run from disembodied officials, passing down orders via video conferences, far from Wendell.

Wendell was a small but notorious cog in the Christian political machine of this fledgling empire of multistate forces, collectively called the Covenant States. The entire machine was run by large corporate concerns, and Wendell was like a Machiavellian city-state. You were either in its good graces or you were dying inside and outside its gates, subject to hunger, thirst and human predators—state-sponsored or freelancer. George was in the power circle. Consequently, so was Janet, sort of. But she was a woman in new Covenant times, so her life was completely dependent on George. Fall out with him, and you might never get up again.

As George entered the outskirts of Wendell, Janet observed the empty houses, listing sideways or collapsing inwards. With each empty house they passed, she wondered if the inhabitants had been lost to the host of viruses that ran rampant in these end times—viruses collectively called God's Righteous Wrath—or if the people had been murdered by their own neighbors after the Covenant governments came to power, neighbors they had once laughed and dined with, neighbors with whom they had once agreed to disagree. What the wars taught Janet was that trusting neighbors could spell death. She learned to keep her ears and eyes open and her mouth shut, for the most part, but Janet wrestled against old habits of having strong opinions and speaking her mind.

As she and George approached the city center, restored white homes with large columns and wide front porches became more commonplace. They passed the Grand Theatre in the center of town where people on sidewalks watched them pass. They turned right past the Wendell New Christ Millennial Church, and parked the car on the street at 208 Victory Lane.

"Home!" George announced. His eyes shone with excitement.

Janet got out of the car, stretched her stiffened muscles, and observed a window curtain fall closed at the house next door.

Their arrival was being announced. She took a deep breath and the air smelled crisp. The November sun warmed her.

As she followed George up the mossy sidewalk to their new house, oak trees arched overhead. Dead, dying and rusted leaves fell softly with an intermittent breeze. The verandah was large with five white rocking chairs on either side of the front door. The front door had an iron cross laid over a circle of emerald-green, stained glass, and a green woven welcome mat lay at the base of it. Janet walked behind George as he pushed open the door. The movers had been there before them and had left plastic yellow crates throughout the house. The house had an odor of fresh paint.

George and Janet's steps rang hollow on the hardwood floors as they crossed the foyer to the stairs that wound to a second story. George wanted to check the upstairs first, since the builders were supposed to have fixed the plumbing in one of the upstairs bathrooms.

They had just begun to climb the stairs when a woman called from the front door. She was an elderly woman, late 70s, and her white and yellowed hair sprung wildly around her pinched face and sharp nose. Her layered clothing and pink sweater had holes. Her intense, mad eyes darted around the room. She had pushed open the door and stood just inside, leaving Janet to marvel at how she seemed to materialize out of nowhere. Of course, the woman smiled, and Janet smiled back.

A smile in these heady days of the pseudo-Christian revival was a subtle tyranny. This was God's government now and you must be joyous, particularly if you were a woman. Beatific even.

The woman spoke in a loud voice as her eyes swept the room and the stairs. "Halloo. You must be the Moores. We heard you'd be here today, so we made you sugar cookies. Everybody loves my sugar cookies." She pulled a teenage girl inside with her. "Me and Sister Mary live down the street. Just call me Aunt Peggy. Everybody does."

George bumped Janet as he hurried past her. He stuck out his big, meaty hands, taking Aunt Peggy's hands in his, and said, "So good to meet you! I told Janet that the folks in Wendell were gracious people. Didn't I tell you, Janet?"

Janet smiled and bobbed, and she and Sister Mary locked eyes for a brief moment. Then Sister Mary looked down under curly rust-colored hair.

As Aunt Peggy pushed passed them, Janet smelled a foul odor and thought Aunt Peggy was probably saving on water.

Aunt Peggy led them from room to room pointing out how the house used to be arranged, as George, Janet, and Sister Mary followed behind. "Jilly kept a piano right there in that corner. You don't have a piano? Such a shame. Oh, I don't play, but it's so nice to have one, don't you agree? Now Robbie, Robbie was my husband who's with the Lord now; he taught himself how to play. Robbie had an ear."

When Aunt Peggy lifted the lid of a crate and offered to help them unpack, George stepped in.

He thanked Aunt Peggy for her offer, but he and Janet would like to unpack on their own.

He took Aunt Peggy's arm in his and gently guided her to the front door. George talked gruff at times but he was gentle overall.

After the women were gone, George turned to Janet, grinned, and winked conspiratorially.

George and Janet unpacked the crates in silence. For George, it was his guns that he took up first, rubbing them with a soft cloth before resting them in his gun safe behind the wall of his bedroom closet. He placed another in his bedside table. For Janet, she must unpack the kitchen items, but it was her yarn and knitting needles that she kept close.

By week's end, they reported to their new church. Everyone in the Covenant States was required to be affiliated with a church, and Georgia's official state religion was New Christ Millennial. Although people had a two-week grace period after a move, George saw no reason to delay. He loved church and he loved people. George was not duplicitous, which was good cover for Janet.

As George and Janet seated themselves in the back pew, Janet watched the good brothers and sisters in Christ carefully. She knew that some of these smiling neighbors were guards at Wendell and some were informers, telling on neighbors who missed too many Sundays at church, who missed their period, who said something cynical about the Redeemers, or who just didn't seem quite right. Today, they wore their Sunday best—even Aunt Peggy—and the blood on their hands was washed clean.

She heard a woman speak clearly above the rest. The woman was standing with a cluster of people next to the pew. "I told you that I talked with him yesterday." A minute later the same woman said, "I told you that…"

"You don't have to get mad."

"I'm not mad. You're not listening to me. I told you that I talked with him yesterday."

"Why don't you just yell at me?"

Someone called back, "Hey Randy. You getting hen-pecked back there."

"She's yelling at me."

"We're in the Lord's house. Let the women be silent." The people chuckled and quieted as the preacher approached the podium, and a member of the congregation spoke from a microphone, "Please take out your hymnals and sing hymn number three hundred and four, "A Powerful Friend." Everyone rose and sang. Janet soundlessly moved her lips while George's voice boomed next to her.

Then the preacher announced that they should shake hands with the people around them, so a white-haired woman in front of Janet turned and smiled as she held out her hand. Her face was creased with tiny lines, her white hair was pulled into a tight bun, and she wore a white turtle-neck top under an orange cardigan sweater. "I'm Sister Emily. So nice to meet you." Janet thought Sister Emily had a kind face, but you never could know about people.

"I'm Sister Janet. Glad to worship with you today." Others wheeled around to hold out white gloved hands, and another hymn was called while Janet glanced sideways at George, smiling widely, happily, and Janet imagined him believing that he always had a friend in Jesus.

Someone called for Deacon Mark Speers to come to the front and lead them in prayer, and Janet watched him closely as he approached the podium. He walked with rigidity in his back and shoulders and was tall and thin, and his face was pale. The prominent bones of his face and strong, straight nose made him almost handsome. Yet the pale, translucent skin made him look ghastly like a vampire from an old movie Janet once watched.

He tucked his Bible under one arm and bowed his head without managing to move his body at all. As he faced the congregation, he coughed slightly to clear the phlegm and began in a deep baritone voice, "Dear God, we gather in your house today to worship together and praise you. Thank you that so many could come to hear your Word today, and we pray that your Word touches each and every one of us, so that we might all be better Christians to our families, our communities, our nation and the Covenant. I ask this in Jesus' name. Amen."

Others in the congregation echoed "amen," and Deacon Speers walked carefully to his seat.

Pastor Wayne smiled as he approached the podium with his big, black Bible, and called out to him, "Deacon Speers. I believe if your back was to get any straighter, we'd be calling you the frozen chosen." Dr. Mark Speers smiled tightly and everyone laughed.

"We have a couple of announcements this morning. First, we need some of you ladies to volunteer for the prison ministry. Some of you have been called to counsel women who are about to meet the Devil face-to-face. Some of you have turned a lost soul to repentance and salvation in their final hours, praise the Lord. But we need more volunteers. Now I know it's not a pleasant task, and it takes someone with a hardy constitution, someone whose armor is fortified against Satan, because the Devil will try to speak to you. Make no mistake. The Devil will speak to you through those inmates who are the worst, most recalcitrant sinners. But if Jesus can offer salvation to the thief crucified next to him in his final hours, then we who love Jesus can continue that ministry at Wendell. To ensure your spiritual safety, you'll receive orientation before each meeting and debriefing afterwards. See Sue Ann Chambers after the service and sign up. God bless you for your service in the Lord, and let's be sure to pray for those already carrying on this great work."

Some people scribbled this onto their prayer lists.

"And mothers. We need soldiers for God's army. So multiply."

Everyone chuckled.

"Also, folks, there will be coffee and doughnuts downstairs after the service. Yes, real, homemade doughnuts! Now I see some newcomers here this morning. Please stand so we can see you."

Janet, George, and another new man stood up. Janet stood and felt she had been served up for dinner. Janet tried to smile as heads turned to look at them, and she was afraid that the muscles around her mouth would quiver and betray her nervousness. Nervousness might as well be a spot of blood on a chicken in these heady days of sharp beaks.

"Is that you, George?"

George's voice rang out a little loud over the congregation, "That's me. George Moore, and this is my new wife, Janet." He placed a proprietary hand on the back of Janet's neck.

"George Moore and his new wife, Janet," Pastor Wayne announced to the congregation.

"What brings you to Wendell, George?"

"We've decided to retire in Wendell where me and some good friends of mine grew up. You know the Chambers and the Camps. I remember Wendell from the old days and well...I just can't say enough good about Wendell, so here we are. Also, my sister will be joining us shortly. In fact, I'd like folks to pray for my sister. Since her husband passed away, she's not getting on so well and has really bad asthma attacks where she can't draw a breath. Thanks for your prayers and thanks for welcoming us back into your church family."

"Well, welcome home. We're real glad you're back. I've heard good things about your heroic actions during the war from Willie Chambers and Warden Camp."

George beamed while Warden Camp said, "Amen to that Pastor. Old George is a good ole boy. I've been knowing him for sixty years now, and we fought together in the Covenant Coalition. He's the kind of man you'd want in a foxhole with you. Yes, sir. We go way back."

"Well George. Real glad you and your wife decided to join us in your retirement. As you know, Wendell's a friendly town, chock full of patriots for Jesus just like yourself."

Pastor Wayne turned to the other new man. "How about you young fella? What's your name?" The man was tall and had a broad back. His close-cropped hair was black and his brown eyes were set in a handsome, chiseled face.

"I'm Sonny Valdez." Sonny spoke in deep, loud voice, perhaps too loud. Janet wondered if he was as uncomfortable as she was.

"You're the Papist who's come to work at Wendell?"

"Ah, no sir. I was raised Catholic, but I've been saved."

"You don't need to call me 'sir.' But you can call me Pastor Wayne. We're all family here, all sinners washed clean with the blood of Jesus. You'll find that the folks at Wendell are open-minded and tolerant when it comes to people of your background. Make yourself friendly and you'll find the people of Wendell friendly, too. Why, I'm just tickled pink to have a Catholic who's turned away from the Catholic cult and put his feet to the path of righteousness. Preach right?"

"Amen," some members of the congregation said.

"What branch of the military were you in, son?"

"Covenant Army, sir."

"Good man. I can tell a military man by the way he carries himself. You got any family?"

"I have five brothers and sisters and my father still living."

"Praise the Lord, and where are they now?"

"New Mexico."

"That a Catholic state?"

"Yes."

"They haven't been saved then?"

"They're still Catholic."

"Well, let's everybody remember Brother Sonny's family in their prayers, so that they might come to know the Lord. And let's welcome Brother Sonny Valdez, Brother George Moore, and Sister Janet. Now everyone, please open your Bibles to James Chapter 1, Verses 5-8.

Janet turned to the requested passage in her New Covenant Bible, which was the only Bible recognized in the southeastern Covenant States, while Pastor Wayne read the passage.

If any of you lacks wisdom, let him ask of God, who gives generously to all without finding fault, and it will be given to him. But when he asks, he must believe and not doubt, because he who doubts is like a wave of the sea, blown and tossed by the wind. That man should not think he will receive anything from the Lord; he is a double-minded man, unstable in all he does.

"Now what does that say? It doesn't just say that the Lord will not give a doubter, wisdom. The Lord won't give him—or her—anything. There's only one way to read this passage.

A doubter can never enter the Kingdom of Heaven, will never see the streets paved in gold, will never listen to the heavenly choir of angels, will never know peace, will never know the Lord, and if you get right down to it, that man or woman is a stumbling block to your brothers and sisters in Christ and to the Covenant. We must root him out and cut him down."

And it seemed to Janet as if Pastor Wayne were looking straight at her, as she felt the heaviness of George's presence next to her.

{3}

Marriageable

D R. SPEERS HAD just offered the prayer for the evening meal with his date, Mary Webber, when he looked down at his hands. He frowned as if irritated, excused himself and explained to Mary that he had to wash his hands. He went to the bathroom off the dining room near the foyer and left the door open. She could see him soaping and washing his hands vigorously under the tap.

After his abrupt departure from the table, Mary wondered if she had done something wrong. She rehearsed in her mind their conversation after he picked her up in his black sedan. She had opened her front door for him, and he had said, "Washed clean," and she had dutifully replied, "By blood." She had been ready to go as soon as he arrived even though Aunt Peggy told her that women should always keep their men waiting. "You don't want to appear too eager."

Aunt Peggy had even allowed her to splurge on a shower, which meant she got two showers within the same week.

Aunt Peggy wasn't Mary's real aunt. She was a widow from the congregation who Pastor Wayne assigned to live with Mary for a while, since they had both lost their families, and single women couldn't live alone. But Mary hadn't really lost all of her family. Not really. Mary was told that her mother had been redeemed and was relocated to another town. The elders determined that she and Mary should not see each other because, at a certain age, it was best to separate some mothers and daughters. Mary ached for her mother, but she couldn't tell anyone about her longing, nor would anyone tell her the name of the town that her mother was moved to.

Though Mary was ready when Dr. Speers arrived, she was far from eager. He was thirty-plus years her senior, and though she had a great deal of respect for Dr. Speers—everybody did—she had not thought of marriage to him until Pastor Wayne broached the subject with her last Tuesday. "He admires you, Sister Mary. You should be proud."

Mary kept her head down with her thick, reddish hair hanging over half of her face and said very little on the short drive through Wendell to his house. In some ways, she still looked like a little girl. She had recently turned fifteen years old, a marriageable age it was said, and some of her friends were married at fourteen. It was only recently that she was placed in the adult Bible study class with Dr. Speers.

Dr. Speers' house was government-issue, an old plantation-style house with a wide veranda that was confiscated from some anti-Christs, along with its contents. The house had high ceilings, and the oak floors gleamed around the edges of expensive Oriental carpets, lovingly selected by the previous owners from a carpet dealer at a trade show, who had gotten them from a government auction, who had confiscated them in a military raid.

She said, "It's beautiful," as Dr. Speers led her quietly over the living room carpet.

"Please sit, Sister Mary, and have some tea while I put dinner on the table."

Mary heard the tick, tock of a grandfather clock, measuring the silence in that opulent room and grew alarmed. "Are we alone?"

"Father is in the back room. If you need assistance, you can scream. He'll hear you."

Mary looked anxiously at Dr. Speers and saw a slight smile playing around his pale lips. "Are you playing with me?"

"Yes. But seriously, he is asleep in the room behind the kitchen and my housekeeper, Katie, is cleaning the kitchen, so you're safe from impropriety. I wouldn't bring you here without some form of chaperone."

Maybe she was handling it all so badly, but Mary had been taught to obey, and to say 'no' to Dr. Speers was unthinkable. Her face was flushed and hot, and she pulled at the collar of her navy-blue, turtle-neck sweater which felt too tight. Her long hair was heavy and damp.

Mary looked at the table laden with pasta, rich spaghetti sauce with roasted cheese, and meatballs that steamed deliciously from large green ceramic plates. Genuine silverware gleamed on the white linen tablecloth, and candlelight flickered on the table, casting a golden light. She was not accustomed to such luxury in these days when food was scarce, and her mouth watered, though her mind shuddered at the thought, the sin of gluttony, in which she knew she would partake this night, praise Jesus. She had been taught that people binged and purged often in the dark days of the secular government, wantonly wasting food. She could not imagine those days. Before tonight, she could not even have imagined this meal.

Dr. Speers returned from washing his hands, sat down, and neatly folded his napkin over his lap. Bow ties were in vogue again, and Dr. Speers adjusted his pink-striped bow tie before clearing his throat and nodding to Mary who asked, "are you okay?" because it was important for a woman to measure the temperature of those around her and because it came naturally to Mary to ask.

"Of course. I'm sitting down to dinner with a beautiful woman. Thank you for joining me."

Mary, a beautiful woman? She still felt like a kid. Mary pulled her hair over her shoulder, sipped her tea, and wondered what to talk about. She said, "Dr. Speers?"

Dr. Speers looked at her gravely as if they were speaking of something of great importance. "Mark. You can call me Mark, except when we're in public. Dr. Speers is too formal for a romantic evening."

Mary was startled. The word, 'romantic,' seemed singularly out of place coming from him, as strange as if the First

Regent of the Covenant States were to break out in song or someone were to dance in church. Romantic. This was not a word anyone used, and Mary temporarily forgot what she wanted to ask him.

Mary imagined that Dr. Speers, Mark, could hear her swallowing. His long, translucent face was practically buried in his salad. He rose from time to time to dab his mouth carefully with his napkin while he seemed to be appraising Mary. It was disconcerting when a piece of lettuce stuck to his pale jaw.

Mary's thoughts turned to the study she passed as she came into the dining room, and she remembered what she wanted to ask. The walls of Dr. Speers' study were lined with high bookcases. That must be why his house had a musty smell, maybe from moldy old books. Mary could smell the mustiness mixed with the aroma of spaghetti sauce, but Mary had a fine nose that could pick out scents easily.

She finally decided to broach the subject, "I didn't know anyone still read books."

"Excuse me? Oh, the books came with the house. Most of them are illegal, you know."

"Won't you get into trouble?"

"I am cleared for them, for my job. I have Internet access for my research as well."

"Aren't you afraid of Satan getting to you through your work and all that knowledge?"

"It's dangerous work, but I'm well-armored against Satan." Dr. Speers smiled and his eyes gleamed.

Mary thought she might like to peek at those books, but Mary had few words to work with, to think with or interpret. She was raised in her formative years with words like Jesus. Damnation. The Devil. Demons. Satan. Propriety. Hell, and fried okra, green beans, and sugar cookies. Be kind. Be chaste. Be modest. Jesus is with you. And so is the Devil. Don't let Satan in. Few books and few words. And grace and fear. Her parents had never directed her to question any of it, until she reached her marriageable age, which got her mother into trouble with the Redeemers.

She said, "I heard that you got a Doctor in Theology at Free Will University in Alabama."

"My doctorate. Yes."

"So why did you never become a pastor?"

Dr. Speers smiled an amused smile. "Shall I wrest the position from Pastor Wayne?"

"No, but there are other towns."

"True, but the work I do now is quite satisfying." Dr. Speers stabbed his lettuce again.

"You know. We've known each other for almost six years."

"Has it been that long?"

"Yes. Remember? Me and my parents moved back home to tend to my brother, Henry, before he died of the cancer, after the First Regent took over. You were home on leave from the war and you took time with Pastor Wayne to bring us groceries. You brought me a lollipop."

"I don't remember." Dr. Speers looked off then, and they both grew quiet; it occurred to Mary that it was the same year that Dr. Speers' wife died. People in the town said she died of a virus or infection. Mary thought it was probably the same virus that killed Mary's father not long afterwards, a virus people called the Wrath. As the bodies stacked up, people were told that there was nothing that could be done about it. It was God's will. Any scientists who argued otherwise were arrested.

After a respectful pause, Mary turned her knife over on the table and took a deep breath. "Dr. Speers, do you know where my mama is?"

Dr. Speers looked at Mary sharply, and she suddenly felt hot as his face transformed and stiffened, and his gray eyes darkened. He said softly, as quiet as a cat's paw, "I'm not at liberty to talk about that. Just know that she's at peace where she is now, and she knows that we are taking good care of you. That's all she ever wanted."

Mary's eyes brimmed with tears and she trembled. "She's really been redeemed? She's not at Wendell prison?"

"Mary. I told you. She's been redeemed and she's safe, but she can never come back. You have to forget about her. She would want you to get on with your life and find happiness again."

"What happens at Wendell?"

"I'm not at liberty to talk about my work, Sister Mary. You know that. And she's not there!" Dr. Speers mouth was set in a tight, angry line, and a muscle bulged on his jaw.

"Oh, yes but...I'm sorry." Mary's face felt hot with shame.

Dr. Speers softened and nodded gravely. "It's okay. Ask me about anything except that, and I'll be happy to answer. Anything else. Ask. Please." Dr. Speers pointed his fork at Mary and bestowed a rare smile that revealed straight white teeth, but his eyes didn't smile.

Two flushed spots appeared on Mary's face. "Sometimes I don't know what it's appropriate to talk about."

Dr. Speers seemed to study Mary for a long pause. "It's okay, Sister Mary. I just don't want any harm to come to you. You're sweet and pure, but even you could come to ruin with too much knowledge. Knowledge weakens one in the fight against Satan, and you must know that I would do anything in my power to protect you from that. No one, but especially not you, can ever know the terrible devils we face at Wendell and what we have to do every day to keep them from rising. I feel very deeply about this, very deeply. Trust me. The less a woman knows, the better for her."

"Sometimes people think I'm too educated for my own good, what with my parents having been teachers and because of my mama. Do you think I'll have to go to the Redemption?" Mary trembled at the thought of being taken away in a Redeemer van.

"No, Sister Mary. Your father educated you on the Lord. That's a good thing, a very good thing. When a man marries, he wants his wife to be his best friend and for that, she'll need to be educated and intelligent in the Word, or else who would he talk to at the end of the day?"

Mary looked down and nodded her head while Dr. Speers continued, "I expect my wife to be a good Christian woman, like you, Sister Mary."

Inwardly, Mary trembled at the idea of being a wife, displeasing God, and losing the fight against Satan. She said, "Of course, we're all Christians, aren't we? Now?"

"Not all, Sister Mary. Not all." He stretched back and set his napkin on the table. "These days everyone professes to be a Christian, even Satanists. Remember your Bible. Many will cry, 'Lord, Lord.'"

Dr. Speers leaned up and reached across the table, patting her arm which rested on the table next to her plate. "But I've never heard an ill word spoken about you, Sister Mary."

Mary felt the room grow darker. "I guess I would just like to believe everyone was a Christian, at least everyone here in the Covenant States."

"We'll get there someday. You're young. You can't know what a terrible time it was before America was liberated, a godless time. When the Redeemers finally got things under control..." Dr. Speers looked at the ceiling, musing, and shook his head. He smiled at Mary. "We overthrew the secular government before they even saw it coming, from the inside. God's Righteous Wrath helped of course. Millions of people came over to God from the viruses, and by that time, the army of God had swelled with a new generation of home-schooled Christians who came of age. But it's your generation that holds the promise of the Covenant."

Mary thought about her father groaning in his hot, damp bed, and she remembered her shock when his breath smelled of decay while he was still alive. As Mary remembered her father and her lost mama, she felt a deep sadness that took her strength from her and left her with a keen sense of her isolation. She looked across the table and had a disconcerting sensation that she and Dr. Speers were the only two people in the world, with a yawning, dark void surrounding them. Reality seemed too glaring.

"The war helped, too," Dr. Speers said. "It gave people a clearer vision of the devils we were fighting, and a purpose, a reason to fight. When you're fighting for God's kingdom on earth, you have supernatural strength, like David fighting Goliath." He smiled again, and for a split second through a trick of the light of the guttering candle, his teeth seemed wolf sharp.

He continued, "Some of our enemies even helped us, because when Satan's minions are not fighting Christians, they're fighting each other. Standing shoulder to shoulder with each other the way we do is a Christian's great strength. Anyway, after the fall of the secular government, the Covenant Peace really began with the execution of at least..." Dr. Speers looked up as if searching his memory. "I'd say at least twenty-five thousand criminals daily throughout the Covenant States. Maybe more. We were washed clean, first with the blood of Jesus, and then with the blood of His enemies."

"And now?" Sister Mary 's eyes were wide with alarm.

Dr. Speers carefully set his fork on the table. "These are changing times, times when it's prudent to be silent about some topics, but I'll answer your question, Sister Mary, because you asked me and because you trust me not to let any harm come to you. I'm flattered that you asked me because of that trust. The official line is that there are still Humanists, Feminists, and Sodomites who are dangerous to our society. Many have joined Satan's army because they hate God and all that's pure. Some cling to illegal Bibles that distort the Word of God, or spread dangerous ideas, damaging to our country, our families, and the Covenant. Some sell contraception in defiance of Christian family values, trying to weaken us from within while our enemies batter the gates of our sanctuaries throughout the South. To safeguard the Covenant—and you know that without the Covenant, fewer people would be saved before Christ's return—those who engage in or assist those engaged in attempts to overthrow the Covenant government are arrested, tried and executed by military tribunals. Others are detained, re-tagged, re-educated, rehabilitated and returned to society as penitent laborers. Some are redeemed, like your mother."

Mary knew about the tents on the edge of town where the penitents lived. Penitents served as "volunteer" labor for the town but couldn't live in town and wore the letter P on their clothing. The redeemed people were relocated to other towns where they were assimilated.

Dr. Speers walked around the table, pulled out a chair, sat beside her, and gently lifted her hair from her face. "But you have nothing to fear, Sister Mary. Your mother was a good woman who became disoriented after your father died. That's all. She's been redeemed."

"What about Seila Lee Campbell on the news? They say she was a Christian."

"The Redeemers are still trying to sort that one out. They don't have all the facts yet, but she is suspected of taking part in the Jacksonville bombing that killed her husband. What they do know is that her sister was a murderer and a lesbian who possibly corrupted her. We hope to get answers soon."

Dr. Speers stroked Mary's face and then quickly pulled his hand back, and returned to his place at the other side of the table.

Mary trembled slightly. "Are we winning against Satan's armies?" Her thoughts grew crowded with demons and ominous shadows.

"Good always triumphs over evil. We have blundered, sure, but I trust that the Redeemers will work out the kinks in time. We definitely need to reexamine some faulty assumptions, like this nonsense of women having weak brains. We need to be a little more realistic about what we're dealing with. Women are some of the most formidable opponents I know."

"Opponents?"

"Only a certain kind of woman, Sister Mary, one who is empowered by dark forces."

Candlelight threw light and shadow across Dr. Speers' face as he watched Mary from across the table.

After a few moments of silence, Mary asked, "What if someone were to accuse me of a dark spirit?"

Dr. Speers guffawed, a short, sharp bark of a laugh, "Is that why you accepted my dinner invitation, so you wouldn't be accused?"

"No, sir," Mary lied.

"I don't want you to ever to feel forced with me. I think that may be the worst thing about the new gender policies. How is a man to know if a woman really loves him if she feels compelled to accept any offer that comes along? It's stupid to push women into this corner. It hurts us all. And what a burden it places on the man. Not only must we pay for a woman's keep, but we can't even be certain of her loyalty and devotion."

Mary lifted her head and looked at Dr. Speers with a mixture of gratitude and doubt, and she remembered Sister Sue Ann telling her that Dr. Speers was more enlightened than most men. She brushed the hair from the side of her face as the candle guttered, strobing its light across the white table cloth.

Dr. Speers smiled, and Mary thought that when Dr. Speers didn't smile, he was almost handsome. Otherwise, Mary thought he was frightening, and how can you marry someone if you don't want him to smile?

It was 9:40 P.M. when Dr. Speers drove Mary to her home in town. As they drove through Main Street in Wendell, Mary noticed a woman hurrying onto 1st Street, but she couldn't see who it was in the dark. A black Redeemer van rolled down the virtually empty Main Street and turned onto 1st Street, following her. As Dr. Speers drove by, he and Mary both looked down the street while van doors slid open. Officers with automatic weapons climbed out. Mary began to tremble and looked at the clock on Dr. Speers' car. All women were to be indoors by 10:00 P.M., but it was too early for curfew.

Dr. Speers said, "I wonder if the Redeemers aren't getting overzealous."

Mary kept quiet.

"It's God's business, anyway, not ours." He glanced at Mary who clasped her hands tightly in front of her, and he said quietly, "Washed clean."

"By blood," she replied dutifully.

When they arrived at Mary's house, Dr. Speers parked the car and walked Mary to her door. It was an unseasonably warm night for November. The crickets were silent this time of year, but the shrubbery was still green under the street-light in front of Mary's house. They stood on the small brick front porch, and Dr. Speers reached again for the side of her face. This time he didn't pull his hand away, and instead, pulled her to him and placed a lingering kiss on her forehead. Mary held her breath until he stepped away.

He said, "See you in church tomorrow?"

"Yes." She turned slowly as Dr. Speers backed down the porch steps, never taking his eyes from her.

Mary stepped inside to find Aunt Peggy in a rocker in front of the fireplace, waiting up for her. A picture of Dr. James Kennedy hung over the fireplace along with a crude pine cross leaning crookedly against the wall. Long nails to signify the nails of the cross lay loosely on top of the mantle.

"Did you have a nice time, child?"

Mary thought about Dr. Speers and the evening at his house and imagined that he held her ideals.

"Dr. Speers seems wise."

"That's because he's a true man of God."

Mary nodded, said she was tired, and climbed the stairs to her room. She carefully changed into her flannel, pale blue nightgown and laid down with her favorite stuffed animal that she clutched to her chest. It was a faded panda that she had since she was seven years old when her father brought it home to her. After he died from the Wrath, it was all she had of him.

That night, she dreamed Dr. Speers took her to him and held her in a tight embrace. And she couldn't break free. When she woke, her face flushed in shame when she remembered Jesus saying that if you think it, then you've already done it. She shoved the image from her mind. "I'm sorry," she whispered in perpetual remorse. Sorry was Mary's word. Sorry. So sorry.

~

When Dr. Speers went home, his father hovered in the doorway of his office. He wore a rumpled and damp cotton

T-shirt and his back was bent so that his neck was twisted up like a stork, thrusting his head of disheveled gray hair forward. He asked gruffly, "Well?"

Dr. Speers placed his keys carefully in a small, right-hand drawer of his rolltop desk, and then settled slowly into a leather swivel chair. He was as straight in his bearing as his father was crooked.

"I think so. Yes."

"Good. We need a woman around here. Is she still trainable?"

"She's young."

"That's not what I asked."

"She'll take direction."

Dr. Speers' father grunted, mumbled something about Mary's mother being a traitorous whore, and shuffled to bed.

Dr. Speers pulled open the center drawer of his desk and took out a folder with photos of the eligible girls in town. Mary's photo was on top and he stared at it for a long time, and then nodded his head as if satisfied about something.

He then rifled through some papers from the prison and selected one, which he held at arm's length so he could see the small print. He held the schedule for inmate # 40072223 who he planned to remove from solitary soon.

When Dr. Speers retired to his bed, he passed over an interrogation manual lying on the closest corner of his nightstand and picked up his dog-eared, black leather Bible.

He felt grim but he didn't know why, nor did he ask. Introspection was a weakness that he couldn't afford.

The next morning Dr. Speers woke to a dawn light. He did not want to get up, and his dream had evaded him, something unpleasant that left him irritable. Was it a woman? Someone had defied him. Was it Sister Mary?

When he entered the kitchen, his father was bent over the counter, preparing the morning coffee. His patchy gray hair was oiled back over his head. Speaking over his shoulder as he readied the coffee, he said, "It's better that a man and a woman marry than risk fornicating. And it gets me grandsons and someone to take care of me in my old age. That last wife of yours was as barren as a dead log. And look at us. A woman should be getting us coffee."

"Do you miss Mother?"

"Darn right I do? That woman could cook."

"Sometimes you got pretty angry with her."

"Spare the rod, spoil the child. Your Mama was a good Christian woman, the best, but she didn't get that way by herself."

Later at the church, Dr. Speers led his father up the stairs, and Pastor Wayne clapped him on the shoulder in the presence of Mary. "Here is a man with all those virtues essential to the purity and peace of God's country. This ol' boy may be straight as a stick, but he's like a brother to me, Sister Mary. You won't find a better man in Georgia, even if he does look like a yam dankee."

Sonny Valdez, one of the new members of the congregation scooted by them, saying, "They call Dr. Speers the Artist."

Dr. Speers frowned while Pastor Wayne turned away to greet other members of the congregation.

Mary asked. "What did he mean by that?"

"Brother Sonny Valdez is a new Wendell correctional officer who needs some lessons in protocol."

"But what did he mean?"

Dr. Speers did not answer right away but pulled Mary behind the church door away from the people milling around and away from the baleful glare of his father. He scrutinized Mary's face. "Do you remember what we talked about last night?"

Mary cast her eyes down. "Don't ask about Wendell?"

"That's right."

Mary blushed as he took her by the arm. "Let's go in."

{4}

Wendell Prison

WENDELL PRISON WASN'T Seila's first encounter with the Redeemers. The first time she was picked up by the Redeemers was just after her husband, Charlie, went missing. She was asleep and dreaming that her house was being invaded and woke to find that it was. Men in dark masks forced her from her bed where she lay naked under the covers, screamed at her, blinded her with bright lights, and jerked her helter skelter while she tumbled down a jarring, confusing cacophony of lights, curses, loud noises, banging, barking, and sirens. And to her "what...how...who...where...and WHY," they only said behind black ski masks, "You know."

She postulated then and continued to put forward that she did NOT know. After she fell down the rabbit hole that dark night, she was more convinced than ever that she could not know anything. They accused her of having something to do with Charlie's disappearance. Then, suddenly, they let her go home, said it was a mistake. She went home to an empty house, and cleaned up the mess that the Redeemers left behind, drawers and cupboards emptied, their aquarium smashed with water and dead goldfish on the floor, and lots of broken glass. She had always been someone who strove for order, so she hurried to pick it up. Then she scrubbed floors, cleaned windows, and dusted furniture to distract herself as she prayed for Charlie to come home. She couldn't sleep for more than a couple of hours at a time and spent nights listening for Charlie or the Redeemers to come back. It wasn't until she knew for sure that Charlie was gone forever that she tried to escape north with her sister, Jim.

When the Redeemers caught Seila on the trail, they took her to Wendell Prison Incorporated. To the Redeemers in Wendell, Seila Lee Campbell was a twenty-nine-year-old white female, inmate #40072223, whose criminal charges were under development, yet to be revealed, but certain to be prosecuted by the Covenant Court. As she shivered in a cold cell before meeting her prison Counselor, she was already stripped of layers of adult ego and persona and had now entered the wide-eyed, vulnerable state useful for confession, salvation, and exploitation.

Prison guards kept her alone for so long, that sometimes she felt intangible. She began to doubt her existence and mused to the cameras that watched her, "If I am my memories, then I am full of holes, gaps, cracks, and falsehoods."

Finally, she was pulled from her cell to meet Dr. Speers, the Counselor who was to help her through the confessional process.

She was led into a small office with neutral gray walls, which seemed to undulate from gray to green and pink to gray again. A tall, thin older man stood behind a cherry wood desk. He straightened his loose, but pressed gray suit, holding one button on his coat as he waited for her to settle into the sunken, black vinyl chair, while chains clinked around her. His face was long with prominent bones, his straight nose large and bony, and his skin unnaturally white, almost translucent with delicate red and blue veins. His hair was gray, but cut close, revealing the pale skin of his shaved head, and his eyes were gray, too, flickering between almost colorless to dark and piercing charcoal.

Dr. Speers' face shifted, too, sometimes appearing larger than it ought to be, while his pale skin slid into unsettled sharp focus and out again, as if he were moving closer and then far away. As his eyes flickered in and out of focus, they pierced her with intermittent episodes of unsettling scrutiny.

Seila's hands were shackled to a waist chain, which was attached to the shackles on her ankles. Her dyed blonde hair was gone and dark stubble grew from her shaved head, and her red prison uniform was a couple sizes too tight—all female inmates wore red. Consequently, she was painfully conscious of every roll, tuck, and dimple of flesh that encircled her stiff and weary body. And she felt like she was swimming in the vinyl chair, a lost little girl, not the woman she once was.

Dr. Speers sat stiffly behind his desk and said not a word. Seila took a deep breath and did not say anything either. They sat for some time that way, neither talking, him scrutinizing, and Seila trying to muster something of her former self, a woman that some had called dignified and elegant.

Seila used to pride herself on her cautious and measured approach to life. When Jim was a teenager and asked Seila to accompany her to New York City for a school project, Seila said, "I don't know. I'm afraid you're going to make spectacle of yourself." Jim grinned, which made Seila smile, too. They couldn't have been more different, but of course Seila would go. Seila was 19 years old when their parents died in a car accident. Despite her grief and the long process of Probate Court, she adopted the role of surrogate parent with equanimity. Hers and Jim's life in those early years mirrored the world in turmoil, but at least they had each other.

Sitting in Dr. Speers' office, Seila prayed that Jim finally found safety.

Dr. Speers' deep voice cut through the silence, "Mrs. Campbell. I am Dr. Speers and will be your Counselor during your stay in Wendell prison. I'm sure you understand that the normal client/therapist confidentiality will be waived in this case?"

"Yes." She thought his voice was familiar. She had heard it before but didn't remember where.

Again, he fell silent, long enough for Seila to collect a great deal of saliva in her mouth, feeling too uncomfortable to swallow, until she was forced to gulp it down in an obvious display of self-conscious feeling.

"What time is it?"

"Time isn't important in here."

"Is it day or night?"

"In Hell's waiting room, there is no day or night."

She mustered a defiant tone, "I won't be going to hell."

"In the latter days, many will cry, 'Lord, Lord.'"

"Are these still the latter days? I thought we were already functioning under God's government," she said dryly.

"We are cleaning up."

"I remember a time when people thought that God's government didn't begin until after Christ returns."

"A delusion inspired by secular fallacy."

At that, they lapsed once again into silence until Dr. Speers sighed, "Is there anything that I can do for you, Mrs. Campbell?"

"How about a breakfast omelet and fresh-squeezed orange juice?" She tried to smile but her lips couldn't muster it.

Dr. Speers' face was immovable, and after another interminable lapse, he said, "We can let you call someone. On the outside. Who would you call, Mrs. Campbell?"

"No one," she said. She wondered if she should call Dan Jackson, Charlie's colleague at work, but she didn't want to bring trouble on him.

"No one, Mrs. Campbell? We understand that you come from an unnaturally small family, but there were in fact two children born to your parents. You have a sister named Ruby."

Seila guessed that the Redeemers and Dr. Speers didn't know about Ruby's nickname, Jim.

A Jacksonville billboard flashed through Seila's mind of a large family, a mother, a father and eight children captured in a group photo and smiling down on the city of Jacksonville with the caption, "God loves large families." A luminescent glow and a host of angels surrounded them.

Seeking to deflect talk of her sister, she said, "It wasn't a crime then."

"Excuse me?"

"Small families weren't a crime then."

"And they're not a crime now, but contraception is."

"It wasn't then."

"No, but that has been rectified, and this is beside the point. Let me try again. We know that your parents are dead, but we also know that you have a sister. Perhaps you would like to call her."

"I was told she was dead." Seila had made a promise to herself not to reveal any friends to these people, but most particularly not to reveal anything about Jim, who she hoped had escaped north. So soon had she been called upon to keep her promise!

"I've looked into that and there is some question about it. We recovered her ID, but we did not confirm that we found her body."

"I don't know about that. If she's alive, I haven't seen her."

"If she were alive, where would she be?"

"I don't know. I haven't seen her in five years."

"Why not?"

"She vanished. I was told she was dead."

"Do you know of any reason she may have vanished?"

"None, except the one the Redeemers gave me. Again, they said she was dead."

"Was she a whore?"

"Oh heavens, no!"

"A homosexual?"

"No."

"An anti-Christ terrorist?"

"No!"

"If you lie, it will go harder on her. For her sake, I hope you're not lying."

Seila thought, large families, lots of hostages, and said nothing.

"You have no friends, Mrs. Campbell?"

"No."

"Who is Jim?"

"Jim?" Seila finally spoke, but her mouth felt like it was full of glue.

"You're recorded calling out to Jim? Who is Jim?"

Seila shook her head slowly, as if mesmerized, "I don't know. I don't know why I would have done that. I don't have any friends, just Charlie."

"But you were active in church. Are you going to tell me that you didn't have any friends in your congregation? Please answer carefully. We have conducted interviews with those you were in fellowship with."

"I don't have friends who I would want to know about this...I don't want people to know. You had no right to contact them."

"Everyone knows that you're here."

"Everyone?"

"It's all over the news."

"What's all over the news?"

Dr. Speers sighed as if weary, but Seila thought his weariness could just as easily be fake.

He said, "Let's don't play games, Mrs. Campbell. I can help you, but I can't if you won't let me. We can sit here as long as you want and waste my time and yours for as long as you have time to waste. Or, we can be honest with one another and make our visits productive ones. I've been straight with you. Now you be straight with me. And believe me, Mrs. Campbell, you need an advocate." He nodded toward the blank wall. "Out there, the media is calling for your execution."

Seila licked her papery lips, "That's a lie."

"I wish it weren't true, for your sake. The media wants you dead, Mrs. Campbell."

"But why? Sure, I tried to go north, but that's not a death sentence, is it?"

"Listen, Mrs. Campbell, I won't argue with you, and I'll do the best I can for you, with or without you, but it would be easier for both of us if you cooperated. I've heard that you have issues with authority, trust issues, and that you may be suffering from paranoia. You need to make an effort to put that aside. That only hurts you, Mrs. Campbell."

"TRUST ISSUES? Someone kills my husband, and you won't tell me anything. You take me to prison, shave my head, strip search me, you...you beat me, you torture me, and never even tell me what I'm supposed to have done to deserve your attention. Who am I supposed to trust?"

It was at that moment that one of the guards, Hal, opened the door, and with a warning glance at Seila, asked, "Everything all right in here?"

"Everything is fine."

Hal closed the door, and Dr. Speers shook his head. "I would hardly call it torture, Mrs. Campbell. In addition..."

"What do you call it?"

"In addition, it is extremely rare for an innocent person to be in prison. Maybe you are rare, but I can't know that unless you talk to me. Tell me what has happened to you. Tell me what you think this is all about."

With that, he sat back and waited again. After a few minutes of silence, he leaned forward, "Do you know anyone planning violence against the Covenant government?"

"No, I'm a simple housewife. I don't know about violence. And let me remind you. I am a CEO's wife, a CEO who headed up a multistate and multinational enterprise."

"Were. You were a CEO's wife. And we don't care who you were. Do you realize it's a crime to withhold information about planned violence or other illegal activities?"

"Yes, of course. But I don't know about any crimes or il-legal activities."

"Who is Jim?"

"I don't know anyone by that name." Seila's head itched and pain spread in her throat and behind her eyes. A tear slid down her cheek. She couldn't hide it, nor could she brush it away, shackled as she was.

Dr. Speers whispered, "Oh, Mrs. Campbell, if you would only let me help you." He stood and walked around the desk as he pulled a folded white handkerchief from his pocket. He knelt in front of her and dabbed at her cheek, which made her cry in earnest as much for her inability to trust his act of apparent kindness as it was for the pain of knowing that she was forced to allow him to wipe her wet face and running nose.

He held the handkerchief over her nose and said, "Here. Blow."

"Unlock me and let me do it for myself."

"Trust," he whispered, "Trust."

Behind clenched teeth, she said, "I can't."

He lightly touched the top of her head. "With or without you, Mrs. Campbell, I intend to help you. However, I think this is enough for today, so I'll leave you with a parting thought. I almost believe that you are innocent, that this is all a mistake, but I'll need your full cooperation to clear you."

And Seila wished that she could believe him.

After that, they kept her up all night, flashing strobe lights in her face until she vomited. She whispered, "Dear God. Protect me," and then she passed out.

When Seila regained consciousness, she was cold. She tried to remember the warm touch of the sun on her skin, and still her arms seemed sheathed in ice. "Heat, more heat," she whispered. That's when she remembered Florida of ten years ago, with soft sand beaches, green, translucent ocean, and a hot, salty wind.

She remembered the red brick building of the dental lab in Florida where she used to work as a teenager and remembered her cracked and bleeding hands as she hunched over a bench inside that building. She had stood next to that building when she was told that she wouldn't get a raise without submitting to the furtive, groping hands of an old man. And she remembered leaving many years ago. When she moved back to Florida five years ago to find Jim, she drove to the small town where she used to live, to the road where she used to work, to the red, brick building from which she drove away. That's when she clearly saw that the building was not brick. It was white stucco and had always been white stucco.

"You see," she said to no one in particular. "We can't even remember the actual facts of our existence." Perception fails, she thought. Memory fails. So how is it that my tormentors want me to tell them what I know? They want to know if I did or did not consort with known terrorists.

I can readily say that I did not. On pondering the matter further, however, I cannot say for certain that there weren't things about the people I've known that were hidden from my sight, inconceivable to me. But if any were terrorists, it was not known. In fact, I am sure that I have never known or met a terrorist, no matter what some might call Jim...oh, Jim, I hope you're okay, wherever you are.

Seila thought that Jim must have escaped or why would they be asking about Ruby?

Seila clung to that hope and the hope that Charlies' friends might still come to her rescue. If everyone on the outside knew that she was there, surely someone would come for her. She just had to survive a little while. And the longer she stalled on answering questions about Jim, the greater Jim's chances were for getting out of the Covenant States.

{5}

Bible Study

WHEN JANET ENTERED her first Bible study class with Dr. Speers, she saw Sister Mary blushing, the same girl Janet met on her first day in Wendell. Something about her troubled Janet but she couldn't figure out why, other than her age of course. She was a child in an adult Bible study.

Janet smiled and said, "So nice to see you in my class," but she did not and could not look towards Dr. Speers, even when she sat in a chair directly in front of him. As she sat, her navy-blue dress caught the edge of the seat, and she had to pull it free before sitting. She was still unused to dresses. They felt unnatural to her, but then, she couldn't remember the last time she felt natural. She felt like an ex-patriot in a foreign country, among but apart.

Sister Mary who sat to the side nearest the door said, "Good to see you here, too." She turned to Dr. Speers and said, "Janet is my new neighbor."

"Sister Janet."

"Yes, Sister Janet," Mary said and ducked her head.

Sister Emily, Aunt Peggy, Sister Sherry and Sister Sue Ann came into the class with a swish of long skirts, and a murmur of washed cleans. The fine, papery wrinkles of Sister Emily's face creased as she smiled, and Janet marveled at hearing that Sister Emily had a teenage daughter. She seemed so old, which could make a woman a suspect in the eyes of the Redeemers. The Covenant government warned the populace about elderly women, saying that they led the way in the dark years, presiding over the most licentious and immoral era since Sodom and Gomorrah. It was said that they went the Way of Eve and led their men to disaster, which the young people believed, and those who knew otherwise did their best to forget.

And then there was Sister Sue Ann Chambers who seemed to enjoy introducing herself as a "woman of faith." Janet already knew her since her husband was Willie Chambers, a friend of George's. Willie was a member of the original Covenant Coalition, and Janet thought that both Willie and Sue Ann were attractive and looked alike, but a little like pedigreed collies. They had long noses, long faces and serious brown eyes. Sister Sue Ann's hair was a silky brown which was always pulled back with neat bows, and Willie had a full head of trimmed, gray hair. Though they had a similar likeness, he was twenty years her senior as most men were to their wives.

When Janet first met her, Sister Sue Ann explained that she and Willie were blessed with five children thus far, all boys. The eldest was only ten and a long way yet from being conscripted for the Covenant wars. And Willie's child from his wife of the dark years had succumbed to the Wrath. "It was God's will," Sister Sue Ann said, and Janet would have liked to tell her that God had nothing to do with it. But these were not the days for truth.

Finally, there was Sister Sherry Hart, a mother of eight children, and hailed by the congregation for doing her duty and for a reputation as den mother for the town. Not all women could give birth, although they were all urged to do so. But something had been happening in the chemical makeup of human beings where sperm counts were low in men and many women were not fertile. Janet was certain that this had to do with the chemicals in their air, food and water, but this was not a safe topic for discussion. Only the Devil himself could be blamed. In Janet's case, she could become pregnant, so she kept a sizable stash of contraceptives in skeins of yarn and hoped that they would last her, and hoped that no one would find out. A simple blood test could reveal her secret. Consequently, she avoided doctors no matter how sick she got. So far.

Janet had been told that there were typically six women to each man leading small Bible study classes. In the old days, women led the classes, but now, each Bible study class must have male leadership.

Dr. Speers coughed slightly and said "Washed clean."

The class intoned, "By blood."

Dr. Speers nodded to Janet.

He said, "Before we get started, I see a new face in class. Sister Janet Moore, perhaps you could stand and say a few words to the class."

Janet stood and straightened her dress, pulling it away from the back of her legs. "My name is Janet Moore, and as you all know, my husband, George, and I recently moved to Wendell from Atlanta and are looking forward to being members of your church family. It's good to meet you all." She looked around at the other women as she sat down, again trying to tuck her dress neatly under her sweaty legs.

The women said, "Amen."

"Thank you, Sister Janet. We look forward to getting to know you as well. Let us bow our heads now and pray. We come here to praise you Father in the name of Jesus, to understand your Word, and to find out how to apply your Word to our daily lives, in our communities, in our families, and in our hearts. And be with us today as we welcome our newest member into our class. We pray that you show us the Way, that you show us how to be obedient and how to listen so that we hear you and follow you in perfect understanding. I ask these things in Jesus' name. Amen."

"Amen."

Dr. Speers shuffled his papers and looked around the room as if he was presiding over a funeral, and perhaps he was. "Our assignment for this week was to think of a time when we made a promise to God that we found difficult to keep. Since this is your first day, Sister Janet, you won't have to speak. Sister Mary, why don't you begin? And remember, God wants personal, feeling stories."

Sister Mary hesitated before she spoke, then pulled her thick hair away from her face, took a deep breath and began. "I want to talk about Henry." Sister Mary turned to Janet and said, "Henry is...was my brother who passed away from the cancer." She turned back to Dr. Speers. "When Henry was dying, he was in so much pain, and morphine couldn't be given." Sister Mary looked up and quickly added, "I know that's right. Morphine opens the way to the Devil. I didn't mean to sound like it should be given. I just mean that he was in so much pain. If you could have seen him."

"Go on, Sister Mary. What happened?"

"First, I prayed for God to save him, but then Sister Sue Ann helped me to see that I was being selfish. So, I prayed that God would take away Henry's pain, and I promised that if God took away his pain, then I would dedicate my life to Jesus and live my life the way Jesus would want me to. Henry died that night, so I knew God answered my prayers."

"And did you keep your promise, Sister Mary?"

Sister Mary nodded but did not look up. "I'm trying."

"And what about your mother, Sister Mary? Shouldn't you have freely let your mother go after she was redeemed and relocated to live a godly life? I'm not sure if you've completely let her go. Aunt Peggy saw you wearing one of her dresses."

Aunt Peggy burst out, "That's right, child! I've seen you wearing that dress! That pretty peach one?!" When Aunt

Peggy opened her mouth, Janet cringed as she saw a bit of glistening saliva loop over Peggy's desk.

Sister Mary looked up quickly, "I keep them to remember her by, and the dress smells like Mama. When I...I keep it to remember her, when I miss her. It's okay to keep something of Mama's, isn't it, even though she was redeemed and sent away?"

Janet wanted to say, "Of course it is," but held back.

Dr. Speers said, "It's not unusual to keep something of our loved ones, but your mother was a special case and I'm not sure if you're keeping your promise to let her go. Perhaps on your wedding day, you'll want to let your mother go. And then it might be a nice gesture to Jesus to burn that dress, too, as a symbol of your commitment to Jesus and to your husband, for doesn't it say that those who marry shall leave their home and cleave to their husband and the two become one?"

Sister Mary nodded and blushed but did not look up from the top of her desk.

"Now, Aunt Peggy, what promise have you made?"

"I promised to be a good Christian woman and to always keep God's word, and I have done it." Aunt Peggy looked defiantly around at the others.

Dr. Speers said, "I think every woman in this room has promised to be a good Christian woman, Aunt Peggy, but as Jesus says, his yoke is light. I think what this assignment asks for is a personal story about a promise you made that was difficult to keep?"

"Well, everybody here knows what that is. I promised to accept God's plan that I be barren, without children. It's been hard. You all know how hard it's been for me, but I have accepted it."

"Yes, it's a terrible shame that you cannot fulfill a woman's role, but I think you might try a little harder to be grateful for what God has given you."

"I am grateful. I'm grateful that God has plans for me. Of course, I don't know what they are, but I'm grateful. There's no one in Wendell more grateful than myself. Grateful! For heaven's sake! Who could question it? God commands and I obey, and I don't ask questions because of what the Bible says about questions. Anyone would be a fool not to listen to the Good Book because if they questioned God and were wrong, well, they'd go straight to hell, so why anyone would take that chance, I don't know. Oh, I'm grateful. You bet I am. And I'll be grateful sitting right there in the bosom of my Lord because blessed are the women who are barren, too."

"That's in the old Bible, Aunt Peggy. You would do well to forget it."

"It is? Well, my memory's not so good any more. Not that I'm getting old, mind you. I just forget things now and then, because God blessed me with a mind that forgets. He surely did, and I am grateful for that, too! No one could ever accuse me of being a woman too smart for her own good. Not Peggy Mackenzie."

Dr. Speers smiled and the women smiled, too. "Very good, Aunt Peggy, and now how about you, Sister Emily?"

Sister Emily looked at Aunt Peggy with a look of genuine sympathy. "Bless your heart, Aunt Peggy. Bless your heart. We've all had such hard times, haven't we, Dr. Speers?"

"To whom much is given, much is required."

"Yes, that's right. We've been given so much."

Dr. Speers spoke gently. "Your promise, Sister Emily, from the heart now?"

Sister Emily lifted her head, which quivered as if she had palsy. "I wanted a girl so badly. The Lord blessed me with strong boys, but I didn't have a girl. A mother wants a little girl, doesn't she? So, I promised God that I would work extra hard to raise my boys as good Christian boys. I promised that whatever God asked of me in regards to those boys, I would do it, and then the Lord gave me Connie, and I was so happy that the Lord answered my prayers. But it's been hard, Dr. Speers, to let go of my boys. I didn't know it would be so hard. I didn't know what God would ask of them." And then Sister Emily wiped her eyes and her forehead with her handkerchief.

"They were fine boys, Sister Emily. They were heroes in the wars against Satan, and you know they're with God now."

Sister Emily nodded her head and tried to smile.

"Very good, Sister Emily. Now Sister Sue Ann. What promise did you make?"

When Sister Sue Ann began speaking, she seemed sure of herself and her place in the world. Under the desk, her feet were tucked neatly to the side and her shiny black shoes were the most pointed-toed shoes Janet had ever seen, but the heel was flat as was required these days. As usual, her hair was pulled neatly back with a white bow, a pony tail curving onto the back of her neck. As she spoke, her sleek pony tail shimmered under the fluorescent lights, while her smooth hands rested easily on the laminated desk top, one on top of the other, contained.

"I promised the Lord I'd do all I could for God's government even if it meant giving up my best friend. I didn't know when I said it that God would call me on it, but when I found out that Tammy was harboring an Anti-Christ Subversive, I thought, this is it. This is what God is asking you to do. Now what are you going to do about it?" Sister Sue Ann looked around the circle of women with wide eyes as if still surprised. "Me and my best friend, Tammy, had known each other since we were two-years old, two! And I would never have dreamed that she would do such a thing, even if it was her brother. But God said that Tammy had broken His laws, and I had no choice.

I prayed all night. I begged Jesus to help me, to intercede. You all know this. I've shared this with you before. You all know that just like His dark hour in the garden when Jesus asked God to take away this cup, I asked, too. But in the morning, I knew that God couldn't take that cup from me anymore than he could take it from his only Son. I called the

Redeemers and then went upstairs and knelt on the floor and prayed while they came and got her. The Devil is wily. I'll tell you right now that the Devil is wily. To the very last minute, he tempted me to go next door and tell her that the Redeemers were coming. But I didn't do it. I didn't give in. It was the hardest thing I've ever done, but I'll tell you the truth. The Lord gave me the strength to keep my promise, and I've been stronger in the Lord since that day." Sister Sue Ann nodded and Aunt Peggy said, "Amen."

"That doesn't mean I have it all resolved in my heart." Sister Sue Ann smiled humbly at the class. "I still haven't forgiven Tammy for putting me through that, but as I mature in my faith, Jesus is helping me to forgive."

As Janet listened to Sister Sue Ann, her heart was a heavy rock in her chest. She thought, 'There are always traitors. Nice of them to announce themselves though.' Still, as much as Janet would have loved to punch Sue Ann, she must be calm. The time for fighting has passed. For now. Now is the time to hide.

The class ended before Sister Sherry Hart could tell what she had sacrificed, but everyone could guess it was her worn out body and a quiet moment, if they were being honest.

Janet noticed that Sister Mary's eyes had tears in them as she was leaving the class, so Janet quickly squeezed Sister Mary's hand and whispered, "I think it's okay to keep your mother's dress." Then Janet hurried away.

~

After the class, Janet joined George and the others in the fellowship hall for the morning service. During the service, Janet saw Sister Mary turn her head to look at the new man, Sonny, whose starched white shirt was stretched across straight, broad shoulders.

Each time that Sister Mary looked Sonny's way, it seemed that Dr. Speers turned his head to watch Sister Mary, which made Janet uncomfortable. Far too many girls and young women were accused of going the Way of Eve and turned over to the Redeemers because of the avaricious desires of older men, and their jealousies. And far too many young men were being sent to their deaths in the border wars of the Covenant States in order to remove the competition.

After the church service, Janet was to attend the knitting circle run by each class, an activity designed to bring the women closer in fellowship and work. They called their work, "knitting souls for Christ."

It was George's idea that Janet join. He'd been reading his news on his cellphone from his brown leather recliner earlier in the week, and from time to time his watery, gray-green eyes peered over the top of his reading glasses to look at Janet who sat on the sofa knitting a baby blue blanket. She tugged the yarn from a skein that rested beside her leg.

When George turned back to his cellphone, a small envelope of birth control pills spilled from inside her new skein of yarn. She quickly slipped it into her sweater pocket and resumed knitting the blanket.

The house was silent except for the hum of electricity that ran as a steady heartbeat through the homes of everyone of means and influence.

George cleared his throat. "Do you know how beautiful you are?"

Janet was startled and her face colored as she wondered how long he'd been watching her. "Don't say that. You'll make me vain."

"You are the picture of domestic bliss, knitting that blanket. Who is this one for?"

Janet studied George's face for signs that he had seen her pills.

"It's, it's…I think Sister Sherry Hart might be expecting again. If not, this will be a donation for the penitents."

"That's very charitable of you, Janet. However, the penitents have received God's wrath for a reason. I hope you don't get too caught up with them. Too many people have gone down that road and become corrupted by misplaced sympathies."

Of course he hadn't seen her get the contraceptives. She knew George. He wasn't sly. If he had seen her, he'd be all over her right now.

"Don't worry about me, George. It's a harmless diversion and practical, too. If we placate the poor and the penitents, maybe they won't kill us. Remember Marie Antoinette."

George chortled, "I think our Redeemers have things pretty well under control, Janet. We have technologies and advantages that Marie Antoinette didn't have."

"You're right, of course. You're the smart one of this pair." Janet smiled through her clenched teeth, stopped knitting, and gripped the knitting needles in tight fists. And she hummed a tune inside her head, 'I got the joy, joy, joy, joy down in my heart.'

George turned back to his cellphone. "You know, Janet. You should think about joining the Wendell knitting circle. They're knitting socks for our soldiers. There's a worthy cause."

Consequently, when Bible study class ended, she left the room to speak with George a moment before attending the knitting circle. This is when a curious thing happened. She took a wrong turn down a church corridor, which was virtually empty. She walked until she heard Dr. Speers in one of the offices talking to someone, saying, "The things that go on at Wendell, the things we have to do for the Covenant are to stay at Wendell. We don't talk about it outside of work, and we certainly don't talk about it at worship services."

Janet stopped and held her breath, listening. She was caught fast between fight or flight, rooted to the spot. She knew she should walk away quickly, but she held fast, choosing a split second of courage that she knew could spiral her downward into a dark plunge. But she had to know more.

"When do we talk about it?"

"Is something troubling you?"

"Inmate # 40072223. Have you seen the prescreen assessment?"

Dr. Speers' sounded annoyed when he said, "Of course."

"She doesn't fit the type for terrorist activity, and she doesn't appear to know anything. What purpose do we have to continue with an interrogation of this woman?"

"Do you accept my authority, Officer Valdez?"

"Yes, sir."

"She's an enemy of the state. The rest is classified. That's all you need to know. Now your job is to follow orders, and if you can't do that, I know there's a soldier in God's Fighting Battalions who would like to switch places with you."

The man spoke low so Janet could not hear his response. She backed down the hall and hurried away, but she turned one last time before exiting the corridor and saw them entering the hallway. Dr. Speers' and Sonny's eyes caught hers before she rounded the turn, and she could almost hear Aunt Peggy saying, "curiosity killed the cat."

She entered the room with the knitting circle, breathless and frightened, while the women welcomed and hugged her, swathing her in their sweet and cloying cologne.

Aunt Peggy stepped back and clapped her hands. "Isn't this wonderful? In the old days, I thought we had lost our sense of community forever, and look at us now."

"Praise Jesus."

As they sat and pulled forth their multi-colored yarn from soft bags, Dr. Speers walked by the classroom and looked in. By this time, Janet had regained her calm and was able to smile and nod, almost naturally as if nothing had occurred at all.

She took a deep breath and fumbled with her yarn.

They had hardly begun knitting when Aunt Peggy got up, peeked out the door, and returned to her seat, glancing sideways at the others with a self-satisfied smile on her sharp impish face. She asked, "So did you all know that Sister Mary had a date last week?"

"Aunt Peggy!" Sister Mary's face reddened.

"It's true. Guess who's come a-courting?'"

Sister Sue Ann said, "Oh, I knew it all along. Pastor Wayne suggested it."

"Who is it?" Janet asked.

"Dr. Speers, of course, the most eligible bachelor in Wendell."

Janet glanced quickly at Sister Mary with alarm, and noticed that as she worked, her fingers trembled and she dropped a stitch.

"Of course, she didn't follow my advice. I told her not to appear too eager. She should have kept him waiting when he got to the door, but did that child listen? The poor thing was ready as soon as he got there."

"Dr. Speers wants me to call him Mark," said a wide-eyed Sister Mary.

"Well, isn't that his name?" Sister Sue Ann asked.

"It doesn't feel right. He feels like a father to me."

"You'll get used to it. Deep down they're all just boys," Sister Sue Ann laughed.

Sister Emily looked around at the other women and spoke gently, tentatively, "Don't you all think Dr. Speers may be a little too mature for Sister Mary?"

Aunt Peggy screwed up her face in disapproval at Sister Emily, "The older men make mature husbands. Isn't that right, Sister Sue?"

"Yes, they do. Look at me and Willie."

Janet tried to speak gently, too, "It's kind of different, isn't it? You and I are older than Sister Mary. She's still very young."

Sister Sue Ann frowned in disapproval and said, "It's not right to discourage her, Sister Janet. She's of age." Then she turned to Sister Mary, smiled and exposed perfect pearl white teeth. "So where did Dr. Speers take you, Sister Mary?"

Sister Mary darted a look at Janet. Janet wondered, 'Was it gratitude? Was it fear for me? For herself?'

Sister Mary said, "He took me to his house for dinner."

"And was his father there?"

"Yes, but he was ill and stayed in the backroom behind the kitchen. I never saw him. Do you think that's okay?"

"Well, with anyone else, you would have had cause for worry. I suppose it was okay with Dr. Speers. I don't believe I've ever met a more honorable man."

"Do you remember when he first came to town? He was straight as a stick, and we were so suspicious of him. We thought he was a Yankee." Aunt Peggy laughed. "Remember that, Sister Sue Ann? You're the one who found out he was from Alabama."

"I don't think anyone believed it until he married the warden's sister seven years ago and Pastor Wayne said, 'Oh,

Dr. Speers is okay. It just takes a while to get to know him.' Pastor Wayne was right about that."

Aunt Peggy exchanged a knowing glance with Sister Sue Ann. "People can't be wrong all the time, can they Sister Sue? And isn't Dr. Speers thoughtful? A beautiful, beautiful man. I don't think anyone can remember a time when he wasn't dropping off groceries for someone in need or giving someone a lift in his car, or praying with them over the loss of someone dear. He earned our respect. He purely did."

Sister Sue Ann furrowed her brow. "I do feel sorry for the poor man though." She turned towards Janet and held her knitting to her lap. "Dr. Speers lost poor sweet Dehlia one year from the day of their marriage."

"Remember how shy Dehlia was?" Aunt Peggy asked. "She stuck to Dr. Speers side whenever they were together and didn't look up."

"It was kind of strange," Sister Sue Ann said, "But men do like modest women."

"What did she die of?" Janet asked.

Sister Sue Ann's forehead furrowed. "I don't know if anyone ever said for sure, but I think it was generally believed to have been the Wrath. I heard that there was nothing anyone could do for her."

"They say that's why he doesn't smile much." Aunt Peggy said.

Sister Sue Ann resumed knitting, "Don't exaggerate, Aunt Peggy. He seldom smiled before that either, but he's a good listener."

An unsettling sensation flitted across Janet's mind, or just an image of Dr. Speers tilting his stiff and formal body forward, much too close to her. Listening. A premonition?

"What did you think of his house, child?" Aunt Peggy asked.

Janet had already heard that Dr. Speers' house was seized from a couple of "Sodomites." Willie Chambers had laughed when he told George and Janet about it, saying, "the only furniture that Dr. Speers replaced was the bed, and I believe he burned that old bed."

All the men got an uproarious good laugh about it, while Janet looked away and pretended that she didn't know what they meant.

Sister Mary stopped knitting and said, "Dr. Speers has a study full of books, stacks and stacks of them."

"I didn't know anyone still read books," Aunt Peggy said.

"He said they came with the house, and most of them were illegal. But he was cleared for them for his job, so that he could understand the enemy."

Janet thought about the books that house must contain. She missed her books, and then gave herself a shake. She bent her head as if to concentrate on the yarn looping over the knitting needles. Her fingers practically flew as she turned yarn into even gray rows, and she was not spurred by fears of supernatural devils but by human devils who are homegrown.

{6}

Secrets

WHILE THE PEOPLE of Wendell worshipped together, Seila huddled in the cold cell. Her back hurt from gripping her knees and her jaw hurt from grinding her teeth. Seila tried to keep moving to stay warm and to keep the cockroaches from settling on her. Her cell was filthy with mold, stains, and a clogged commode. She choked on the stench and recoiled in horror when she felt something crawl on her. At times she imagined papery legs and wings scuttling across her braced arms, brushing, whirring, tickling her goose bumped flesh. So, she moved. She braced. She locked her arms; she rubbed up and down, from bicep to elbow and elbow to bicep. She prayed, but the words that dumped into the frigid air seemed mechanical words, devoid of spirit. I'm too tired, she thought, dear God end this. End me. Fatigue ran its clammy hands down her neck and spine. It covered her face with a veil. It thickened her tongue until her own voice sounded coarse and unreal.

It was surreally quiet, and in the wall above the cell's metal door, cameras watched unceasing in their housings.

Where was everybody? She was told that Wendell was over-crowded with women.

The silence unnerved her and she ached for Charlie. Her mind was on a continuous loop, going over again and again what happened when she found a note in her mailbox that said Charlie was dead, and she needed to get somewhere safe. She thought it must be a mistake.

She called the Redeemers for Christ headquarters begging for information about her missing husband. She even went in person to the imposing white building where a sculpture of a man's arm, a fist, and sword towered over the lobby with the caption, "Mark 10:34 Do not suppose that I have come to bring peace to the earth. I did not come to bring peace, but a sword."

Seila approached one of the women behind the glass windows in Redeemer headquarters, but a guard screamed at her, "DO NOT approach the desk until your number is called!"

That's when she saw the sign and the kiosk where she was to take a number. She had to select a category on the screen first, but nothing seemed to fit...General Information, Report a Crime, Report to Debt Relief, Visitation... Seila finally selected Report a Crime and took a number. Forty-seven.

She sat for two hours on a hard, gray plastic chair with a somber group of people who dared not speak. The sign warned them against eating or drinking in the waiting room, but Seila saw a woman sip through a straw tucked out of the top of her jacket. Seila wouldn't have dared, but Jim would have. The chairs faced the wall in front of a plaque with large black letters, "Redeemers for Christ. Covenant Peace is Now!

They appeared to be calling the numbers out-of-order, and Seila wondered if she had already been called and had somehow misunderstood. She finally resolved to approach the guard. She pulled her hair from her wet face, "Please, I've done nothing wrong. I'm a Christian woman. I just want to find out if it's true, something happened to my husband."

"You're hostile."

"I'm not. Really, I'm not. Please. Can you find out what happened to my husband? I got a note that said..."

"Who sent you the note?"

"I don't know."

"Let me have the note."

Seila took a step backward. "I don't know where it is now. I was upset. I might have thrown it."

"Get in your seat, Ma'am, and wait your turn like everyone else."

The guard looked past her to the others who crowded the lobby with worried faces, and the next number was called. "Sixty-three."

"This is all a misunderstanding."

"You'll force us to arrest you if you do not SIT DOWN."

Seila smiled a tremulous smile. "I'm sorry. Of course, you're right. I'm sorry. Am I cooperating now? Is this good?"

A woman called from the window, "Fifteen."

Headquarters closed to the public before Seila's number could be called, and she and the others were told to return the next day to begin the process anew.

She went home, worried and exhausted, and fell onto the pale silk sheets of her empty bed. She could not forget the sign at Redeemers for Christ headquarters. "Do not suppose that I have come to bring peace to the earth. I did not come to bring peace, but a sword."

That was the night that the Redeemers first came for her and then released her, and before she tried to run.

~

Alone in her cell now, except for the scrutiny of the cameras, Seila clutched at disjointed memories, examining them one at a time and dozed off. She dreamed of Charlie rescuing her, but the fantasy turned dark in her sleep as Charlie kissed her. She looked up at his amber-colored eyes after the kiss, and saw his eyes turn black and his face twist into something loathsome. Then she knew he wasn't the real Charlie. He was someone masquerading as Charlie, and he was evil. Seila woke up terrified, listening for the sounds of someone coming down the corridor, but only heard the thud, thud, thud of blood pulsing in her ears.

A loudspeaker shattered the silence, a passage from Mark, "For I have come to turn a man against his father, a daughter against her mother, a daughter-in-law against her mother-in-law, a man's enemies will be the members of his own household. Anyone who loves his father or mother more than me is not worthy of me; anyone who loves his son or daughter more than me is not worthy of me."

Seila's thoughts turned to Jim. She remembered telling Jim, "It isn't pretty, but Jim, we're smart. No matter what. We will change this system from within. It will be slow but it'll happen. Just lay low. No more rainbow flags or belts. You have to tone it down. Don't be...you."

Seila thought she heard Jim speak as clear as a bell in her cell, just like she did that day long ago, "Hah!"

Seila looked wildly around her cell. "Jim?" Nothing but silence and the steady hum of lights answered her.

Seila remembered the night Jim showed up at her house after Jim ran away from the Redeemers and their "cure" for lesbians, which they called abomination. Jim had scaled Charlie and Seila's subdivision wall. She crawled in the basement window while they were hosting an employee party above. If she had been caught, the Redeemers might have picked up all three of them.

Seila found Jim laying on an old plaid couch in the basement when she went to get some supplies. Jim was wet and shivering. "Jim, what's happened?"

"The Redeemers happened. What do you think?"

Then Seila saw that Jim was not just wet with water, but also with blood. "You're hurt!"

"It's not my blood."

And that set Seila back on her heels, but she was afraid to know more. She said, "Charlie has work friends upstairs. They can't be trusted."

"I know. I won't be here long, just a night."

Seila felt Jim's forehead and whispered tightly, "You're sick. You need to stay here. Not just a night. We can hide you."

Jim's voice was weak and she flopped out her hand wearily. She said, "You better get upstairs."

Seila went up and found her jewelry box and scooped it all out, 18 karat bangles and necklaces, sapphire rings, and her favorite tanzanite. She took all of the cash from her purse. She tucked the jewelry and cash into a felt cloth bag and carried them downstairs along with a bottle of water and a change of clothes. It seemed that Jim was asleep, so she put the bag into Jim's sleeping hands and pulled a blanket over her. She was scared but Jim was her sister, and she was in trouble.

She whispered, "Don't go, Jim. But if you do go, take the jewelry and the cash. Get safe."

In the morning, Seila went down and found Jim gone and the tanzanite ring on the table with a note that simply said, "Florida." She tore the note into bits and flushed it, and she burned with shame and anger and fear. She should have stayed with Jim and kept her from leaving.

The Redeemers came by her house a few days later, asking questions about Ruby who the Redeemers did not know by the family nickname of Jim. Did they know where Ruby was? Had they seen her? Did they know she had killed a man? The only thing that saved them was Charlie's position in the corporation, but it terrified and haunted Seila. Jim would never kill anyone. Would she?

Seila and Charlie moved to Florida after that, checking out some of the places they used to go near Jacksonville, trying to find her. Charlie had been so patient. Seila didn't think many husbands would move house and risk everything to find her sister, a fugitive and enemy of the Covenant States.

Not long after they moved to Jacksonville, the Redeemers informed Seila that Ruby was dead. Seila grieved and wrestled with guilt and self-loathing. For years! But Jim turned out to be alive and came to her after Charlie was killed. And she's alive now if she got away.

Seila looked frantically at the cameras. Had they heard? Was she speaking out loud? She lay down on her hard pallet with her hand over her mouth. I'll keep Jim's secret. I won't tell them where I last saw her.

'A little while,' she thought. 'I only have to survive a little while.'

∽

When Seila met with Dr. Speers again, he had a thick file with her name on it.

He said, "We have quite a history here. Your associates have been sloppy."

"What associates?"

"Please, Mrs. Campbell."

"You mean my husband, Charlie?"

Dr. Speers looked intently at her with those awful gray eyes.

She said, "Charlie was not an associate as you call it. He was a respected man and just the kindest man I ever knew."

Seila had met Charlie after the Covenant States were formed. Each state held a vote for their state religion, and Georgia chose New Millennial. Afterwards, all Georgians were required to convert. Seila and Charlie had been raised Catholic, and they attended the same conversion orientation. When the conversion facilitator referred to Catholicism as a cult, Charlie and Seila exchanged an amused smile. Charlie wore a starched white shirt and burgundy silk tie with dress pants, and his dark hair and amber eyes, like honey, mesmerized her. When he bent near her, she smelled a pleasant fragrance of men's cologne. She joined him for coffee after the orientation and felt something familiar and comforting in his presence. More importantly, she discovered over time that he shared her sentiments that it was best to go along with the new government while trying to make small changes from within.

Together, they converted and soon married amidst the turmoil of the new government. She knew she couldn't control what was happening outside her home where people were rounded up by Redeemers, and her own sister might be captured in their dragnet. At first, she watched the news daily, hoping that she wouldn't see Jim on television. But the news threw her into uncontrollable shakes and she felt so cold that she stopped listening.

Slowly, she became enveloped in the safe cocoon of Charlie's world, but she could never shake the feeling that by going along, they were also complicit.

Now, in the quiet of Dr. Speers' office, the metronome ticked louder. It was the first time she really noticed it, TICK TICK TICK TICK. She didn't know why she didn't notice it before. She was just so tired. She said, "I need some sleep. If I could sleep, I could think. I could remember. What time is it anyway? It must be the middle of the night."

"Forget about time. When we have the information that we need, we can let you sleep. Until then, there is nothing I can do."

"I just want to know if it's day or night."

"It's not important."

"How can you do this? You're supposed to protect women."

"That's what I'm trying to do," he spoke insistently, urgently. "I'm not out to get you. I don't like having to do this, but it's God's work to save your soul and that's what I mean to do." After a pause, he asked, "Mrs. Campbell. Who is Jim?"

"I don't know anyone by that name?" She cast around in her mind for quickly evaporating trains of thought that vanished like soap bubbles. Finally, she said, "I remember a time when we sat on porches sipping coffee or tea and talked about books and ideas, our families, philosophies, science, discoveries. What did your people do to us? You inserted terror into our lives. People don't talk now.

They sip your bitter coffee and don't talk. It's not even real coffee anymore, is it?"

"All those ideas are what brought you terror. They belong to Satan, Mrs. Campbell. You should have stayed in your lane, taking care of your home, having children, reading your Bible."

"Charlie was sterile."

"It won't work, Mrs. Campbell."

"What won't work?"

"You/re changing the subject. I asked you who Jim is."

"I don't know anyone by that name?"

His eyes narrowed and he asked, "Are you aware that they've brought back execution by burning for women found to be in league with the Devil?"

Seila paled and asked, "What can you possibly mean?"

"I want to save you from that. Who is Jim?"

"I don't know."

"I'm calling the guard now, and he's going to put you into The Tomb. Would you like to change your mind?"

"I don't know anyone by that name."

Seila was hustled down corridors into more corridors. There were moments where her feet barely touched the floor, as they lifted her by the arms, squeezing them so tight she gasped.

Seila was thrown into blackness. It was so dark that she could not see her hand in front of her face. She hugged her knees and was haunted by Dr. Speer's threat about fire.

Surely, they don't do that; but inside her, it felt like her blood froze. Anything was possible.

After days or weeks in the dark, she doubted her existence, and then her brain seemed to stop. Suddenly, she couldn't think a single word, and her terror grew as she touched for the first time that existential emptiness that cannot be grasped by thought. She felt she needed something solid, something real, so she threw herself at the cell door, leaned on it and pounded her head on the door until she could think again. In doing so, she was dimly aware that she missed a chance to sense the sacred, to feel blessed detachment, to escape the confines of her fleshly body and the lonely travail of her anxious mind.

Sometimes she thought she was in prison because it was one of God's lessons, because Seila was one who sought a reason for things. Sometimes she sewed cause and effect together, whether the fabric matched or not.

Not like Jim, Seila thought. Jim didn't believe in reasons or free will. She would say. "Biology and social conditioning, not free will. Free will is an oxymoron, and stop looking for magical reasons for the world sucking. It sucks because people made it so."

Seila thought that it was biology that got Jim in the end, and Karen Seawell. Seila remembered Jim showing Seila a photo of her and Karen holding hands, and Seila was worried. What would it mean for Jim's future?

Seila could still see Karen tossing back her thick, black hair and folding her arms against the taunts that came.

"Dyke! You're going to hell, dyke," and then Jim punched one of the teenage boys who tormented Karen, and they knocked Jim flat on the ground. Jim said she regained consciousness in the principal's office with the school nurse bending over her and Jim kissed the nurse on the lips as a joke. She was suspended for fighting on school property and lewdness. And that was before the Redeemers gained control.

One night, when Seila and Jim lay side by side in the dark, resting on soft pillows and talking before sleep. Jim told Seila that she and Karen were going to get married someday.

Seila said, "They are making marriage illegal for you, Jim."

Jim didn't speak for so long that Seila thought she had fallen asleep, but then Jim asked, "Do you believe I'm going to hell, too?"

"No, you're not going to hell."

Then Jim seemed to fall asleep for real, and Seila turned on her side and slept.

In her cell in Wendell, sometimes Seila slept and sometimes she couldn't tell if she were awake or asleep. One time, a wild-eyed lunatic came to her and squeezed her in an inescapable embrace, coiled tight around her as he said, "You have the Jesus fire in you." Then he vanished and she knew she was hallucinating. Seila felt her way to the cell door and screamed over and over, "LET ME OUT!"

She thought she heard Dr. Speers say, "You know what you need to do," and Seila fell to the floor, huddled in the dark corner of her mind, cut loose from certain moorings, from the familiar, from the sanctuary of her beliefs, where any touch, ANY TOUCH from enemy or friend was welcome.

That's when Dr. Speers' disembodied voice began visiting her down in The Tomb, speaking softly through an intercom system. Seila looked forward to his talks, which always began with a prayer. And then the day came when Dr. Speers said, "You know that sometimes we redeem women and release them. I have permission to do that. Together, we can get you out of here, but I need you to take this pill for me."

Someone slid a tray through the door slot with a cup of water, and her trembling fingers fumbled with the pill as she lifted it to her lips, spilling the water over her chin as she drank.

"Is it done?"

"Yes," Seila rasped.

In a little while, Seila's teeth were on edge. She vibrated, the walls vibrated, and she thought she was in a coffin and couldn't get out. Soon she was blinded by a light so intense that she was in pain. She screamed, unable to understand that it was merely the cell door that was open, letting light pour in from the corridor. Guards grabbed her, thrust her in a cold shower, and left her shivering in the black vinyl chair in Dr. Speers' office.

She noticed something behind her chair and she jumped. Dr. Speers said right next to her left ear, "What's wrrooonnngg?"

"Who are you?'"

"It's Dr. Speers."

Then he was at his desk again and seemed so far away, it was as if Seila saw him at the end of a long tunnel. A few minutes later he was so close that she could read the map of his pores. "Ruby was your sister."

Seila nodded.

"You loved her very much, didn't you?"

Seila shivered and ground her teeth. Suddenly Dr. Speers shifted before her eyes, and he looked like Satan himself. His eyes seemed dark and menacing and was he leering? This was all wrong. "Get away from me."

"What's wrong, Mrs. Campbell."

"Drugged."

"Yes, you took the pill yourself. Remember."

Seila found her voice and yelled, "GET AWAY FROM ME!"

"Okay, Mrs. Campbell, I'll have the guard take you back to The Tomb." Dr. Speers rose, smoothing his dark jacket.

"NO....no...no." Seila shook her head, and she felt that her head swung way over to one side of the room and way back to the other. Her head felt huge, as big as the room.

Dr. Speers shrunk into himself again and was no longer Satan.

"When did you last see Ruby?"

And Seila remembered what she was supposed to say. "Five years ago." Seila held up her hand and examined her fingers. She could see the veins throbbing under her skin and scabs on her knuckles. Her hands were ugly.

"What happened five years ago?"

"Jim was in the basement."

"Who is Jim?"

"Ruby is Jim."

"Ruby is a man?"

Hot fear spread through Seila slowly, and her teeth chattered.

"Of course, we know that Ruby is not male because she was sent for the Cure, wasn't she? What does God say about lying?"

"Thou shalt not lie."

"And yet you lied to me, didn't you? You said you didn't know anyone named Jim, and when I asked if your sister was a homosexual, you said she was not."

Seila's body shook violently.

"God sends liars to hell, doesn't He?"

"I'm saved."

Dr. Speers appeared contemptuous, "No, you could not be a member of God's church. You must be lying about that, too."

"No." She shook her head in terror.

"I repeat. God sends liars to hell. Why did you lie about your sister?"

"Because she is my sister."

Dr. Speers recited from Mark, "Anyone who loves his father or mother more than me is not worthy of me; anyone who loves his son or daughter more than me is not worthy of me."

He said, "That applies to sisters, too. Your sister joined Satan's army a long time ago, and yet you still protect her? Do you love God, Seila?"

Seila didn't answer.

"I ASKED IF YOU LOVE GOD?!"

"Yes."

"Well, God is here in the room with you, and He knows about every lie you tell. Is your sister a homosexual?"

"Y-y-yes."

"Who is Jim?"

"Rub...ee...nick...name."

"Is Ruby still alive?"

Seila was freezing and thought she felt the earth slide away under her feet. She swung her head from side to side.

"Then why were you protecting her?" Dr. Speers came over, crouched down in front of Seila, and yelled, "WHY?"

Seila jumped, and her eyes rolled wildly around the room.

"And why do you speak of her in the present tense."

When Seila spoke, it was the grunt of an animal, "I....c-c-c-can't....h-h-h-help...mmm m-me..."

"IS YOU SISTER ALIVE?"

"I c c c can't......t t talk."

"Why can't you?"

"D d d dying."

"You're not dying."

"D d d dying."

"You are not dying."

Seila looked at him and shook. She couldn't breathe, and she made loud guttural sounds. She had lost her capacity for speech.

Dr. Speers called the guards and a nurse to administer a sedative. It took two guards to hold her down while she bellowed. Then they dragged her to the Tomb and left her with the tremors.

At irregular intervals, Dr. Speers voice was piped over the speaker, "You have power over your body, but the Lord Jesus has power over your soul.

{7}

Jephthah's Daughter

THE FOLLOWING WEEK, after Dr. Speers finished the opening prayer for the Bible study class, he asked about the week's lesson. "Have we all read Jephthah's vow? Would anyone like to venture the meaning behind this story?"

At first the women didn't speak, and the room hung suspended in a long silence. Janet focused on Dr. Speers' pink-striped bow tie or the speck of paper on his charcoal-gray sleeve but didn't look into his eyes. Or, she looked at his lower jaw and thought his skin looked a little gray. Maybe he would die soon. A faint hope.

Finally, Sister Mary said, "Sacrifice."

"And?"

Sister Emily shuddered. "It's just hideous isn't it, that poor child burnt for a sacrifice?"

"It had a purpose," Aunt Peggy snapped. "That child set an example."

Sister Emily shook her head, sadly, "But that poor child. What she must have felt when her own father set her on fire!"

"Well, I'm sure he killed her some other way first so it wouldn't hurt so bad."

Dr. Speers fixed his eyes on Emily. "Sister Emily. I think you're missing the point of this lesson. Do you know why Jephthah offered his daughter as a burnt offering?"

"He was keeping his promise to God," Sister Emily said.

"That's right. We've all heard, 'be careful what you wish for.' Jephthah teaches us to be careful what we promise."

"That poor, poor child." Sister Emily said.

"Sister Janet, would you please read Judges 11: 30-39?"

Janet pulled the book to her slowly. Her mouth felt dry, but she swallowed and read the passage.

And Jephthah made a vow to the LORD: "If you give the Ammonites into my hands, whatever comes out of the door of my house to meet me when I return in triumph from the Ammonites will be the LORD's, and I will sacrifice it as a burnt offering." Then Jephthah went over to fight the Ammonites, and the LORD gave them into his hands. He devastated twenty towns from Aroer to the vicinity of Minnith, as far as Abel Keramim. Thus Israel subdued Ammon.

When Jephthah returned to his home in Mizpah, who should come out to meet him but his daughter, dancing to the sound of tambourines! She was an only child. Except for her he had neither son nor daughter. When he saw her, he tore his clothes and cried, "Oh! My daughter! You have made me miserable and wretched, because I have made a vow to the LORD that I cannot break."

"My father," she replied, "you have given your word to the LORD. Do to me just as you promised, now that the LORD has avenged you of your enemies, the Ammonites. But grant me this one request," she said. "Give me two months to roam the hills and weep with my friends, because I will never marry."

Janet stole glances at the women in the class. Poor Sister Emily shook her quivering head sadly.

Dr. Speers said, "Thank you, Sister Janet. And yes, Sister Mary, this is first and foremost about a sacrifice. Jephthah's daughter willingly went into the fire for her father and for her people. And in doing so, she became pre-eminent among women. What a triumph!"

"What was her name?" Janet asked.

Dr. Speers turned to Janet, and she felt his eyes boring into her now. "Her name is not important."

"I'm sorry. I thought I saw it here somewhere and forgot it."

"She has no name."

"Oh."

Dr. Speers surveyed the women who were rapt and quiet. "Now let's talk about Jephthah. Why does Jephthah show poor judgment by making such a rash vow in the first place?"

"He was the son of a prostitute," Sister Sherry said.

"He was an adventurer," Sister Sue Ann said.

Sister Emily, who couldn't say a bad thing about anybody, said nothing.

Dr. Speers said, "That's right. He was both the son of a harlot and an adventurer, the product of a broken family. So, although he delivered Israel from the Ammonites and led Israel for six years after that, he was flawed. And that flaw revealed itself in the rash vow before God, teaching Jephthah and the people of Israel that you don't play games with God and get away with it. So, Jephthah suffered a great loss by tempting God, and his daughter redeemed him just as the women today redeem their husbands and their children through faith, piety, and selflessness. Jesus loves the women of today. He surely does."

It appeared to Janet that there was quite the difference between Abraham's Isaac and Jephthah's nameless daughter. With Isaac, God stopped Abraham at the last minute and told him it was just a test. Isaac was saved by divine intervention. Janet thought wryly, 'No divine intervention for a girl though.'

Dr. Speers said, "Would anyone like to share a time when they made a rash vow before God?"

No one spoke.

"How about a sacrifice?"

Again, no one spoke, and the women shifted in their chairs. Finally, Sister Emily coughed and whispered something.

"What's that?" Dr. Speers asked.

"I sacrificed...I'm sorry, Dr. Speers. I can't talk about it. Please, excuse me..." Sister Emily hurried from the class-room.

Sister Mary whispered to Janet, "She lost all of her sons in the Covenant wars."

Dr. Speers who overheard Sister Mary said, "Yes, she gave her sons to God. She should be very proud. Now, how can we compare Jephthah's daughter to the feminists of the dark days in America? Sister Janet?"

Janet hesitated before she spoke. "I was only 16 years old when the Covenant wars started. I didn't know any feminists. I'm sorry." But Janet did know. She'd considered herself a feminist and counted feminists among her friends and her parents' friends.

"What have the Redeemers taught us about feminists? Janet?"

"Feminists were angry and bitter complainers." Janet felt dirty and could say no more.

Sister Sue Ann said, "Feminists are the very opposite of Jephthah's daughter. Where his daughter self-sacrificed, feminists were selfish."

Aunt Peggy said, "They were more than selfish. They were murderers, isn't that so, Dr. Speers? Babies had to be hidden from their feminist mothers when they were born or they'd cut off their heads."

Dr. Speers pressed on. "Janet, you were a teenager during the dark days, old enough to remember. Is that true?"

Janet hesitated, afraid that her voice would give away her rage. Consequently, she spoke in slow, measured tones. "I never knew any who killed their babies."

"Once they were born?" Dr. Speers prompted.

"Once they were born," she said and felt a cold chill pass over her.

"But you said you didn't know any feminists personally?"

"I didn't."

"So, you can't answer with authority on this issue."

"No."

"Thank you, Sister Janet. That was very enlightening. Whether the rumors are true or not, what we do know is that the feminist sowed discord wherever she went. She tried to compete with men, thereby violating God's natural laws. Nor was she willing to sacrifice her lustful and perverse pleasures for her children. She was the Great Whore who placed multitudes in danger of God's wrath and eternal damnation."

Dr. Speers clasped his hands together as if to pray. "Praise Jesus that the Redeemers have rooted her out and banished her from our flocks."

The women said, "Amen."

Dr. Speers surveyed the room. "Sometimes, someone must be sacrificed for the good of the flock. God demands this of his Chosen. And it may not always make sense, and it may be the hardest thing that we do, just like when Sister Sue Ann had to give up her best friend." But if we love God who sacrificed his only begotten Son for us, then we can sacrifice one of ours when we're called to it."

The room fell silent.

"Has someone been called?" Sister Mary asked with alarm.

Dr. Speers smiled a tight smile. "No, Sister Mary. Is that what you all think?"

No one spoke.

"Forgive me ladies. I didn't mean to frighten you. I'm only saying that we can't allow sick sheep to poison the rest of the flock, so if someone becomes sick with devils, we may have to call that sheep to the sacrifice, remove it before the rest of the flock is destroyed. But I doubt that anyone in our flock is afflicted. I've never seen a finer bunch of ladies than those in fellowship at Wendell. Not one. Now let's look at this passage again. Why do you suppose that Jephthah's daughter's last request was to weep with her friends over the fact that she will die without ever marrying?"

"Because God wants women to be mothers." Sister Sue Ann said as she glanced at Aunt Peggy who had never borne children, and never would.

Janet noticed that Aunt Peggy looked down and didn't speak for once.

Dr. Speers said, "That's right. A virtuous woman is a mother, first and foremost. Were you ever a mother, Sister Janet?"

"No."

"Why not?" Dr. Speers asked with a trace of menace.

"I don't know why God has never given me a child." Janet said with downturned eyes. Aunt Peggy looked at her with sympathy, while others in the class echoed Dr. Speers' sentiments. It was a shame.

Janet could not look again at Dr. Speers, and she left the class shaken. When she found her husband, George, he was talking to other worshippers, saying, "The Covenant government is strong. Look at it. Practically zero unrest among the masses! Only God has the power to make that happen. It's a good God we have."

Men stood around him, saying, "Yup," "Praise the Lord," and "You got that right. Amen, brother."

Janet listened quietly and remembered last night's dream where a hungry lion took up residence in her house, and though she fed it to keep it from eating her, the lion just got hungrier.

People began to drift to the pews. Someone called for them to sing, and they stood and opened their hymnals and sang together, with gaping mouths open.

Janet noticed a baby hefted to the shoulder of Sister Sherry Hart in the pew in front of her, and the baby smiled a toothless smile. She smiled, too, and then turned her attention back to the fellowship hall.

Pastor Wayne, who was already at the podium with his Bible under his arm, was saying, "Lord, our prayers and love go to all who have lost and suffered in the terrible attack in the Covenant wars yesterday. Let us rally to the flag and God, and show what the Covenant States of Christ the Redeemer is about in these years of stress and danger as we fulfill our Christian mission of bringing more souls to Christ."

"Amen, Pastor."

It seemed to Janet that the war was lost a long time ago. There was no fighting back. What group could get together without being filmed by some street-side camera or drone, or whose voice wasn't broadcast on some hidden transmitter, or who couldn't be found anywhere with GPS and thermal imaging? And what group, no matter how innocuous, wasn't already infiltrated by some informer? No one talked about anything serious. No one. Gloom settled over Janet, perhaps wafting over the walls and barbed wire from Wendell prison.

She turned and looked at the people across the aisle to find Dr. Speers watching her.

The next Sunday was a warm December day, so they held the knitting circle outside on church grounds. Since people couldn't tell what each day would bring, whipping up cold and violent windstorms one day and the next day, a warm and gentle breeze, they took advantage of the good days, seeing it as a personal blessing from God.

When Janet arrived, Sister Emily was the only one there and sat on a large blue and red patchwork quilt, smiling broadly at Janet. Despite her grief over her sons, Sister Emily typically appeared cheerful.

Janet smiled in contagion, a real smile, an easy smile. "Sister Emily, how are you today?"

Sister Emily grinned and said, "I could complain but it wouldn't do no good."

Janet chuckled and said, "Truth." Janet liked Sister Emily more every day and began to feel something thawing within her when she was in Emily's presence, like Emily was someone with whom she could drop her guard a little.

Janet nodded as the other women arrived and dropped their blankets and knitting baskets on the ground, and then it was a hustle of activity as the women burst into 'washed cleans' and 'by bloods' and 'it's such a pretty day.'

After they were settled, Sister Mary plucked a clover from the dead grass that surrounded it and gave it to Janet. "Some luck for Sister Janet."

Janet took the moist green clover from Sister Mary's hand, and Sister Mary said, "I always wanted a sister to talk things over with when I was growing up. Henry was nice, but not the same as a sister would have been."

Sister Sue Ann said, "I didn't like my sister."

Sister Emily pulled yarn from her basket, saying, "Well, we're all sisters here, aren't we?"

Sister Sue Ann and Aunt Peggy exchanged glances while Sister Mary said, "That's true, Sister Emily. I have sisters after all, but much older sisters." Sister Mary smiled to show she was teasing them.

The women chuckled and settled down to knitting, but Janet found it hard to sit still. Janet had taken up knitting so

that she might look and act like other women in the Covenant States, and she had found some quiet comfort in looping the yarn over the needles and the clicking of the needles.
But she would rather be up and moving, today especially.
She felt anxious and the sun was brilliant and a rare bird
song called from the woods.

Janet said, "I didn't know there were any birds left. Is
there a walking path nearby?"

"I'll show you." Sister Mary stood and held out her hand
to Janet, helping her up from the blanketed ground.

"Stay together," Aunt Peggy said.

Sister Mary showed her the walking path on the far side
of the church. Janet stood at the entrance to the path and
said, "You can go back with the others. I'd like to be alone to
pray for my...brother."

"Aunt Peggy said we should stay together."

"It'll be perfectly safe. Go on now. I won't be 15 minutes."

"But Wendell prison is there."

"Where?"

"About ten miles that way, through these woods."

"Ten miles is a long way. I'll be fine."

"Sister Janet? We never got time alone until now. I just
wanted you to know that I won't tell anyone where I saw you
before." Sister Mary looked with worry at the woods, and
then she hurried away as Janet watched her, puzzled.

And then Janet recognized her. Sister Mary was the girl
in the woods with her mother. Janet felt her stomach drop.
'Fuck, fuck, fuck!' When the shock of recognition subsided,

she turned to call Sister Mary back, but Sister Mary was already halfway back to the other women. She wondered if Sister Mary could be trusted. Could anybody? And Janet felt sick with the added realization that the child would be married to her mother's murderer.

With a renewed urgency, Janet allowed herself to think of Seila, her sister for whom she had come. Janet's position was compromised, and where was Johnny? He was supposed to have a position in the prison by now, but Janet had not seen or heard from him. She knew that every day was an excruciating delay for Seila, and she had already taken too long just getting to Wendell. With time running out, she thought about how she might get more messages to contacts in Jacksonville and Atlanta. And then there was Sonny. He might be sympathetic based on conversations that she overheard. Could he help? Would he?

{8}

Where Is Your Sister?

THE NEXT TIME that Seila was brought before Dr. Speers, he pushed a button from his desk and played back an earlier conversation:

"Where is your sister?"

"I don't know. I haven't seen her in five years."

"Why not?"

"She vanished. I was told she was dead."

"Do you know of any reason she may have vanished?"

"None, except the one the Redeemers gave me. Again, they said she was dead."

"Was she a whore?"

"Oh, dear God, no. You can't say things about people like that."

"A homosexual?"

"No."

Dr. Speers appeared angry and jammed his finger down on another button to rewind and hit Play again, "A homosexual?"

"No."

Seila said, "I was afraid."

"The commandment did not say, thou shalt not lie except when it's inconvenient to tell the truth."

"Abraham did."

"What?"

"Abraham lied when he told people that Sarah wasn't his wife. He was afraid that they would kill him to steal her, so he told them she was his sister."

"Are you trying to compare yourself to Abraham?"

"No, no, I'm just saying…"

Two red spots appeared on Dr. Speers' pale cheeks. He pressed a button on his desk. "Mrs. Campbell is ready for the Conviction."

"I'm sorry…I didn't mean…"

"If you had been honest with me, I could have helped you."

"I'm sorry…I won't lie again…I promise."

"Smart-mouthed women are just smart enough to be dangerous. It's a loathsome trait in the female sex."

"Please, Dr. Speers. I'm not a smart woman."

She was still saying, "I'm not a smart woman," as they carried her down a series of corridors and into a concrete courtyard that opened to the sky. The sky! It was day! With the sky so bright, Seila could only see a dark silhouette in the brilliant light. As her eyes adjusted, she could see that the silhouette was a naked elderly woman fastened to a pole on a wooden platform set up on kindling and wood. The woman's head was shaved, and her aged breasts and skin drooped. The poor soul opened her mouth to scream, and Seila saw that something was wrong with her mouth. She could only emit strange noises, while her eyes frantically swept the yard. Oh my God, she has no tongue. Seila tried to shrink backwards but was held fast by guards.

"This woman has sinned before God. She's a liar and an unrepentant fornicator."

"Oh, dear God!"

The guards stood behind Seila, holding her shoulders.

She said, "You can't."

Dr. Speers ordered the guards away and stood behind Seila himself, speaking calmly over her shoulder. "She's about to join the rest of Satan's elite where she will burn for eternity. We'll give her a proper send off."

Seila shook her head. "No...no don't. I won't lie...I won't lie."

One of the guards was a freckle-faced, beefy man with a thick neck and shaved head. "Let me burn this bitch." He was the guard called Hal, and he was there the night they caught Seila in the woods with the girl and her mother.

"Go for it, Hal."

Hal turned to one of the other guards and said, "Sonny, douse her," but the young guard didn't move. Hal grabbed the gasoline can from him and doused the woman. He climbed up on the platform and poured the gas over her.

Seila tried to shrink from the scene, to fall away, but Dr. Speers gripped her shoulders and held her up. "You stand up there. Stand up or I'll throw you on the fire myself. Now

I'm going to let you go and unfasten you, and you'd better stand."

All the time that it took for someone to unfasten Seila's handcuffs, Dr. Speers said, "If you run, you die. If you fall, you burn." Then they lit the fire which crawled and leapt up the wood, the platform and the woman's flesh as a ghastly sound issued from her empty mouth and the stench of burning flesh suffused the courtyard. Dr. Speers pressed a gun into Seila's hand and yelled, "Spare her!"

He pushed Seila forward until she thought the heat was burning her own flesh. "SHOOT HER! PULL THE TRIGGER."

The woman on the platform writhed in flames.

Then Dr. Speers reached around Seila and helped her hold the gun in her hand, and he forced her fingers on the trigger.

Seila squeezed the trigger under his relentless fingers, and the woman slumped forward, still held fast to the pole. When the pole burned through, she collapsed into a charred ruin. The stench was sickening, and Seila dry heaved and hyperventilated.

Someone took the gun from Seila and pushed and pulled her down more corridors, until they shoved her into her cell where a voice played repetitiously from a loudspeaker, "You have power over my body, but the Lord Jesus has power over my soul." A small muscle over her right eye twitched.

～

When Dr. Speers called for her again, the same two guards, Hal and Sonny, led her down the corridors to the office. Sonny lowered her carefully onto the chair, and Hal muttered, "Inmate lover."

Seila didn't comprehend it, shocked as she was.

Dr. Speers brought her orange juice in a plastic cup and held it to her chapped lips. She said, "No," but he pressed it to her lips. It was the sweetest tasting drink she'd ever had. It had been so long since she tasted oranges, but she was as much afraid of his kindnesses as his cruelties.

Dr. Speers smiled gently. "You've been through a lot, Mrs. Campbell. It's almost over now. Tell me something. Would Ruby, Jim, want you to go through all this because of her?"

Seila shook her head.

"What would she tell you to do right now if she were here?"

"She would tell me to talk to you."

"Of course she would. So why have you been denying what you know would be your sister's wishes?"

"I don't want her to die."

"Then she's alive." Tears rolled down Seila's face. She hadn't meant to say.

"Who has power over your body, Seila?"

"You do."

"Who has power over your soul?"

"Jesus."

"Remember the fire? Remember shooting that woman? You're a murderer, Seila, just like your sister."

Dr. Speers came around his desk to crouch beside her. "Who has power over your soul?"

"You do."

"Very good. Now who can offer you and Jim redemption?"

"You can."

"That's right. I can give you eternal life or eternal hell. It's your choice really, what you shall have. God gives you free will, doesn't he? Now tell me all about Jim, and you can both be sentenced as penitents. I'll even get you a job cleaning and landscaping national parks, both of you. You want to save your sister, don't you?"

Time seemed to stop as an image of Jim sitting on a log in the woods and holding out a granola bar flitted across Seila's mind. Seila could hear Dr. Speers breathing near her face and the ticking metronome on his desk, and she could smell his cologne.

She said, "My sister is dead."

"You just said you didn't want her to die. So, you've seen her. Where? Did you see her after she was reported dead?"

No." Seila could feel her pulse thudding in her ear.

"Your failure to cooperate will make things far worse for Jim. What kind of a sister are you?"

Seila didn't answer him.

"You should have reported her five years ago. By hiding her, even for one night, you were aiding and abetting a murderess. You were an accomplice."

"When she came to my house five years ago, I didn't know about any murder. I didn't find out what she went through. I only knew that she had run away from the Cure, and she was sick. She was gone by morning. It wasn't until after she was gone that I heard about the murder. She would never have murdered anyone, unless she had to." Seila did not feel as strong as the words that she uttered. She felt weak and light, as if she might float away.

Dr. Speers got an inch from Seila's face. "I can see right into your soul at the dirty lie that's still there. You know she's alive. You've seen her. Where?" For an instant, he looked like a black crow. "You know something and I'll root it out. But the longer it takes me, the worse it will be for Jim."

Dr. Speers walked around to his chair and sat, speaking now in an almost jovial voice. "Did you know that Charlie was with a woman the night before he died. A woman who appeared to be in her twenties. Who was she? Was that Jim?"

"I don't know. I didn't know he was with anyone. It was probably an employee."

"Does Jim have any distinguishing marks, blemishes, moles, and the like?"

"No."

"All we have is this photograph for now, but there's a large birthmark on her chin." Dr. Speers lifted up a photograph of Seila and Jim as children, sitting together on porch steps in frilly, sky-blue dresses. Seila at six years old sat with her legs together and tucked neatly to the side. Three-year old Jim sat forward with legs splayed and feet ready to leap from the steps, frowning because she didn't want to wear a dress. Today, Jim was still small and scrappy.

Seila almost smiled. Jim had long ago paid to have her image scrubbed from servers, but sooner or later, some were bound to resurface. But this. A sense of relief flooded Seila. Dr. Speers still didn't know what Jim looked like, and that birthmark had been removed long ago.

Dr. Speers mused, "The woman Charlie was with did not have a birthmark, but she could have removed it.

He sighed and looked up. "How would you feel if you knew that your sister got Charlie killed?"

"She didn't." But Seila was uneasy.

{9}

Temptations

ON THE NEXT Sunday, the knitting circle was canceled, so Dr. Speers asked Sister Mary to go for a walk with him after the service. "Do you think it's okay?" she whispered.

"You're safe with me."

By this time, Sister Mary had accepted what Aunt Peggy and Pastor Wayne said about Dr. Speers being a suitable match for her. They were supposed to spend more time getting to know one another, and she agreed to go on a walk with him. Still, she felt an incessant anxiety during the service. What will I say to him? What will we talk about?

She also made a conscious effort not to look at the new man, Sonny, since her attraction to him was certainly machinations of the Devil himself. But he was certainly beautiful. She prayed to God to lead her from temptation, and she put a rubber band on her right wrist so that she could snap herself to attention if she ever thought of him.

After the service, she popped the rubber band on her wrist and waited for Dr. Speers at his black sedan, resisting the impulse to kick rocks and leaves in the parking lot. Ladies did not kick things. She frowned at a rock near the curb with pink and black veins that ran through it, and wished she could pick it up and turn it over in her soft hands, something she liked to do as a child when she was looking for fossils. It would roughen her hands too much now.

When Sister Mary turned 13 years old, she was no longer allowed to play with the 12 and under kids. Starting at 13, girls were in training for marriage, and some of Sister Mary's friends had married already. Sometimes, she passed younger girls playing hopscotch on the sidewalk and wished she could join in. They usually stopped playing to watch her pass, and she wondered what they thought. Did they not like her now because of her mother? Did they miss playing with her like she missed playing with them? Did they look up to her now because she was older and soon to be married? Sometimes they waved and she waved back. She felt better when they waved, but she missed them even more.

Sister Mary looked down at her feet as she waited for Dr. Speers. How could she possibly walk in these pointed shoes that bent her toes so? She turned her foot this way and that, looking at the black suede shoe. Her feet were small and her ankles were delicate and pretty.

As Dr. Speers walked towards her, it seemed as if a light emanated from him. It was true that he was an older man, but he had an energy around him that drew Sister Mary to him, and scared her at the same time. He has a quiet assurance, she thought, something that she lacked.

But he wasn't Sonny. When she saw Sonny in church, she felt a thrill in her chest.

Mary popped the rubber band on her wrist nervously and asked, "Dr. Speers? Mark, I mean? Could we go by my house so I can change into walking shoes first?"

Dr. Speers smiled, showing even teeth. "Of course. But wouldn't it have been smarter if you had brought them with you?"

"I'm sorry. I didn't think of it. So stupid."

Dr. Speers chuckled and went to the passenger's side of the car, opening the door for her. Sister Mary smiled as she scooted in. She fumbled with her seatbelt as Dr. Speers got into the driver's seat, and then he leaned over her, saying, "Allow me." He took the seatbelt from her hands and pulled it around her waist slowly, clicking it into place while a frightening shudder went through her.

At Sister Mary's house, she put on her walking shoes while Dr. Speers waited in the car and Aunt Peggy, who was already home, watched from an upstairs window. Afterwards, he took her to the trail that she had shown Janet, the one that wound around a small pond, shimmering in dappled light, and edged by rust-colored scum.

Sister Mary hesitated.

"You're safe, Sister Mary."

Sister Mary followed Dr. Speers down the trail. She watched his shoes step over the soft ground. How quietly he walks. He stepped softly, gliding under the trees like a wolf.

She felt pride in the fact that he had picked her, an important man like him, and at the same time, she was afraid of him. She reminded herself that all the men around Wendell worked at the prison, and they were good, decent God-fearing folks.

As Dr. Speers stepped over the soft ground, he explained differences between men and women because Dr. Speers was always teaching. "Women are prone to think subjectively, circling the wagons around their families—as they should—whereas men think on a broader scale, weighing cause and effect to the community as a whole. We need both ways of thinking to exist harmoniously in this world, a world that should never be too masculine or too feminine. That's why marriage is so critical to the human family. Male and female become one."

Sister Mary thought he spoke with authority, like her own father when she was young. Her father, who had taught in a Christian private school, began teaching her about Jesus while bouncing her on his knee. Sister Mary felt lucky to have had such a father, and then she thought that the only thing that Dr. Speers lacked of her father's character was joy. Aunt Peggy had assured Sister Mary that Dr. Speers would be joyful after they married.

In time, Dr. Speers fell silent.

"Dr. Speers? I mean Mark."

"Yes, Sister Mary?"

"If you could be anywhere in the world, where would that be?"

Dr. Speers stopped, turned, and smiled at Sister Mary. "Right here on this very spot, with you."

Dr. Speers reached out and pulled Sister Mary to him, embracing her, and she felt the warmth of his chest through his starched shirt. Her heart beat faster. Dr. Speers had always been slow and staid, so this sudden move frightened her and excited her at the same time. With his hand, he lifted her chin so that she was looking up at him, and his sober, dark eyes looked deep into hers. He whispered, "Sister Mary, I can feel you pulling me in. What have you done to me?"

Sister Mary felt her legs trembling and didn't know if it was love, fear, or the wind that made her tremble.

Dr. Speers stepped back, pushing Sister Mary gently away. "And I don't trust myself with you right now. We should go back."

Sister Mary nodded dumbly, and when Dr. Speers walked by her to retrace their steps, she turned to follow him, still trembling. There was this terrible anxiety, too, leaving her painfully vulnerable. What had she done wrong?

She watched Dr. Speers step carefully, slowly.

"Mark?" Dr. Speers did not answer and walked more quickly. "Dr. Speers, have I done something wrong?

"No, Sister Mary." He walked faster still, until Sister Mary was practically running to keep up with him. She was out of breath by the time they got to the car. Dr. Speers opened her car door for her, but he didn't help her with the seatbelt this time.

They rode to her house in silence, but when he parked the car, he turned to her, taking her hand. "We need to be more careful. I almost lost control back there, Sister Mary. It would have been a terrible, dishonorable act. You deserve better than that."

"Oh, I don't think you could do anything dishonorable."

"I'll see you next week, Sister Mary."

Sister Mary got out of the car and was painfully conscious of walking down her concrete walkway and up the stairs to her porch, fumbling with her keys, and knowing all the time that Dr. Speers was still idling in his car, watching.

{10}

Conviction

SEILA WALKED IN tight circles around her cell, counting as she walked, 23, 24, 25. Or, she recited childhood rhymes, 'one, two, buckle my shoe, three, four, shut the door, five six, five six, five six, lay them straight, lay them, straight.'

But she couldn't get the image of the old woman out of her head while she recited other words, other thoughts, anything but the image that seared her mind. And she couldn't remember whether she had told Dr. Speers about Jim being alive or dreamed it. 'A little while,' she told herself, but the word 'while' sounded very strange to her. She repeated it. While. Wow. A little wow. While.

When she saw Dr. Speers again, she said, "A little while."

"What's a little while?"

"In a little while, it will be 3:30."

"It's 5:30."

"Would that be A.M. or P.M.?

"Ah, I see what you did there. Very clever. Now Seila, I'm going to tell you a story about myself."

Seila imagined smashing his skull with a crowbar and her mind skittered away like a magnet repelled. She told herself that she was not a murderer.

Dr. Speers spoke again. "Did you know that I was a soldier in the Covenant army?"

"No."

"I was near the ruins of a bombed-out compound, fighting Satan's army."

Seila understood that Satan's army included any member of the United States military who fought on the side of the former United States against the Covenant States and any citizens of secular border states that didn't opt into the new Covenant. The war was ongoing as the Redeemer army sought to take more territory from neighboring states.

Dr. Speers said, "We were fighting in a wicked storm that Satan had thrown up to obstruct us. We were in the middle of it, and I was wild for God's work, hollering, and singing, praising Jesus, and blasting every demon that rose up against us. We had drones mostly but I loved the close combat. The adrenaline of God's work gives you power, Mrs. Campbell. Power. Listen, because you're only the second person who's heard this story. I tell you this because I think that it's important for you to understand me, to understand my conviction. Are you listening Mrs. Campbell?"

"Yes."

"Out of this hellish smoke rose a brick wall. I didn't see it until I was almost upon it. Crouched down at the foot of the wall was a small, big-eyed, blonde-haired boy. He must have been about six years old. The boy enraged me. What kind of parents would have their child out in a war zone like that?"

Dr. Speers stood up, walked around his desk to Seila and bent down. His warm breath was on her cheek as he asked, "What kind of parents, Mrs. Campbell?"

As he talked, Seila could picture the little boy and she had the disconcerting sensation that she was the little boy, so she could both see him and be him.

Dr. Speers stood and straightened his steel gray suit jacket and towered over her. "I hate weakness, Mrs. Campbell. Weakness is the door to corruption, and I was almost corrupted in that dreadful moment when I saw that boy. I was weak. For a split-second, I forgot that the boy was a child of Satan."

Seila looked straight in front of her at the creases in Dr. Speers' gray pants.

Dr. Speers spoke softly, "I hesitated, and out there, hesitation can kill you."

Dr. Speers bent down again, gripped Seila's chin, and forced her to look at his pale face and stormy eyes. "Praise Jesus, I recovered and blasted that little, teary-eyed demon straight to hell."

It seemed to Seila that his face was drained of all color while hope, if there ever was any, drained out of Seila. He rubbed her wet face with his thumb. "The only real tears are the tears of salvation, of conversion, and of righteousness. Anything else is a Devil's manipulation." His eyes narrowed. "Are you crying, Mrs. Campbell?"

"No."

"Good."

He let go of her face and stood. Then his voice seemed to catch, just a little, or maybe she imagined it. "I rarely dream, but once in a while, Satan sends that boy in my sleep, and I have to kill him all over again."

"And us?"

"Us?"

"Us, the old woman, the people you counsel."

Seila looked up to find Dr. Speers staring at the wall of his office, as if he were far away, perhaps seeing the boy again, eternally crouching. A tremor flickered across his face, and then his face recomposed as if nothing had moved at all.

Dr. Speers straightened his jacket. "I did what I had to do in service to the Lord then, and I do it now." Dr. Speers bent down and whispered, "Do you see?"

Seila didn't answer.

He stood up. "You killed a demon, nothing more. You see how easy it is to do the right thing?"

"I didn't kill her," she said softly.

Dr. Speers said, "You did," and stood over her for an uncomfortably long time and she flinched when he bent over her again and moved his hand towards her, taking ahold of her chains. He said, "And you have a demon in you. I can see it."

She looked up at him and saw a look of utter hatred and revulsion, as if he were indeed looking at a demon and not at an innocent young woman from Jacksonville, Florida.

"It must be awful for you," she whispered.

"What is?"

"Seeing devils everywhere where there are none."

His eyes flashed and he grabbed tight on her chains, and then he let go. His face went flat again and he walked back to his chair. He said, "It's a great battle that goes on in a godly man's soul."

Dr. Speers sat down with a long sigh and said, "I like patterns and study them. I wander around in the details of a person's mind until an entire landscape emerges. That's why they call me the Artist. I discover patterns and annihilate them, so that sinners can come to God as a child, no longer ensnared by the trap of knowledge. You, too, have patterns and false beliefs. For example, you say you're not a murderer, and yet you killed your husband."

Seila felt a bolt of adrenaline shoot through her body, and she cried, "Charlie?! I didn't kill Charlie!"

"We have it on good authority that it was you."

"That's crazy! It's a lie! Is that why...? There's been a mistake, Dr. Speers. I haven't killed Charlie. I couldn't."

"You never wanted to kill anyone before you killed that old woman?"

"No."

"Not even me."

"N-no." Seila's eyes became vacant again and she said, "Yes."

Dr. Speers called Sonny in and barked, "Remove her chains!" Sonny released the chains, and it seemed to Seila that Sonny looked down upon her in sympathy. She later thought that she must have imagined it.

When Sonny left, Dr. Speers pulled a pistol from his desk, walked around the desk, and held it out to Seila. "It's loaded. All you have to do is pull the trigger."

Mrs. Campbell held the gun in her shaking hands and tried to hand it back. "No, you take it."

Dr. Speers got on his knees and helped guide the pistol to his forehead. "Shoot me," he whispered. "I'm a sinner before God, and I can't stop in my sin. Shoot me."

They stared at each other as if their bodily identities were gone. All they had left were their dilated eyes watching each other while Seila's breath came fast and shallow. Dr. Speers' eyes pulled her in like whirling black holes that she struggled against.

"I can't kill you, Dr. Speers." She saw a terrible need in him, something dense and magnetic, a death wish?

"Shoot me," he urged.

"I can't." Her hands trembled, and she thought, 'he's mad.' She didn't breathe, didn't say a word. What she didn't notice was that Dr. Speers' hands didn't tremble at all as he took the gun from her.

He chuckled and returned it to the desk, saying, "Sometimes, we have one shot in life."

Maybe she should have killed him. But she held on to hope that she could get out of Wendell, that Charlie's friends might come to her defense and that she might still retain her humanity.

Dr. Speers snapped his fingers and said, "You must try harder to concentrate, Mrs. Campbell. But you are a woman, so...still, do try, Mrs. Campbell. Do you know why your husband Charlie was seen with a woman at Tabernacle Square the evening before he was killed?"

"I don't know." But she did know. Jim had told her that Charlie helped her that night when the Redeemers cornered her.

Dr. Speers asked, "Was Charlie having an affair? Is that why you had him killed?"

"No! Of course not. If I could kill anyone, I would have killed you, just now."

Seila wondered if this was how Jim killed a man, and inwardly she groaned. She should have stayed with Jim that night in the basement, when Jim needed her most. She should have asked her about Karen.

Dr. Speers asked, "Where was Charlie the night before you saw him last? Was Charlie home the night before you last saw him?"

"Yes...I don't know. I don't remember."

"Yes, you do remember. You just don't want to face it. Think back. Charlie was gone for three hours that night." Dr. Speers waited without speaking.

"How do you know that?"

"We know. Three hours was a long time to go to the store, and you wondered about it that night, didn't you? You wondered where he was, and who he was with."

"I wondered if he'd been in a car accident."

"Sometimes when we are tired of someone, we imagine them having all kinds of mishaps."

"Not me."

"Don't antagonize me. We're too close to a breakthrough here. Up until now, you haven't admitted that Charlie was gone the evening before he disappeared."

In her fatigue, Seila accepted the truth of his statement instead of realizing that she had never denied it. She hung suspended in a soupy world where dreams and reality merged, and she could no longer ascertain fact from fiction, the real from the unreal, day from night.

"You do admit that now, don't you? You admit now that Charlie was gone for three hours the night before he disappeared, and you imagined a violent end for him?"

"No, wait. You're putting words in my mouth. I admit that he was gone for several hours the night before he went missing, but I didn't imagine a violent end for him."

"Is a car accident a violent end?"

"Yes, but..."

Dr. Speers shouted, "Then you did imagine a violent end for him! Just say it, Mrs. Campbell. Say that you imagined a violent end for your husband! Confess that much before God!"

"Alright! If you mean a car accident, then I imagined a violent end for my husband." Seila felt like her body was swaying, either that or maybe the ground was moving up and down.

"Okay, I want you to ponder this. If your sister was alive—and you knew they were together the night before Charlie disappeared—what were they doing together? Ask yourself: Where was Charlie? What were they involved in?"

But Seila knew they weren't involved in anything. Jim said it was a chance meeting, and Charlie got Jim out of harm's way when the Redeemers were questioning her on the street. Isn't that what Jim said?

He said, "I want you to think back five years. Why didn't you stop Jim from leaving when she showed up at your house?"

"I wanted her to stay."

"The truth."

"Maybe I was afraid of me and Charlie getting arrested. People were disappearing."

"Or maybe because you knew for a fact that she was a murderer?"

"I didn't."

Dr. Speers said, "Okay, let's look at this from a different angle. You told me that your sister was alive. How do you know that your sister is alive?"

Seila's lips parted, and at first no sound issued forth. Her mouth was dry and her lips were chapped. She tried again. "I don't know. It's a feeling."

Dr. Speers had a bemused expression on his face. "Feelings? Women and their feelings. False prophets."

He seemed to shake himself from reverie. "Feelings are nothing to me. I need facts. And you almost had me there.

I almost believed you. But you know what? I've been going about this all wrong, all wrong. I see that now. Where do you think Jim is right now? She would have heard about you on the news. What would she do when she heard that you were under arrest? What do you think she would do?"

"I don't know."

"Don't you?"

Seila's mind blanked for second, and then she said, "She'd go to Vermont."

"And leave you here? Abandon you? Maybe we know what kind of a sister you are, but suppose she didn't abandon you. True, it's hard to believe that secular homosexuals have family values, but it is possible. Why, she could be in Wendell right now."

"Did the media say that I was at Wendell?"

"No, but I can't rule out that she somehow knows. If she were able to disappear under the Redeemer's radar, she would know how to get information, and it just so happens that a new woman has moved to Wendell, a woman approximately the same age as your sister. Would she dare?"

{11}

Gossip

JANET HATED WHEN George led her around with his hand clasped around the back of her neck or by her upper arm. He had her neck in his hand now as they walked up the sidewalk of the Wendell Dance Hall. The Dance was one of the big events of the year, outside of Resurrection Day and Christmas, and the only time that dancing was allowed. The Dance was the day that marriageable girls were paraded before the eligible men and boys under the watchful eyes of the town's men and women. Some of the girls would be claimed on this day and would find their life altered forever, for better or for worse.

Dr. Speers was expected to claim Sister Mary at this dance, and Janet could see no way to stop it. If she warned Sister Mary or told Sister Mary about her mother, it would put both Sister Mary and Janet in a more precarious situation, and jeopardize her mission of getting Seila out. It's not like Sister Mary could refuse Speers anyway. Ignorance was her only shield, as weak as it was.

As George steered Janet up the walk, Janet noticed the large black Covenant flag flapping over the front lawn. These flags were first displayed to the American public the same day that the office of the President was dissolved and the new office of First Regent was created. Most of the Constitution was dissolved, too, and along with it went her friends' already-vanishing hopes. When they announced it on television, Janet and her wife, Karen, and their friends cried like there was no tomorrow, and for most of them, there wasn't. Janet remembered that Karen tried to cheer her up, saying, "This will change some day and things will be back to normal."

Janet had wanted to say, "It's not going back to normal," because she tired of people not facing facts, too afraid to see things as they are. That was Seila's problem, too, who preferred to think good thoughts. Well, who wouldn't? But on that day, Janet lied to Karen and agreed that things would get better because Karen needed to believe it, too.

But their world was collapsing and no longer resembled the life that they knew as young teens, back when Janet was called Jim and girls could have cellphones. They met in history class and exchanged phone numbers. They talked all evening after school and the next night and the next. And whenever Janet saw Karen, she felt a thrill in her heart and it was strange. It didn't happen with anyone else.

Then Karen came to spend the night on a sultry Friday night in May. They camped out on their balcony with Seila, and they all studied the night sky together. Seila pointed up, "That one looks red to me."

Karen said, "I see it! Oh look. There's a blue star. Look there."

They laughed and talked until about 1:00 am, and then Seila said, "This sleeping bag is too hot and the balcony is too hard. I'm going in. I want my bed."

Janet said, "Goodnight princess."

"Goodnight shrimp."

After Seila went inside, Janet said, "Seila used to play in the ocean with me and go roller skating and stuff. Now she doesn't want to do anything except paint her nails and try on clothes."

Karen said, "She's nice though. I wish I had a sister."

"We can be sisters."

Karen said, "I have to tell you something, but I'm afraid you'll laugh at me."

Janet rolled to face her and said, "I won't," but she was already smiling.

Karen said, "I've missed you, like I've missed you all my life and didn't know it until I met you. Is that weird?"

"Yeah, you're weird," Janet said grinning.

"No, you're weird!" Karen smiled back and picked up a pillow and swung it. And Janet grabbed a pillow and swung it, and pretty soon they fell together in a giggling heap.

Then they quieted and stared again at the night sky, and Janet whispered "I think I love you. How's that for weird?"

Karen held and squeezed Janet's hand, and tears welled up in Janet's eyes. It felt like the best day of her life. But that was long ago, before Karen was lost to her forever.

Janet closed her eyes tight against an image of Karen when she last saw her in the Redeemer camp, emaciated and bruised, with damp black hair spilling over a dirty mattress on the floor of a Redeemer shack. As Janet closed her eyes against the memory, she thought, 'I am poison. Know me and you will die.' And then Aunt Peggy brought her attention to the present, to the Dance, and George's hand on her neck.

Aunt Peggy, in a long, blue dress and bonnet, waved to Janet and George from the porch of the dance hall. Everyone was supposed to dress like early revolutionaries, in whatever they supposed revolutionaries wore. George was dressed like George Washington and Janet was Martha.

Aunt Peggy stumbled and righted herself, saying, "Get thee behind me, Satan." For Peggy, there were no accidents. Satan was surely obstructing her personally, maliciously and deliberately. Peggy is not insane, Janet told herself. You're not crazy when most people have the same delusion as you, are you? Isn't that what normal is no matter how crazy it seems?

"George! George Moore. Get in here and straighten Willie out. He's going on about them dawgs again." Football was one thing the Redeemers hadn't changed. Football teams could travel in order to compete, and it was some of the most exciting events of the season, more exciting than the Dance.

Sister Sue Ann, also in a long blue dress and bonnet, came to the door and took Janet by the back of her arm to steer her away from the men, saying, "The women are on the left." Chairs were set up along both sides of the dance hall.

Women from the Bible study classes stood in groups, chattering, holding plates with bits of precious celery, carrots and apple, and Janet could smell home-baked bread and cinnamon. Cinnamon was so precious these days. Many foods and spices had become rare or intermittently available. Sanctions against the Covenant States had limited imports. Furthermore, beneficial insect populations had declined, and many plants weren't getting pollinated. Crops might be destroyed by unpredictable weather before they could be harvested, or enormous hurricanes sprung up quickly and swamped container ships at sea. A brain drain didn't help. Scientists in the Covenant States were killed by the Redeemers, and the ones who were not killed, escaped or were able to keep their past and knowledge to themselves. Besides, people thought that if these were hard times, then this was God's will, and the rapture might be right around the corner. God's chosen would be whisked into the sky and saved. Most people believed that they would be among the select few.

The women at the dance stopped talking momentarily to say, "Washed clean," and waited for Janet to answer, "By blood," before their chattering resumed in exaggerated, high-pitched girl voices. Janet thought she couldn't bear to hear their squeaky squeals of pleasure. She noticed Sister Mary sitting by herself in a corner and approached her.

"How are you, Sister Mary?"

"Just fine." Their eyes locked and flitted away, neither one giving away the fears, the knowledge that weighed them down.

Sister Sue Ann excused herself and then returned a few minutes later and told the women in a conspiratorial whisper that Brother Sonny had come. Brother Sonny joined the men on the right side of the hall, and his eyes seemed to linger on Sister Mary.

Sister Emily said, "Oh, he's a handsome one, Sister Mary." Sister Mary blushed and flicked a rubber band that she wore on her wrist.

Aunt Peggy shook her finger at Sister Emily. "Now Sister Emily, you know that Sister Mary is spoken for. Besides, why would she be interested in a Papist anyway?"

"How can he be a Papist when he goes to our church?" Sister Emily asked.

"Well, he can't be a scriptural Christian, can he? He doesn't carry his Bible to church. Besides, I don't believe in crossing racial lines."

"What race is that?"

"Well, for goodness' sakes, dear. He's from Mexico."

Janet kept her voice casual and said, "He's from New Mexico. He's American."

"Well, he might as well be a Hindu as far as I'm concerned." Aunt Peggy lowered her voice. "They say he's crossed Dr. Speers."

"How so?" asked Janet. Was there hope?

"I don't know. The men don't talk about their work, but Dr. Speers is an important man down there, a very important man, and I've heard that Brother Sonny is behaving like a disgruntled employee, not following Dr. Speers' orders. I also heard that someone broke into Brother Sonny's house and wrecked it. Now I ask you, what sort of man gets his house vandalized?"

Janet shook her head puzzled. "What sort of man is that?"

"Evil attracts evil, I always say."

Some of the women nodded.

George's voice boomed from the across the room, "Julius Caesar was the greatest man who ever lived."

Someone else yelled, "We'll soon be the new Roman power, only better. We'll usher in a Christian empire the likes of which this world's never seen since Constantine the Great, but this time, with Jesus himself marching at its head."

Janet thought wryly, 'I think the Romans killed Jesus.'

The women giggled while the men sang a fight song. When they were done, Aunt Peggy whispered conspiratorially. "Anyway, Brother Hal calls Brother Sonny an inmate lover. I say if he loves them so much, he can join them."

Janet thought again that Sonny might be persuaded to help her. Dare she risk it?

Sister Emily said, "We shouldn't gossip about things we don't know about, should we?"

Aunt Peggy laughed and looked knowingly at the other ladies. "I expect you wouldn't like gossip, Sister Emily."

"I don't know what you mean."

"Well, if you don't know, neither do I?"

Sister Emily reddened. "Judge not lest ye be judged, Aunt Peggy."

"Isn't that from an old Bible?"

Sister Emily's daughter, Connie, entered the kitchen. "Mama, I need some ice. Tommy Lee hurt his knee." Connie was fourteen years old and wore a dark cloak over a long dark blue skirt, and a red cross was embroidered on her cloak. She had long blonde hair cascading down her back, brilliant blue eyes, and the red, full lips of a young woman. Janet felt an abrupt pain in her heart seeing Connie. So young, yet they will marry her and Sister Mary off to someone at this dance. What kind of life could they have? Besides the obvious trauma of their wedding night, and the other nights to come, she guessed that she need only look to poor, exhausted Sister Sherry Hart for an answer as to what the rest of their lives would look like. Sister Sherry was in a back room at that moment trying to corral the children. And that was a best-case scenario. For Mary, it would be quite a bit worse with Dr. Speers.

Aunt Peggy said, "That's very sweet of you, Connie, helping Sister Sherry with the young-uns like that."

"Yes, Ma'am," Connie said softly.

When Connie had gone, Aunt Peggy said, "You really should pull her hair back, Sister Emily. The hair makes the person I always say, and that hair is swinging too freely."

"My Connie's a good girl."

"Well, no one said she wasn't dear."

"That poor girl's been through enough. She's lost her three brothers to the war, and you know it. It's not right to talk about her as if she were..."

"As if she were what?"

Sister Emily left the kitchen and Janet wondered what kind of trouble the girl was in.

Frowning, she excused herself to find the restroom. As she quietly opened the bathroom door, she heard a man's voice speaking in hushed tones from one of the other rooms down the corridor. "I don't know about all that, but I've been a correctional officer for twelve years. Trust me. It's not your place to get rid of bad counselors or bad guards. I don't like Dr. Speers and Hal Wayne any more than you do, but it's best to just do your eight and hit the gate. You don't want these guys as enemies. You just don't."

"I can take care of myself."

"No, you can't. If you could, you wouldn't have been dumb enough to go to Warden Camp with this."

"Get out of my way."

"Hey wait a minute. I'm just looking out for you. These guys are crazy here. Don't put your neck out for an inmate. Just pray, Sonny. Christ will make things right. You'll see."

Janet wondered how she might get a few moments with Sonny, and then she heard the music stop. Pastor Wayne was telling everyone to find their seats with unmarried girls and men taking the front rows. Then the music restarted as everyone found their seats. Sister Mary was on the front row and so was Connie. Aunt Peggy, with great shame and embarrassment must sit on that front row, too. Even the widows must find a man, if they can, so they wouldn't be a continued drain on the church budget and risk having the Redeemers finding them in need of redemption, which the older women might not survive. Redemption required a hardy constitution.

Janet watched Sonny in the front row. His face was unreadable.

The men and women broke out in cheers as Dr. Speers, looking like Abe Lincoln, approached Sister Mary, whose face was flushed scarlet. She was the first one chosen. One by one, girls were chosen, which was followed by their first dance. Then their parents collected them for their final months at home as they prepared for their new life. They needed continued training in cooking, cleaning, and how to stay friendly and joyous. They also had to formally accept the proposal after they had time for prayer and reflection.

But Connie. Connie was not chosen, and there was much whispering and side eyes.

{12}

Accusations

JANET WAITED THREE agonizing days before she saw an opportunity to visit Sonny. George attended a men's Bible study at the Camp's house and Janet was alone. She threw a black wool shawl over her head and coat, and went out through the back door. She could be back before curfew, but in reality, there was an unofficial curfew—dark—and it grew dark early on winter days. She had a pot of chicken soup in her hands as an alibi if she were seen and questioned.

Janet learned to cook in the Redeemer camp, back when she was Jim and selected for the so-called Cure. Karen was there, too. The Cure involved an initial exorcism, and then they paired the women with Christian elders in marriage who would 'tame' them and teach them how to be good Christian wives.

Janet's elder had wild, stringy hair around his disheveled head and a long, straggling brown beard that he couldn't keep food out of. His false teeth were manufactured incorrectly so they were too big for his mouth. He towered over

Janet, with long arms and big hands, and he was fast and violent.

He caught her the first time she snuck over to Karen's shack in the woods. He slapped her open-handed across the face and pulled her hair, and dragged her down to the tabernacle where he tied her to a wooden pole. She was left there overnight, and in the morning, she was whipped in front of the 'congregation' of elders and their 'wives.' She didn't cry out at first, so they kept whipping her until she did.

To this day, she made sure that George never saw her without a shirt on her back, even during sex, but she had a lie ready in case he did. This was something else he mistook for modesty.

The second time that she tried to sneak over to see Karen, they whipped Karen instead, and she'd never forgiven herself for that. She tried to stay away, to wait for a time when the elders might let their guard down. But then when she heard Karen was sick and dying, she ran to the shack anyway and found Karen on the dirty mattress, in a fever. Karen's elder was already dead with wide open, unseeing eyes, lying on the floor where he must have fallen. And the foul smell of death and vomit choked Janet.

And Janet saw that Karen had been starved, and she had bruises all over her body, and when she held her, she was so thin that her bones jutted sharply from her body. Janet said, "I'll get you some water. I'll make you some soup. You'll get better."

"No," Karen said and her voice was labored, "I'm dying."

"No, no, you can't. You won't."

Karen coughed weakly, so weakly. When she finished coughing, she said, "I love..." And that was it. She was gone and Janet remained kneeling on the floor and holding her and crying, deep heartrending sobs. Someone rapped at the back window and said, "You gotta get out of there. They're coming." Janet dimly heard the commotion in the camp and didn't care and didn't move. She was ready to die. She wanted to die, to join Karen wherever she was. So she stayed and they beat her and whipped her and kept her tied to the pole for three days. At the end of those three days, she realized that, as much as she wanted to die, she still had to live. Seila would need her to live.

She dully went through the motions of living after that, and then one day when her elder was on top of her, she watched his fleshy face turned up toward the pine beams, praying for 'the woman,' and grunting over her naked body, 'duty, submission, obedience.' The sweat rolled off his nose and chin onto her, the hot drops on her flesh, his disgusting weight. The violation!

Her elder said, "Submit and be saved, repent, you'll repent before the whole damned congregation, make me look good. I didn't used to be Christian you know, but these days Christians have their perks hahaha. You were a tough old dyke and now you're my sweet dove, praise the Lord. That's why the Devil took that bitch Karen and I still got you."

And the rage she felt for Karen's dead elder and all the elders and Redeemers and believers cracked open.

As her elder sat down to his last supper, he said, "A song, give us a song, I got the joy, joy, joy, joy down in my heart, down in my heart, down in my heart, sing it! And then give us some good ole pork ribs. What's this? Get that knife outa your hand, sweet Jesus woman!"

Janet remembered that it wasn't easy. The flesh is hard and slippery when bloodied, and she plunged that knife over and over before he slid to the floor. But his warm blood on her hands felt like relief, and she remembered asking him as he slid, "Can't I get an amen, brother? What are you sliding out of your seat for? Ask Jesus to help you rise and walk again, you sick bastard."

Janet could still smell her escape and feel it and hear it in song. There was vomit in the weeds. She could never forget the smell of pork ribs and cornbread and vomit, and didn't know how she got to Seila's house, walking, feet slipping off curbs, hiding in bushes, hiding in ditches, breathing hard, heart pounding, just like, 'I got the joy, joy, joy, joy down in my heart...'

Janet shuddered and tried to shrug off the memory, as she hurried forward to Sonny's house with the soup, panting in the frigid air. She must remain focused. For Seila.

She turned right on Magnolia Street and stole glances at her neighbors' front porches and tried to look natural for the 'eyes of God.' She knew that Sonny lived at the end of Magnolia, on Bachelor's hill in a small wood frame house on a corner lot. Aunt Peggy had pointed it out to her that morning.

When she arrived at his front porch, his house was quiet, and she dreaded the walk back home. Still, to be sure he wasn't at home, she tapped lightly on the front door. When she didn't hear anything, she turned to leave and found herself face to face with Sonny who had stepped from the side of the house, "What do you want?"

Janet's stomach leapt into her throat. "I brought you some chicken soup."

Sonny didn't speak and Janet couldn't tell from his face what he was thinking. His wide, open face was closed to her.

"I said I brought you some chicken soup."

Sonny still didn't answer her.

"For heaven's sake, let me in before someone sees me up here."

Sonny stepped around her and pushed his front door open. She turned, stepped inside and nearly tripped on a thick string stretched across the living room floor. Sonny steadied her and shut the door. He moved around her and turned on a small green lamp.

"What's this about?" Sonny asked.

"I was told that you were in trouble with Dr. Speers."

Sonny crossed his arms over his chest. His face looked green in the glow of the lamp. He said, "That's interesting. I was told that the things at Wendell stay at Wendell."

"They call you an inmate lover."

"Maybe you'd better leave," he said and he moved past her to the door.

"I need help," she said, and she stood very still.

Sonny stopped and turned, and then pointed to a small wooden table. "Sit down, ma'am."

She settled the pot of chicken soup onto the table and sat.

He asked, "Do you know how many cameras are on the street tracking you?"

"I brought soup."

"It was a stupid, female thing to do, taking a risk like that."

"Which I had to take." They were talking low as if someone were right in the room with them listening.

"What do you want with me?"

"I've come to ask about Seila Campbell, Charlie Campbell's wife."

Sonny looked long and hard at Janet.

"Alright. Get out." He took her by the elbow as if he were going to yank her up.

"Don't do this. What's wrong with you?"

He asked, "Who sent you here?"

"No one. Seila Campbell's a friend of mine."

Sonny let go of Janet's arm but continued to stand.

"I'm an old friend of Seila's and the reason she's in there."

"How so?" Sonny looked puzzled and dubious.

"I don't know exactly. All I know is that I was out late, just before curfew, and the Redeemers cornered me on the street. I don't know how her husband, Charlie, knew it was me. I hadn't seen him in years and I...well, I was different. Charlie came up to me and put his arm under mine, pulling me away from them and saying that I was a friend and that he was late. They let us go, but the next morning I had him followed. That's how I found out that the Redeemers shot him in cold blood. They killed him. THEY did!"

"You had him followed. Who takes orders from you?"

"No orders. Just a concerned friend."

"Right." Sonny looked severe as if he might haul her away to a Redeemer van.

"Seila committed no crime, and if you've seen her, you know that."

"I don't care who the hell you are. And this lady, Seila Campbell, is none of my business either."

"None of your business?" Janet chewed on her lip. "She's still there, isn't she? In Wendell?"

Sonny sat down and stared at the pot of chicken soup lying on his kitchen table while Janet waited him out. He frowned as if troubled. Finally, his face softened and he sighed. "You can't help her."

"Why not?"

Sonny fell silent again, and Janet pulled her black shawl tighter around her. She said, "I've got to see Seila."

He sat up and placed his large hands on the table. "The only way I know is through the prison ministry, but you'd have an escort."

"Would you be that escort?"

"This is none of my business. I'm not sticking my neck out for you or her."

Janet stood silent for a few minutes, and then she asked, "What if she were your sister or your mother or your wife? What would you do?"

"It doesn't matter what I would do. Go home, Mrs. Moore. Go home right now and maybe I'll forget about this." A shadow seemed to cross Sonny's face and a severity returned.

Janet turned one last time as she left him. "Even when there seems to be no hope, we must act as if there is. We have to do what's right where we can. Even here. Even in hell."

Janet sweated through Saturday, not knowing if Sonny would turn her into the Redeemers. She took deep breaths whenever she heard the rare sound of a car engine turning down her street or a drone hovering nearby. By Saturday night, she told herself that the Redeemers always come in the night and so she slept very little. By Sunday morning, she was exhausted and no longer cared whether they came to arrest her or not. She dragged through the morning, boiling eggs for George and baking biscuits. The hungry beast in her house must eat.

On Sunday, George and Janet dressed and arrived at the church late. Most of the class was already in the room when Janet hurried in, breathless. "I'm so sorry I'm late."

"We all have days like that, dear," Sister Emily said.

Janet looked for evidence in Dr. Speers' face that he knew she'd gone to Sonny Valdez's house or that he knew who she was—and found none. She removed her orange and brown-striped sweater, draped it over the seat, and sat down.

Dr. Speers turned to Aunt Peggy. "You look joyous today."

"Oh, I'm still laughing about the Chambers' boy, Lauren. He was out back with the little ones and commenced preaching like he was the pastor. 'Forsake your sins and turn back to God.'"

"Out of the mouths of babes," said Sister Emily.

"When you hear the young-uns saying it, you know that God is speaking through them."

"Or their parents," said Janet.

"You don't believe God speaks through the little children, Sister Janet?"

Janet looked at Dr. Speers in alarm. "Oh no. I mean, yes, of course God speaks through the children. I just meant that they learned it from their parents, too. Role models for Christ."

"Oh yes. They used to call it 'the hand that rocks the cradle.' It's the most important job a woman can have, teaching her children about Jesus. Isn't that right, Dr. Speers?" Sister Emily nodded sagely at Dr. Speers and around the room. Then she smiled brightly at Sister Mary, "I guess you're looking forward to having some little ones of your own one day?"

Sister Mary blushed and glanced hurriedly at Dr. Speers, and Dr. Speers appeared pleased.

Aunt Peggy gave Sister Sue a sly look and asked, "What about you, Sister Emily?"

"Me?" Sister Emily asked.

"I hear tell that your daughter, Connie, was seen with one of Pastor Wayne's boys. Any grandchildren in the picture?"

Everyone in the room gasped because everyone knew that Connie hadn't been chosen. Sister Emily reddened and stammered. "How can you say such things?"

Aunt Peggy's sharp face and mad eyes hadn't a trace of malice in them, but she was a friend of the Chambers and knowledge was growing that the Chambers' wanted Pastor Wayne removed. If Pastor Wayne couldn't control his household, he could be voted out by the congregation.

Dr. Speers asked, "Aunt Peggy? Who makes those accusations?"

"I'm sorry, Dr. Speers. I didn't mean anything by it. I just meant that Sister Emily should be looking after her family, that's all. We—me and Sister Sue Ann—saw them coming out of Henson's woods after the last Warriors for Christ picnic. It's not proper. And then, she wasn't chosen."

"Gossip is the Devil's tool, Aunt Peggy. Pastor Wayne's boys are good boys, and there's a rational explanation for what you saw."

"And my Connie is a good girl!"

"Of course, she is. But even good girls are susceptible to the Way of Eve."

Janet felt something dark creep over her. She felt an impulse to move forward as if to reach for Aunt Peggy, but she caught herself and stayed still, forced to sit in silent witness. The shame of her silence hung over her like a slick sweat, but she had no choice, not if she had any hope of helping Seila. Or surviving this.

Sister Mary looked stricken, too.

Aunt Peggy was relentless. "And I heard that your Connie admitted in Bible study last week that you don't watch her close enough, that sometimes you take a nap in the afternoon when she gets out of school."

"I took one nap two weeks ago, one. I was feeling poorly and had to lie down. I had such a headache." Sister Emily looked beseechingly to Dr. Speers. "It's okay to lie down when you're sick, isn't it?"

"We all have our infirmities, Sister Emily, but we push on. Look at Sister Sherry," said Sister Sue Ann.

Dr. Speers said, "Ladies, sisters, what does the Good Book say about the lilies of the field, how they toil not? I think that it's fine for ladies to rest now and then, so long as it doesn't become a habit of idleness. However, our need for rest should never overwhelm our duty to remain vigilant over our children, especially girls, and especially with the Devil so close at hand to turn our girls from the path of righteousness."

What are they doing? Janet wondered about Peggy and Sister Sue Ann. Do they know what they're doing? But then she remembered Sister Sue Ann's friend, Tammy, and thought, of course they do.

"Sometimes a headache is the work of the Devil," said Aunt Peggy.

Sister Emily's face quivered as she fought to hold back tears, and her head shook more than ever. "Why don't you tell them, Aunt Peggy? Why don't you tell them why you never had children? Can't that be the Devil?"

"Good heavens!" Sister Mary burst out.

Sister Emily convulsed. "I'm sorry. I'm sorry, Peggy...I'm sorry...I was just upset..."

"There's nothing to be sorry about Sister Emily, because I've done nothing wrong. Me and Robbie tried to have children. And maybe it was a devil, but I didn't stop trying. I didn't give in to it like you did. Shame on you for taking naps in the afternoon, when your daughter is in the hands of who knows who!"

Dr. Speers said, "Ladies, sisters. Before we go into this any further, let's bow our heads and ask for God's guidance." The agitated women bowed their heads on command.

Janet was afraid for Sister Emily and her daughter; fear felt dark and oily inside her skin. She knew better than any of them where they were headed, and they were all plunging down into murky, brown, cloying and deadly depths.

"Dear God, we humbly gather together today to learn your Word in Jesus name, and to learn how to apply it to our lives so we might all be better Christians to our families, our communities, our nation, and the Covenant. We have special problems here today and need your guidance now more than ever. Remove the veil of deception that may be hindering us in our faith. Help us to walk in truth and compassion today and for all our days to come. I ask this in Jesus' name. Amen."

Dr. Speers continued, "Now as to Aunt Peggy, some women have been cursed with…"

"But I couldn't help it…"

"Barren wombs. It's God's wish that they remain childless, and it's their cross to bear. It only becomes the concern of the State when there is a reasonable suspicion that contraceptives are in use. Aunt Peggy has already submitted herself to the medical community for review and was proven innocent in this matter. And she's long past childbearing age anyway. Now let's turn to First Corinthians, Chapter 5. Sister Janet, will you read from verse one through five."

Janet flipped through her Bible, turning pages deliberately slow as if fighting against profound inertia, but she drew herself up. For Seila. She read the passage as directed.

It is actually reported that there is sexual immorality among you, and of a kind that does not occur even among pagans: A man has his father's wife. And you are proud! Shouldn't you rather have been filled with grief and have put out of your fellowship the man who did this? Even though I am not physically present, I am with you in spirit. And I have already passed judgment on the one who did this, just as if I were present. When you are assembled in the name of our Lord Jesus and I am with you in spirit, and the power of our Lord Jesus is present, hand this man over to Satan, so that the sinful nature may be destroyed and his spirit saved on the day of the Lord.

"Thank you, Sister Janet. Now what does this tell us to do in our lives?"

Sister Sue Ann said, "Give the sexually immoral people to Satan to destroy their sinful nature."

"And what is the sinful nature?"

"The flesh."

"Very good. Now why should we hand over the sexually immoral people to Satan to destroy their flesh?

"Well, because God says so right here."

"But why does God say to do it?"

Sister Sue Ann said, "So that the spirit might be saved in the day of the Lord. We deliver them to Satan to destroy their sinful nature and save the spirit of the Church."

"We kill them to save ourselves?" Janet asked.

"To save the congregation. Sometimes, it's the most merciful thing we can do," said Dr. Speers.

"You say sometimes?"

"Sometimes a soul can be redeemed through redemption camps, such as the Way of Eve camps. If they are redeemed, we don't hand them over to Satan for destruction, but they must still be purged from the community, lest all perish for the sin. In that case, we relocate the redeemed to other towns where they are assimilated back into society, or we relocate penitents to the outskirts of town."

Sister Emily pleaded with Dr. Speers and the women in the room, "My Connie's all me and Edward got left. Our boys have gone to the Lord."

"We know Connie's a good girl, Sister Emily." Sister Mary said.

Sister Emily's voice shook as she trembled, "She was one of God's miracles. You know I was 48 years old when I had her. My boys were already grown."

"Sister Emily, we need to focus on the lesson now. Sister Mary, please read verses six and seven."

Sister Mary's voice also shook as she read.

Your boasting is not good. Don't you know that a little yeast works through the whole batch of dough? Get rid of the old yeast that you may be a new batch without yeast–as you really are. For Christ, our Passover lamb, has been sacrificed. Therefore let us keep the Festival, not with the old yeast, the yeast of malice and wickedness, but with bread without yeast, the bread of sincerity and truth.

"What do you think, Sister Janet? Is God's command clear?"

Janet played dumb and said, "Yes, don't make bread with old yeast. Of course, the bread won't rise with old yeast, will it?"

"We're not talking about bread, Sister Janet. We are talking about corruption. So, if Sister Emily's daughter has gone the Way of Eve in fornication, what should we do about that?"

"But she hasn't!" Sister Emily wailed.

"Quite so. This is hypothetical. If she had, what should we do, Sister Emily?

"I can't think of that...I can't possibly..."

"Sister Mary?"

Sister Mary's face turned completely red and she stammered, "I-I-I don't know. Can't she be redeemed?"

Dr. Speers looked at her for what seemed the longest time before he spoke. "Of course, she can. She can marry, so her husband can redeem her. Or she must be put aside and redeemed through the camps. There is always hope, even for sinners, but they can't be allowed to pollute the community and place a stumbling block before others. Would it be fair for some to burn in hell for another's transgressions?" And then he turned to Janet, asking, "Sister Janet?"

"No," she said and deep inside her, a song welled up. I got the joy, joy, joy, joy down in my heart and she was sickened by a phantom odor of pork and vomit and song. Her right hand twitched.

Dr. Speers said, "No. Of course not. It's good that we remain compassionate, but we cannot suffer an unrepentant sinner to remain in our midst. Sometimes kindness means surgically removing the tumor that's destroying the body. Now this has been a difficult class this morning, and I think we may feel a little wounded from this process. Consequently, let's all stand and hold hands and pray for healing and understanding. Sister Janet, come stand by me."

"Why?" she asked and curious faces turned to look at her. "Please."

Janet went and stood to the right of Dr. Speers, and he reached for her hand. She allowed him to take her hand, and his hand felt rough and cool to her like a snake winding through her fingers. The other women lined up and joined hands. Sister Emily kept her eyes cast down and could not look at any of them.

After the prayer, they filed out except for Janet who Dr. Speers asked to stay and whose hand he had tightened his grip on when she first tried to pull away. "Such soft hands," he said as he turned them over, tracing one finger down the line where Janet's incision had once been. Fortunately, Janet had been to a master plastic surgeon who had sewn her up with thread like gossamer after he replaced her ID chip and changed her identity. It was all but impossible to see the scar from the typical palm lines.

"How long have you and George been married?"

"Three months. Why do you ask?"

"You look very comfortable together, like you've been together for many years. I just wondered."

"Yes, well, from the time I met George, I felt like I'd known him all my life."

Dr. Speers smiled a tight smile and let go of her hand. "See you in the service."

In the morning service that followed, Janet listened dully to her brothers and sisters in Christ sing Christ Lives in Families. Her thoughts drifted to poor Sister Emily and her beautiful child, Connie, and then to Dr. Speers tracing the line of her hand with his finger. Her heart pounded.

Pastor Wayne got her attention when he announced a new member of the congregation. "Please welcome John

McMannus. John, can you please stand so everyone can see you?"

Janet turned and saw Johnny at the back of the church. Tears of relief nearly spilled from her eyes, but she blinked them back.

He said, "You can call me Johnny Mac."

"Johnny Mac everyone. I understand that you've started work at Wendell prison."

"Yes sir, and I'm grateful for the opportunity."

"Where did you move from, Johnny Mac?"

"Jacksonville, but I grew up twenty miles from here. My mama's still there." Johnny Mac's eyes swept the congregation, and his eyes briefly caught Janet's.

"Well, we are tickled pink to have you here. Everyone, be sure and welcome Johnny Mac back home. It's almost back home anyway."

Janet could hardly contain her sense of hope, but Pastor Wayne caught her attention when he read from Thessalonians. He was no longer beaming as he had when he was introducing Johnny. His voice thundered, "For we hear that there are some which walk among you disorderly, working not at all, but are busybodies."

He looked around the congregation and said, "Now what He's telling us is that an idle mind is the Devil's playground. Satan starts whispering, insinuating...that's what the Devil does...he insinuates...tells tales out of school and turns brother against brother and sister against sister..."

Someone shouted, "Well, maybe we need to talk plainly preacher!"

"Something on your mind, brother Billy?"

Janet looked around her. Some people grumbled and others shook their heads.

"Has Connie Mobley gone the Way of Eve?"

"My Connie's a good girl!" Sister Emily cried out.

{13}

Cellmate

BEFORE SEILA WAS sent back to her cell after another interview with Dr. Speers, he said, "You didn't tell me Jim was alive when I first asked, and for that, I withdraw the offer of sentencing her as a penitent. I will, however, make you another promise. If you can provide me with the information that I need, I promise that her death will be quick and you'll be released as a penitent. I'm going to send you back to your cell now, so that you can think it over. I need three things from you: a description of her from the last time you saw her, where you saw her last, and the names of anyone who helped you, from the time you left your home in Jacksonville until the time we found you in those woods."

Seila couldn't remember if she told Dr. Speers if Jim was alive or not. She said, "I don't know if Jim's alive."

"Yes, you do. You do."

He added, "Tell me what I need, and if your answers are complete and you are genuine in your desire for redemption, we can begin transitioning you to cells with others prisoners slotted for penitence. In the meantime, as a show of good faith, we will begin acclimating you for this change by providing you with your first cellmate today. I trust you'll make the right decision, but you're running out of time. Jim may already be in Wendell, but I'm looking for confirmation from you."

As Seila was escorted back to her cell by the guard, Sonny, she felt a flicker of that devil, hope, which died a quick death when she thought about what Speers was asking. And then it occurred to her that it was hope, a simple twist of thought that robbed her of her chance to kill Speers. The hope that she could still get out of this prison, that they could both survive. But it wasn't just hope, was it? It was also her belief in her own humanity.

But what good was saving herself if she couldn't save Jim? She should have killed Speers when she had the chance. If she had killed him, wouldn't Jim be safer? She relived the moment when she had the gun, and Dr. Speers was urging her on. She imagined a second chance at pulling the trigger, and the thought soothed her.

When Sonny opened her cell, she found herself standing face-to-face with a gaunt, pale young woman, who introduced herself as Lily. Lily had dark, purple circles under her large, brown eyes, and her head was also shorn.

After Sonny was gone, Seila asked, "How long have you been in Wendell?"

"A year. You?"

"I don't know exactly. Months, I guess. Not a year."

Seila lowered herself to the floor of her cell and asked, "Why are you here?"

"You mean in your cell?"

"Both. In my cell. In Wendell."

Lily rubbed her nose with her red sleeve. "My brother was labeled a subversive. After they took him, they came back and got the whole family, Mom, Dad, sisters, Grandma, the whole family." She hissed, "I hate him for doing this to us."

"Was he a subversive?"

"I don't know. No."

"Then why do you hate him?"

"Who else can I hate?" Lily asked blankly. "Anyway, they didn't tell me why they brought me to your cell other than to say that I might become a penitent, and I would be transitioning. Seems too good to be true." Lily laid down and stretched out on the floor and asked, "How long have you had your own cell?"

"As long as I've been in here."

"You must be really important to have had a cell to yourself. I hope you're not a serial killer or anything." She sat back up and said, "We couldn't stretch out like this in our cell. There were thirty-one of us in a cell as big as my old dining room. We slept slumped over someone's shoulder. And the piss bucket. Ugh, I don't want to think about it."

When Seila didn't respond, Lily asked, "So. What did you do to get in here?"

"Nothing," Seila said as she looked up at the camera.

"Lily sat up and looked at her, "There's gotta be something. Are you a witch?"

Seila smiled faintly and shook her head, "No. Not a witch."

"Too bad. If you were a witch, you could put a curse on the one who put us in here. I think it was my neighbor, Teri, who turned us in. Teri could be all syrupy sweet when she wanted something from you, but she got downright vicious if you ever turned her down. And my brother said his little thing would shrivel up like a turtle when she showed up. Well, he didn't call it a little thing, but you know what I mean. No part of him wanted any part of her. And she knew it. I know she turned him in. She turned in a lot of people. The Redeemers would come for somebody, and you'd see a smug little smile on her ugly, flat face. Wish I coulda wiped that smile off her before they got me."

The more Lily talked, the more afraid for her Seila became. The Redeemers wouldn't tolerate this kind of talk, particularly from a woman. Didn't she know that?

Lily laid back down and said, "It's too late now. In here, we're already ghosts. I doubt they'll let us be penitents or anything else. We'll die in here, and no one on the outside will know or remember us."

"My sister will remember me."

"If you got a sister, they'll get her, too."

Seila realized her error and said, "My sister died five years ago."

"Then how's she gonna remember you?"

"From heaven," Seila answered hurriedly.

They both laid down under bright lights and the cameras. After a while, Lily said, "I can't sleep in this place."

Seila turned to face her and whispered, "What do you know about Speers?"

Lily also whispered, "Nothing. I'm not from this town, but one of the women in my cell was."

"Did she know him? Did he have a mother, sisters?"

"She said he didn't, not when she knew him. He had a mean daddy though." Lily cupped her hand over the side of her mouth and after a quick glance at the camera, Lily said, "She said that he must have come fully-formed out of the crack of his dad's ass."

Seila laughed and nearly choked at the same time.

Lily's eyes got big and she said, "I shouldn't have said that. Don't tell them I said that. They cut that woman's tongue out for that."

Seila looked somber and said, "I think I saw her. They burned her at the stake."

"What the fuck!?" Lily mouthed silently. She looked cornered and fearful and curled into a fetal position. Then she started to cry, at least Seila thought she did. Her shoulders were quaking and she was sniffling.

Seila said, "Crying only makes it worse. Dr. Speers doesn't like it."

They stopped talking and Seila's thoughts circled wearily around Lily, and Jim, and killing Speers. She said, "I can't think straight anymore," and then she realized that she had spoken out loud.

Lily seemed to be sleeping by then, and Seila curled into a fetal position, too, and thought about when she and Jim were teens.

Before their parents died, persecution and harassment were not yet overtly, legally sanctioned. But they became more commonplace. Teenage boys showed up at Seila's work sneering about her dyke sister. A man called up late one night and spoke in a chilling but quiet voice, saying that he saw Jim at the pool and was going to rip her bathing suit right off her and teach her a lesson she wouldn't forget. It scared Mom half to death. That's when Seila first urged Jim to pretend to be straight. She told Jim she had a premonition that things could get worse.

Seila had looked at the near-naked actresses that covered Jim's walls and ceiling, the feathered wings, feather boas, Mardi Gras faces and beads, a stuffed lion on the bed, and the photo of her girlfriend, Karen, on the bedside table. Seila said, "You're not just doing this to yourself. You're putting everyone you love in danger."

Jim's eyes dilated and she yelled. "Get out! I hate you!"

Later, when the Redeemers came to power and dissolved the secular government, the violence came from all directions, militia, neighbors, and Redeemers. It was almost a blessing that Mom and Dad died when they did. They didn't have to see what happened to their daughters.

All this time, Seila tried extra hard to be extra proper to survive and with the hopes of helping her sister to survive. But Jim never could hide who she was, and Seila never could help her. Seila rubbed her cracked and bleeding knuckles and turned to the wall. Lily's words chilled her. "Who else could I hate?" And Seila knew that, although she had never hated Jim, she hadn't been fair to her. None of it was her fault. And in the end, it was Jim who came back to try to save Seila from the Redeemers.

After a while, Seila fell into a fitful sleep and dreamed she had helped hide a body many years past, and the police were now catching up to her. The body would be dug up and she would be implicated. This was a recurring dream since she'd been in Wendell, and each time, it was a different body. Sometimes a teenage boy. Sometimes a young woman. Then she'd wake, with deep shame and fear that gradually subsided as she realized that she had never done such a thing. Relief flooded through her, but it was short lived because she was still in Wendell.

Lily groaned in her sleep, and Seila wondered what dreams haunted her in this place.

And through this bleak night, Seila wondered if she should tell Speers where she saw Jim. Surely, Jim was long gone by now, so it wouldn't matter.

{14}

False Tales

AFTER CHURCH, SISTER Mary walked all the way to Dr. Speers' house. She slipped a note under his door, but before she could walk away from the front porch, an old woman hurried up the street toward Mary at a speed that seemed to defy her age. She had a dirty green and brown, army-issue blanket slung around her shoulders. Her face was a scarred and wrinkled net across her hollow skull, and her mouth was sunk in. She wore a black knitted cap, dirty white tennis shoes that were clearly too big, and a filthy black dress. Sister Mary feared she was a witch, and her heart flipped into her throat. Then she saw the letter P stitched on the woman's dress. The woman was a penitent.

She stopped in front of Mary and asked, "Is this Dr. Speers' house?" Her voice was harsh and angry.

Sister Mary nodded but couldn't speak.

"Who are you?"

"A friend," Sister Mary said.

"A friend of this devil?" she demanded, incredulous.

At that moment, a Redeemer van careened around the corner, startling both women. The old woman tried to hurry to the side of the house, while the van's black doors opened and the Redeemers poured out.

Before they knocked her to the ground, the old woman screamed, "You tell him I put a curse on him! He'll be dead soon! Tell him!" Then she let out a tremendous howl as they pulled her into the van, and Sister Mary thought she heard her shout, "he's the Anti-Christ!" but it was so incoherent that Sister Mary wasn't sure if she heard it or imagined it.

As soon as they were gone, Dr. Speers arrived home. He looked at Sister Mary quizzically as he came up the steps. "Sister Mary, are you okay?

"I came by to...a woman came by here. She was horrible."

"Did the Redeemers come?"

"Yes."

"Good. I'll check into it later."

"She said she had cursed you."

Dr. Speers frowned and said, "Sister Mary, we're at war with the agents of darkness. Never forget that. In my line of work, I work with the worst of Satan's agents who know this is the final battle and will pervert any truth and attempt things that the rest of us can't even imagine. But with God on our side, they can't hurt us."

Sister Mary looked at the gray, painted-wood floor of Dr. Speers' porch and nodded.

Dr. Speers turned to his front door. "Good girl. Now come inside, and I'll get you some tea."

"Wait!" Sister Mary cried out.

Dr. Speers stepped back, puzzled. "Sister Mary?"

"I slid a note under your door. Please just give it back to me without reading it."

Dr. Speers opened the door, bent down, and picked up the letter. "This letter?"

"Yes, please don't open it. Just give it back."

Dr. Speers smiled as he held it from Sister Mary. "Now wait a minute." He turned his back on her as he opened the letter. She tried to get around him to grab it, but he spun around and eluded her. "Hold on, Sister Mary. Just hold on," and he held out his arm to bar her from coming any closer.

"Your father will hear."

"He's at a senior's fellowship."

After he read the note, he gave it back to her smiling. "Let's don't have secrets, Sister Mary, and I don't blame you for this. My behavior was inexcusable last week. I hope you can forgive me."

"I know you wouldn't hurt me. I can't imagine you hurting anybody, but..."

"But what?"

"What's the difference between our walk in the woods and young Connie's?"

Dr. Speers stopped smiling, took a deep breath, and let the air out slowly. "Connie's been to a doctor. Someone got a copy of her report and has circulated it around Wendell. She's no virgin, Sister Mary."

"That can't be true. It's not true. Someone's made a mistake."

"I wish things were different, but our hands are tied on this one."

"And Luke Wayne?"

"He won't marry her and claims he never touched her. The town is split now. Some people think he's lying, and they want Pastor Wayne to step down. Others think he's telling the truth, and Connie has lain down with someone else."

"What does Connie say?"

"She says it was the Wayne boy. She says he forced her."

"No! But what about DNA?"

"DNA won't change the fact that she committed a sin against God. She went the Way of Eve. It would be wise to distance yourself from Sister Emily."

"Oh, how could I? She's such a dear person. We can't do that. Please say you won't do that?"

"What do you want me to do, Sister Mary?" He took her by the hand and led her to a rocking chair. "Come. Sit. I'll get you some tea and we'll talk."

"No!" Sister Mary glanced uneasily at the cameras on Dr. Speers' front porch. "People will talk."

He spoke to her as if he were speaking to a child. "We're on the front porch. In broad daylight." Dr. Speers took her shoulders and pressed her lightly into the rocking chair.

Sister Mary noticed all the cameras on Dr. Speers' porch, on light poles, and even in the oak in front of his house. At home, she had Aunt Peggy bursting into her bedroom unannounced or admonishing her for forgetting to soak the beans. Intrusions were a fact of life. Everyone knew that evil grew large in secret, so it was best that everything and everyone remain open to the community's inspection, like young Connie, but sometimes it was just too much.

Dr. Speers brought Sister Mary a cup of hot tea, and the steam rose and warmed her nose as she brought it to her mouth and sipped. The tea was too sweet, but Sister Mary would not be rude.

Sister Mary held her tea in her lap and said, "They taught us in school that the Devil liked secrets."

"Yes."

"But there are secrets everywhere."

"You mean Wendell prison."

"Yes."

Dr. Speers sighed and rocked back in his chair.

Sister Mary kept her eyes cast down. "I know I'm not supposed to ask you about Wendell, but I have to know what you do there."

"Yes, maybe you do."

Sister Mary looked up fearfully and expectantly.

Dr. Speers sighed. "My job is to destroy an inmate's capacity for resistance and replace it with a cooperative attitude. Once that's done, I gain confessions and gather information needed to prevent further attacks on God's elect. We save lives, Sister Mary."

"How do you destroy an inmate's capacity for resistance?"

"Kindness. We kill them with kindness and reasonableness."

Dr. Speers quoted scripture. "If your enemy is hungry, feed him; If he is thirsty, give him a drink; For in so doing you will heap coals of fire on his head."

"Does that really work?"

Dr. Speers chuckled. "The Bible also says, 'If anyone among you seems to be wise in this age, let him become a fool that he may become wise.' So, if inmates refuse to answer our initial questions honestly, then we have to strip them of the ego that's holding them back. When they are fully broken down, they become innocent again, empty vessels. Then, they are finally ready to cooperate and are most open to suggestion."

"Suggestion?"

"Deprogramming. Most Anti-Christs have been conditioned to believe monstrous things about the Redeemers. This enables them to commit atrocities on innocent civilians. Consequently, we don't want to just gain confessions, we want to change hearts and minds. After we get their attention, we assail them with logic until even they can see through their former delusions. Then we reintroduce Jesus into their lives. We want converts, Sister Mary, so we can save their souls, and in some cases, release law-abiding, God-fearing believers back into society; and naturally, there are some who cling to their delusions. Satan is formidable. Make no mistake about that."

Dr. Speers raised his teacup to his lips. "This is between us. You understand?"

"Yes," Sister Mary said but she felt uneasy. They watched a Redeemer van roll by and someone on the passenger side waved to Dr. Speers, who waved back.

Sister Mary asked, "What kinds of questions do you ask the prisoners?" And Sister Mary wondered about her mother, what they might have asked her before she was redeemed.

"The basic stuff at first. For example, have you ever known a feminist, Sister Mary?"

Sister Mary's heart beat faster as Dr. Speers fixed his eyes on her, and she wondered about Janet. "No."

His questioning came in a rapid fire and her heart felt faint as she answered.

He asked, "Have you ever known a homosexual?"

"No."

"Have you ever known a Satanist?"

"No."

"Have you ever known anyone plotting or urging violence against the Covenant government?"

"Enough, enough. I'm the kind of person who feels guilty when I'm innocent." Her face was warm, and she hurriedly took a drink of warm tea. "But if anyone were any of these things, they would lie."

"Exactly. My job is to expose the lie. I ask questions, watch for body language. Suspects tend to leak physical clues to what they really know or feel. They turn toward the door in a natural flight response, or cross legs and arms if they're feeling defensive. If so, I'll calm them down and help them relax. I'll also notice if she's rubbing the back of her neck?"

"She?" Again, an image of Sister Mary's mother flitted across her mind.

"We house some women at Wendell. As I was saying, humans instinctively protect their neck when cornered in questioning. Does she put her hand over her mouth when answering? Avert her eyes?"

"I avert my eyes sometimes, but just because I'm embarrassed about something."

"We keep those things in mind. Sometimes, a suspect sits back with her feet apart and her hands open, palms upward. That indicates that she's telling the truth."

"A woman would never sit back with her feet apart."

"We don't look at just any one thing. It's the whole picture. During the course of the interview, I'll gradually move my chair forward to get inside the suspect's defense space." Dr. Speers turned his chair and moved it forward until he was almost touching Mary. "If the suspect is female, I won't touch her, but I'll be close enough to where our knees are almost touching. Like this." Dr. Speers smiled gently at Sister Mary, and a tremor went through her.

"When I feel that she's ready to confess, I might reach out and touch her on the arm as if to say, 'I'm here. Talk to me.'" Dr. Speers lightly touched Sister Mary on the arm and she felt a rush of energy travel up her arm and through her body. He let his fingers linger on her forearm, as he looked into her eyes. And she wondered if she should tell him about Janet.

"The human touch sometimes triggers the confession because most people want to confess. They feel bad about what they've done." Sister Mary felt bad about keeping secrets and that she let him leave his fingers on her arm, so she looked guiltily at the camera on the post by the stairs.

Dr. Speers removed his hand and pushed his chair back. "Of course, it doesn't work on everybody. Those whose hearts have been hardened don't feel remorse for what they've done, and in their case, we have to go through the softening up process first. But I'm making you uncomfortable." Dr. Speers lowered his voice. "I do it to keep people like you safe, Sister Mary."

Sister Mary whispered, "I think you're a brave man," but she allowed herself to wonder if her mother was really safe in another town.

Two little girls walked onto the porch of the house across the street. They were singing, "Yes, Jesus loves me...the Bible tells me so."

"What did the woman who came to my house today look like?" Dr. Speers asked. "Did you know her?"

"I've never seen her before. She looked wild and old, like a witch."

"What did she say to you?"

"She said to tell you that she put a curse on you. She said you'd be dead soon. And I think she called you the Anti-Christ."

Dr. Speers laughed and leaned back again in his chair. "She did?"

Sister Mary smiled because Dr. Speers smiled, but she didn't know why.

"These people will stop at nothing."

The Chambers' black sedan came down the street and Aunt Peggy leaned her head out of the rear passenger side window. "Washed clean."

"By blood," they said in unison.

Aunt Peggy asked, "Did you hear about Connie Mobley?"

Sister Mary wondered if one day Aunt Peggy would ask, "Did you hear about Sister Mary?"

"Yes, Aunt Peggy, but what does God say about gossip?" Dr. Speers admonished.

Inside, Sister Mary smiled. She was so proud of Dr. Speers for saying that.

"Evil grows in the dark, Dr. Speers."

"And in false tales, Aunt Peggy."

"Well, there's nothing false about this. The Redeemers took Connie straight after church."

"What will they do to her?" Sister Mary asked.

Dr. Speers said, "As a kindness to the family, they'll re-educate her and release her as a penitent, unless of course, Luke Wayne relents and agrees to marry her. In that case, they'll re-educate her and release her to him."

"Humphh," Aunt Peggy said. "Well, I'm on my way to the Chambers for lunch. See you at home, Sister Mary."

"Yes, ma'am."

Dr. Speers leaned forward and whispered, "The Camps and the Chambers have wanted Pastor Wayne to step down for some time. They want one of their own as Pastor, and between their two families, they're half the church. I'm willing to bet they've been staking out the woods around the Wayne's family farms for quite some time. You watch. This won't end with Connie Mobley."

"That's awful."

Dr. Speers shrugged. "What can we do?"

{15}

No Medals

THE NEXT DAY, Dr. Speers received a call on his cell phone from Warden Camp, asking him to come to the prison. They needed to talk. As Dr. Speers pulled his car from the driveway, he saw Sister Sue Ann waving him down from the sidewalk.

He braked, eased to the side of the road and rolled down the window.

"I'm glad I caught you, Dr. Speers. With all that business about the Mobley girl, I forgot to give you the list. Sister Sue Ann's soft brown hair was pulled back with a red-checkered bow, but she wore no cosmetics now that the Redeemers forbade it

"The list?"

She held out a printout. "The Calgary list. You know. The list of women who volunteered to counsel at the prison."

"Sister Sue Ann. Always on top of things."

Dr. Speers smiled, took the paper, and rolled his window up waving the sheet at her to say good bye as he pulled away. At the next red light, he pulled his reading glasses from their case. He put them on and scanned the list to find Janet Moore's name on it.

Dr. Speers drove the long, winding road to Wendell Prison wondering what business Warden Camp had that couldn't wait until morning. Surely not the Mobley matter. That would be routine.

He took a right onto Zachariah Road where someone had placed a small white cross. As Dr. Speers turned onto Zachariah, dun-colored prison buildings, tall fences, and barbed wire rose from the pines. Wendell Prison Incorporated.

Dr. Speers paused at checkpoints, saying, "Good morning, brother," to the guards. Gates slid open and he passed through, while automatic scans passed data from Dr. Speers' ID chip to a central database deep inside the prison.

When he arrived in Warden Camp's office, Camp was poring over some records. A photograph of Warden Camp's wife and children was displayed in a silver frame facing outward instead of toward Camp. His wife was a small woman, and his children, both boys, knelt in front, frozen in this posture since the photo was taken and arranged on Camp's desk to be viewed by prisoners and guards alike who waited in the hard chair for their orders. "It's all about family," Warden Camp liked to say.

Dr. Speers sat in an antique wooden seat in front of Camp's desk and waited. His mouth was a tight, straight line and he frowned. He hated to be kept waiting, and he didn't like having his back to the door.

Camp finally looked up, his spectacles reflecting two circles of light, and smiled. "Washed clean."

"By blood."

Dr. Camp was a short, stocky man with a round, baby face and light-brown hair. Today, like any other day, his face was creased in a deceptively benign smile. "Thanks for coming down on the Lord's Day. Very sorry to have called you away."

"What's happened?"

"Seila Lee Campbell."

"Yes?"

"I'm looking through these records, and it seems to me that we don't have a lot on her."

Dr. Speers looked at Warden Camp thoughtfully, but did not speak.

"Cameras and mics are off."

Dr. Speers looked up at the camera above Camp's desk, and the red light was off. He cleared his throat. "She may be innocent in regards to the bombing, but she has a homosexual sister who was tried for murder, and found guilty in absentia. Her sister stayed at least one night at the Campbell home before vanishing. She was listed as dead at one time, but Mrs. Campbell indicated that she's still alive. I have a hunch that Mrs. Campbell has seen her since her death certificate was signed and can tell us where she was last seen. In any case, we've got her on charges of aiding and abetting a murderer and known terrorist."

Warden Camp sighed. "That may not be enough. Charlie comes from money and he had powerful friends, and people are asking questions about that Tabernacle Square bombing. The Redeemers know they screwed this one up, and now..."

Dr. Speers interrupted, "What do you mean the Redeemers screwed this one up?"

"Some folks on the Redeemer task force got trigger-happy and killed that old boy, and instead of putting down the shovel when they found themselves in a hole, they blew up his office a few days later to make it look like a Subversive action."

"They what?"

"They found a woman on the street after curfew. Before they could question her, Charlie Campbell hustled her away, saying that he was late picking her up. They let them go, and then had second thoughts."

"Yes, that's in the record."

"What's not in the record is that the Redeemers killed him the next day. Then when Mrs. Campbell started asking questions, they put his body in his office and staged the Tabernacle Square explosion as a cover-up."

Dr. Speers looked at Warden Camp, studying him. "Why would they do that?"

"Oh hell. You give a city boy a gun, some plastic explosives and a little authority, and he gets overzealous. I don't know. They said they thought Campbell was a Subversive."

"Was he a Subversive?"

"No. Now we gotta help them cover the whole thing up. His death. The explosion. I don't need to tell you how bad this would look for the Covenant government. A Christian nation has an image to uphold."

Dr. Speers rubbed his forehead and kept his hand there for a moment. Idiots. He took his hand away. "And so they leaked the story to the press about Mrs. Campbell being the bomber?"

"Yup."

Dr. Speers fell silent again until Warden Camp cleared his throat and said, "Sometimes someone has to be sacrificed for the good of the flock."

Dr. Speers unbuttoned his suit jacket and sat back, a posture that he was not prone to take. Dr. Speers wanted to believe that everything he did was for the right reasons. Of course, he had killed Sister Mary's mother, but she would have poisoned Sister Mary with her doubts. He saved Sister Mary.

Warden Camp interrupted his musings, "So, I gotta ask and you gotta give it to me straight between the eyes. Are you quite sure she's not involved with the Anti-Christ Subversives or something else we can use to tie her to the bombing, something with a little more ummph than aiding and abetting a sister?"

"What do you need?"

"We need her to confess to the Tabernacle Square bombing, and we need it public. We need a televised confession and public apology. We need a televised execution."

Dr. Speers sat straight in his chair while Camp spun his paperweight. The paperweight was a miniaturized image of the Statue of Accountability, a glass bauble given to prison officials by a banking consortium in appreciation for their role in processing debtors. "They're a bunch of darn fools, but you and I both know that if this sort of thing got out, it would be a blow to the credibility of the Covenant government. You know that. The almighty God doesn't make mistakes."

Dr. Speers still didn't speak while he weighed the problem on his relative scale of right and wrong and justification.

Warden Camp appeared annoyed with Dr. Speers' silence and his voice was tinged with irritation. "If you don't think you can handle this, we can get someone who can."

Dr. Speers nodded once as if bowing, "It's going to take some time."

"How much time?"

"Two months."

"That won't do. Charlie Campbell had friends in high places, and they're asking questions. There's talk about getting together a commission to look into Mrs. Campbell's status down here. We can stall them a little while by citing national security concerns, but sooner or later they're going to want to see her. We don't have much time."

Dr. Speers sighed, "Six weeks then. That's going to be pushing it, so I trust I have permission to conduct a vigorous interrogation—medical, chemical, electrical."

"Make that four weeks, and you're the artist. You do your job, and I'll work out things on my end."

Dr. Speers rose from his chair and buttoned his suit jacket. "What do you know of George Moore's wife?"

"Not much. They met in Atlanta and married a few months ago. Why?"

"Has anyone ever done a background check on her?"

"She's been scanned."

"Has anyone matched the information on the scan with her actual DNA?"

"No and no one's going to. That old boy's a real buddy of mine and a great patriot. Now what would it be like if we go sniffing around his wife?"

Dr. Speers held the back of the chair as if he were bracing his body against a strong wind, then he nodded. "I'll keep you informed on my progress."

As he turned to leave, Camp called after him. "Hey pee-casso."

Dr. Speers turned slowly.

"You stay away from Janet Moore."

"Of course."

"Another thing. What's that foreign boy's name? Sonny something."

Dr. Speers smiled slightly. "He's from the Catholic State of New Mexico. The name's Valdez."

"That's the one. That young fella was in here with some crazy story about a fire and an old woman. Just thought you'd like to know."

Dr. Speers frowned and said, "I've heard."

"Good. By the way, pull this one off, pee-casso, and you'll be awarded the Covenant Medal of Honor."

Dr. Speers turned and said, "No medals."

He drove home, turning over thoughts on the Campbell case, which made him think of Warden Camp's request, the entire Camp clan, and then the Camps and the Chambers' growing feud with the Waynes. The Camps' and the Chambers' desire to replace Pastor Wayne with one of their own was a real problem. Hal Wayne was his right-hand man, and it wouldn't do to lose him now.

On Monday morning, Dr. Speers called a conference with Officers Sonny Valdez and Hal Wayne. "Gentlemen, sometimes our measures and procedures for bringing inmates to accountability are hard; however, it's crucial to the safety and well-being of our society, especially at a time when we are besieged by enemies. That said, I do understand that some of our procedures are difficult to employ if one is not fully aware of their purpose. One must be clear that it's for the greater good. Brother Sonny, I have been deeply troubled by your concerns of the past couple of weeks, particularly now that I have to call on you for an extremely sensitive assignment. So, I'm going to put my cards on the table."

Sonny sat up straighter, and Hal cast a malevolent glance his way.

"Mrs. Campbell is suspected of being involved in the Tabernacle Square bombing, where her husband and two other people were killed. We're trying to save lives here, not just the lives of Believers, but the lives of our fellow Redeemers. We need to know who she got her explosives from and what they're planning next. Then, we need her confession on this, and we need it public. We're going to make Mrs. Campbell a priority project now. Can I count on your cooperation, Valdez?"

"Yes, sir."

"Everyone, please take a copy of the revised project plan for Mrs. Campbell's confession. Mrs. Campbell is becoming acclimated. That will work against us. Look over this schedule. Let's step up the unpredictability of her interrogation sessions. As you can see, after our meeting today, she will be left alone for two days, brought to me on Wednesday, returned to her cell, and allowed a five-minute sleep. Then she is to be brought back to me. Act as if she has had a full night's sleep. Also, vary her meal schedule. At no time is anyone to let her know the time or the day."

"And we want to fear up our inmate. Valdez, strip inmate Campbell and escort her through Sodom & Gomorrah."

Dr. Speers' face was, as always, deadpan. He slid a file over to Sonny. "And I need you to finalize Hal's report on last week's accidental death. Fix it and make it sound good. Sign it. Date it. Bring it to me when you're done. When I approve it, you'll enter it into the system."

While Dr. Speers watched by remote camera, Sonny escorted Seila by caged men who engaged in howls, catcalls, and open masturbation. Seila stumbled repeatedly, and

Officer Valdez reached out to steady her. Every time he touched her, she flinched.

Someone yelled, "Bring the bitch over here. I love the bitches."

When Sonny returned Seila to her cell, Lily was gone. Seila didn't seem to notice her absence. She moved wherever Sonny led her, without resistance, sat wherever he placed her, and her eyes were glassy and distant. Sonny backed out of the cell slowly.

{16}

Family Ties

JANET FOUND HERSELF alone and saw a note from George that he had gone to Ed and Emily's house. Conveniently enough, Sister Emily's house was just past Bachelors' hill where Sonny and Johnny lived. She thought this was an opportunity for her to check on Sister Emily under the pretext of joining George, and if she happened upon Johnny, they had good cover to speak for a few minutes. She walked with a brisk, cold wind at her back that hurried her along. She slowed as she passed Bachelors' hill and looked up the hill. She didn't see Johnny, so she kept walking to Sister Emily's pale green farmhouse set back from the road.

Before she could knock on Sister Emily's door, she heard a man's voice through the open living room window, saying, "But Connie was a gift from God. He wouldn't let the Devil take her away. Something happened, something that wasn't her fault." It was Edward, Connie's dad speaking.

"God is testing your faith, Brother Ed, just like He tested Job's faith before you, just like He tested Abraham when He commanded him to take Isaac up on the mountain for a sacrifice."

Someone else said, "It's God's will, Ed. The Lord gave and the Lord took away."

"If I knew it was the Lord that took her away, I might be easier in my mind. Then I'd know the Lord would take care of her, too. But I don't know that, do I? The way I see it, the Camps and the Chambers have taken her away, and if you get right down to it, the Waynes and this feud they all got going took her away. Seems to me that the Devil's working in Wendell alright, but it ain't through my little girl."

"Now hold on a minute, Ed. That's not fair. The Camps and the Chambers are good people, and you might not like to hear it, but your daughter wasn't a virgin. Like it or not, she went the Way of Eve. Now how are you going to say the Camps and the Chambers had anything to do with that?"

"It might have been Luke who did it, but the Camps and the Chambers were sure quick to jump on this and have her taken away. I don't know. I don't know what I'm saying anymore. And besides, how do we know she ain't a virgin? We just have Doc Perry's word on it."

"Now Ed."

"And if she ain't a virgin, Luke forced himself on her. And if I find out for sure that he done it..."

"Well, that Wayne boy did come out of the woods with her. We can talk to him, see if we can reason him into marrying her?"

Janet realized that it had been George speaking, and then Ed said, "They aren't going to let you near that boy."

Janet took a deep breath and tapped at the door. The men stopped talking. She thought she could hear someone getting up from a creaky chair, and then Brother Ed was at the door. He was stooped over like he was carrying a great load.

"George left me a note that he was here. I thought I might see him and check on Sister Emily."

"Sister Emily's feeling too poorly today." Ed turned his head and said, "George, it's your wife."

Janet said, "Maybe I can help. Maybe I can sit with her for a while."

"I know you want to help, but there's nothing you can do here. Connie was all she had left in the world. She won't see anyone. Won't eat, and as far as I can tell, won't sleep neither. Just keeps rocking herself, rocking herself and praying. You come back another day."

George came to the door behind Ed and said, "Go home. We'll talk later." He shut the door and left Janet standing on the porch.

She turned and walked down the porch steps to the sidewalk. The sky was too bright and the cold wind bore down on her as she pushed forward.

≈

Before attending the next knitting circle, Janet stared into her reddened and worried eyes in the bathroom mirror of the church restroom, and she focused her attention

on the heavy feeling in the center of her chest. She remembered Karen resting a smooth hand over her heart, asking
"If you gave it a color, what color would you give it?"

"Black and blue."

"What's underneath that?"

"Rage."

"And underneath that?"

"Fear."

Janet thought about Dr. Speers turning over her hand
and tracing his finger down the line at the center of her
palm. She should have thought about a background check.
How could she be so stupid? Of course, they'd check out the
volunteers. Maybe they would just question her about her
past and be done with it. She considered the critical details
again. She was christened Janet Nell Horne and was born to
John and Barbara Horne. She was the only girl with seven
brothers, and she was the sole family survivor. She always
intended to dedicate her life to Jesus, and consequently,
didn't marry until she met George and fell in love for the
first time in her life.

And the only way the background check can cause a
problem is if they match the DNA on my chip with my actual
DNA. They have no reason to do that. Inside, Janet did not
feel so confident. All chips have data about the DNA of their
owner, and Janet had someone else's chip.

Janet felt certain that Dr. Speers knew something. Would
there be time to rescue Seila?

Janet ran into Johnny after she left the bathroom. She dropped her yarn and Johnny bent down to retrieve it, speaking low, "Got a job as a driver for the prison transport, but Seila's in a special wing. Can't get near her."

Janet said, "Sonny Valdez might be sympathetic. He's wavering, but watch yourself. He can go either way. And Johnny, you should know that Mary Webber knows who I am. She says she won't tell anyone, but I don't know. You want to back out?"

John handed her the yarn, and said, "I think that rocket is already launched. I'm in." Then he quickly walked away.

Janet went outside to join the knitting circle, and the women were already settled down and knitting. It was a cold day and they were all bundled up. Sister Emily was not with them.

Janet had hoped to get Sister Mary alone, perhaps to feel her out some more. She worried for Sister Mary and wished she could warn her about Dr. Speers, but it was too risky, and she worried about what Sister Mary might tell him. She walked across the dead winter grass and had the strange déjà vu experience that she had been there before, walking across the grass to these women on this day, and when Aunt Peggy asked, "Did you hear about Connie Mobley?" she knew the exact inflection that would be in Aunt Peggy's voice.

The strangeness slackened her jaw and her concentration sharpened to a single blade of grass that rested on Sister Sue Ann's pale blue jacket.

Janet shook herself from the strangeness.

Sister Mary spoke softly as if she were afraid of being overheard. "If it's true about them being in the woods, is anyone asking the Wayne boy what he was doing there?"

"Sister Mary's got a point there. If a preacher can't keep control of his own house, he ought not be preaching."

"I didn't mean..."

"Of course, you didn't. You're too sweet to say it, so I'll say it for you."

Janet had not even taken out her knitting, so she stood and left her unopened orange knitting bag on the ground. "If you all don't mind, I'd like to find a quiet spot on the trail to be with God."

Sister Sue Ann said, "Now you be careful, Sister Janet. Women shouldn't be alone on that trail. Look what happened with Connie Mobley."

"I thought you said that Connie was with the Wayne boy?"

"You know what I mean."

"I'll be fine. I'm older than Connie, and I know how to keep safe."

She left the women and found the trail again, walking further down the path this time, around the foul pond and beyond it until she found a twisted trunk of an old fallen and decaying tree and the ravine on the other side of it. It was well-hidden from cameras that hung from poles evenly placed beside the trail. Here, tucked into a depression in some brush in the ravine, she was truly alone. Here, she could clear her mind so that she could think about the way forward.

An icy wind stirred her hair and she lay still, listening, forgetting, until Seila's anxious face intruded on Janet's mind once again. It was before the Redeemers took power, but they were getting closer to it and Seila had asked Janet to hide things a little better. Seila was saying, "You didn't give us any choice in the matter. Aren't you the one who's always talking about fairness? Is it fair to risk us like this?"

Janet remembered asking her, "Is it fair to ask me to never know love?"

"You can love who you want; just hide it. And that's not all it is and you know it. Everybody knows about the birth control pills and condoms you sell. If you're not calling attention to yourself one way, there's always another, isn't there?"

"I just happen to believe that it's better to take a risk for justice than sit back and be rolled over anyway," Janet had replied. But now in Wendell, Janet didn't know if she believed that anymore. She turned her head, seeing the shadow of a branch bouncing lightly in the wind. She remembered that night in the dark when Seila told her, "You're not going to hell." She never loved Seila more than that night. She should have listened to Seila, been better at hiding her heart. Karen might still be alive. Seila might be safe.

Janet took a deep breath. If only I could trade my life for hers.

Janet's thoughts were interrupted by the sound of footsteps on the trail, which grew louder until they were almost upon her. Janet sought to flatten herself against the side of the ravine. When the steps stopped, she held her breath.

Someone jumped into the ravine, crashing through small branches, and she stifled a scream.

"What are you doing here?" It was Sonny.

"I could ask you the same question."

"I saw you walk into the woods and followed you. Come. Let's walk."

Janet and Sonny scrambled up the ravine and stood together on the trail. Janet said, "The Eyes of God are right around that turn."

Sonny turned to look down the trail. Janet could see the pistol holstered under his blue suit jacket. He said, "Speers had them turned off along this trail."

"Why?"

"I don't know. Look, if you're any friend of Sister Mary's, you should talk her out of marrying Speers."

"Does she have a choice?"

Sonny looked away and grimaced, and it seemed to her that as he peered down the path, he struggled to tell her something. She didn't press. Instead, she stood and they watched each other, unsure.

Janet listened to the living and dying trees that raked the sky or knocked against one another in the brisk wind until Sonny broke the silence. "I put on the Redeemers uniform for a reason."

Janet heard anguish in this voice and waited.

He said, "A society can't sustain itself without order. Families were being torn apart. They needed water and food. They needed oil."

"Yes, but who first tore them apart? Who brought them to this?"

Sonny shook his head. "I don't remember what it was like before. I was sheltered from most things when I was a boy, so you tell me. What was it like before, when the women were in charge?"

"You can't be that much younger than me. In your childhood, did you see women in charge? Other than your mother or your grandmother? The women were never in charge, no more than anyone else. And from what I understand, men controlled most of the high offices in business and in government. Do you remember any of your childhood?"

"Not much. But I remember the start of the wars and the looting. We lost our home. We lost people. And people were starving."

"Yeah, they still are, but they're corralled now so that you don't have to see them die. The so-called dark days were never as dark as things are today. Before the wars, we had saner laws, and torture was illegal."

"Torture is still illegal."

"Is it?"

Sonny winced and asked, "What about the sex traffickers, the satanists and the witches, the soddomites?"

"Sex traffickers? Are you aware that the Redeemers are involved in the sex trafficking of women penitents? I've seen it. And in the urban cities, what do the poor sell when they have nothing left to sell? And what do you think marrying off teenage girls to old men is? As to satanists and witches, I never met one, but I know that no one had any special magic or power. It's just lies used to frighten people, so people cling more tightly to the churches. And your Redeemers surpass anything a satanist is purported to do."

"Careful, Mrs. Moore."

Janet shrugged again.

"And the soddomites and lesbians?" Sonny asked.

"You mean men who loved men and women who loved women? I was taught that Old Testament stories were handed down by word of mouth for thousands of years before they were written down. And no one wrote about Jesus until two hundred years after his death. Then the stories and accounts were chosen and interpreted by men for two thousand more years. Plenty of room for error and biases there. Even with that, I don't see where Jesus concerned himself with who people chose to love. He concerned himself with people who lent money on interest, people who were bad hosts, and those who committed adultery. And even when a woman was being stoned for adultery in the New Testament, Jesus stopped the stoning."

"You're lying," Sonny said but his eyes darted aside as if he were uneasy.

"Well, you won't find any books on the subject, unless you're welcome to Dr. Speers' library. Most books have been destroyed. And I know you men have internet access, but you know that information is controlled, too."

Sonny clenched his fists, and Janet felt his tension. "Is Satan talking or Mrs. Moore?"

Janet wondered how she could possibly explain. There were so many variables and she'd been so young herself. And she was just bursting to let loose with more impassioned speech that she'd held back for too long, but it was like the water from an entire dam only had one quarter-sized hole to spring through.

She sighed and took a deep breath to slow herself down. She spread her hands, "My dad said that when times get tough, unsavory leaders give people scapegoats who don't have the power or numbers to fight back: women, gays, minorities, outsiders. And powerful people exploited the scapegoating to hide the fact that they themselves were the source of people's despair. And they used religion to do it. When enough people bought into this mythical, magical thinking and divided different types of people into good and evil, the religious, political, and business leaders aimed them like a gun at the rest of us. Instead of feeling powerless, people felt important and righteous. They became proud of their sacrifices and sacrificed their rights, their country, their wives, sisters, daughters, and friends. And they washed themselves in the blood of their neighbors. And you can watch it happening right now in Wendell, with little Connie Mobley."

Janet noticed a vein pulsing in the middle of Sonny's forehead and thought she should stop talking, but there was so little time.

She continued, "Let me ask you something. Do you see many elderly people these days?"

"They didn't escape the Wrath."

"And many who escaped the Wrath, didn't escape the Redeemers. They were witnesses to the actual past. You can't have too many witnesses. And you weren't so young then that you can't remember what actually happened when the Redeemers came to our towns. You were a teenager when the Covenant governments came to power. You have to remember the terror. How could you not?"

Sonny frowned and Janet could see the muscles in his jaw tighten.

Janet asked, "Why haven't you had me arrested? That's the real question, isn't it?"

Sonny's voice cracked, "I don't know. Maybe because I don't like what's going on in Wendell, with Sister Mary and Dr. Speers. And Connie."

Sonny looked over at Janet and she saw the pain behind his eyes, and then he drew himself up and said, "And maybe I don't like what's going on in that prison."

Janet's mouth felt dry and the hairs on the back of her neck stood up. "What's going on in the prison."

"It's better that you don't know. But. They're preparing Mrs. Campbell for a public confession. She'll confess to the Tabernacle Square bombing."

Janet felt rage rising in her. She said, "Seila plants gardens, not bombs! Posies."

"And she'll confess to knowing that her husband would be there, that she killed him and the others because the Devil told her to do it. And she had an accomplice."

Janet shook her head, rhythmically. "Those are lies. All lies."

"I believe you, but they'll never release her. They've gone too far."

"What do you mean?"

His eyes and face reddened as if he were about to cry, but he didn't. He said, "We've done everything to her. We're burning her out."

"You?"

Sonny didn't answer while something in Janet fell away. She was in free fall and the plunge would be deep. She stared vacantly at Sonny and then spoke so softly that Sonny almost didn't hear her. "What part does Dr. Speers play in this?"

"He's her counselor directing the confessional process. He tells us what to do. I tried to file a complaint against him, and now I'm a pariah among the guards." He spread his hands. "He'll get away with this. And Sister Mary? God help her."

"Did you know that Dr. Speers killed Sister Mary's mother?"

"No. What? How do you know?"

"Don't ask. The less said, the better."

Sonny shook his head slowly as they stood beside the path, each lost in their own terrible realities that had collided in Wendell.

Janet said, "I'm going inside. I volunteered to offer last minute salvation to women facing execution."

"If you meet with her, your session will be recorded on camera and with audio."

"Could someone turn off the camera and audio like they did on this trail?"

"Not there. Look, I'm risking too much even being on this trail with you. You should just pack some things and get as far from here as you can. There's nothing you can do for her now."

"We have to do something."

"I have a family back home. I can't risk it." Sonny turned and strode quickly down the trail, away from Janet while helpless rage consumed her.

She started to call after him, "Seila is my family!" but caught herself. She didn't know who else might be in earshot, and she'd said too much already.

{17}

False Memories

SEILA SAT LISTLESS in the vinyl chair and watched Dr. Speers. She thought that he looked smaller than the man who sat in that chair the day they first met in his office. When she first met him, she thought he might have some moral authority, but she learned pretty quickly that he had none. He could kill her now. So what?

"What happened to Lily?" she asked.

"We've had a change of plans. It's possible that she is beyond redemption or eligible for a penitent life," he said as he shuffled some papers in his file. Then he fixed his eyes on Seila and said, "God is displeased with you, Seila."

"Is he?"

When Dr. Speers didn't answer, Seila no longer felt that he could see right through her. In fact, she thought probably he couldn't see her at all.

"I should think that if I were in your position, I would show a little respect."

"I don't see a lot of respect in this place."

"Has someone been talking to you besides me and Lily?"

"God," said Seila and she shifted in her chair, rattling chains.

"Many people who thought they were talking to God were actually talking to the Devil."

"Yes, yes. As long as we believe that the Devil is so clever that even reason or reasonableness is a trap, who could argue with us? Jim was right about that."

"Shall we add heresy to your charges?"

"Do whatever you like."

"What did I tell you about smart women?"

"I don't care anymore. You see. I'm free now. You freed me of that."

"How so?"

"When you asked me why I believed there was a reason for my suffering, I began to see a little. And now, I finally understand that there is a reason, but not a good reason. I'm not suffering because I've failed God or because God wanted me to learn some great lesson. God has nothing to do with any of this. I'm suffering because you're torturing me. That's all. You, this prison, the Redeemers, the Covenant government—a colossal, monstrous delusion."

"I believe you've forgotten where you are."

"Oh, I know perfectly well where I am. I'm in the hands of wicked men who do the dirty work of a corrupt government. And I'm outside your control now. You can't stand that, can you, Dr. Speers? And you. You had the power of life and death over a child. Aren't you the big man killing a terrified little boy?"

At that, Dr. Speers jumped up and over his desk, and then everything went dark as his fist hammered her face. When she became conscious again, he stood over her, breathing hard, and his eyes turned to black coals. His nostrils flared.

Her voice was weak and her mouth and tongue felt thick. She mumbled, "Go ahead. Kill me. You've lost, Dr. Speers. You've lost, because I don't care what you do anymore."

Dr. Speers called the psychiatric team in and told them that the inmate had attacked him, which was ludicrous since she was still shackled and it was her face that was no longer recognizable.

The psychiatric team gave her an injection that stung her arm so bad that she passed out again. When she regained consciousness, she was paralyzed and rigid, with her teeth ground shut and her body locked in pain.

When they were gone, Dr. Speers watched her sullenly. "You torment me at night. How do you do it?"

Even if she knew what he was talking about, which she didn't, she could not speak. She was a seething still-life. And through her swollen eyes, Seila could only watch an approximation of Dr. Speers.

He said, "Temptations to sin are sure to come; but woe to him by whom they come!"

Then he called for the guards, Hal and Sonny, and ordered them to take her to Sodom & Gomorrah and leave her there for the night.

It was a night darker than any that she could imagine.

Her flesh stank where they burned her.

And the pain mounted but reached no peak.

And when Seila begged for death, the depraved men of Wendell's most notorious cellblock only laughed.

Damnation was eternal.

The next morning, Seila was in shock as they carried her to the prison hospital.

At one point, she thought she had risen from her body and was floating. She heard two men talking and one man was furious, He said, "If that commission comes down here and sees the shape she's in, you're on your own."

And then she was back in her body, in agony. Seila shivered in a hospital bed that week and felt the throb, throb, throb of heat that came in cyclical waves of pain. Blisters formed over her chest and swollen red belly, which had become one vast, bloody and blistery wound that broke, oozed, and crusted over.

They pulled her broken teeth and she put her tongue in the holes, tasting blood. Sometimes she dozed, woozy from a pill the guard gave her. For once, the drugs were a welcome release from the pain, and she looked forward to them.

She was half aware sometimes that Dr. Speers sat in a chair next to her bed. He held a hand over his eyes as he sat. Was it remorse?

Every morning or maybe it was evening or maybe it was at some other regular or irregular interval, Seila heard a detached voice reading from the Bible over an intercom system. When she was finally moved from the hospital bed to her cell, she listened to a passage from Job:

Behold, happy is the man whom God reproves; Therefore despise not the chastening of the Almighty. For he wounds, but he binds up; he smites, but his hands heal...

And then things were back the way they were.

She visited Dr. Speers' office again and again, and they never spoke of his rage or his actions. It was still about her and her evasions, so they went round. Reality became fluid and she began to feel that she really did help to hide a body. And if she did that, what else might she have done? Dr. Speers could be right about her. And she no longer knew whether she had turned Jim out or let Jim go because of fears surrounding the Redeemers or because Jim was a terrorist. Sometimes her reasoning mind said, neither. Neither are true. And curses came unbidden to Seila's mind.

During this time, the drugging and sleep deprivation ploughed the field of her malleable mind. And every day for several weeks, Dr. Speers repeated and repeated, piling up "evidence," displaying pictures of the Tabernacle Square bombing, and asking questions, questions, questions until he had Seila thoroughly confused.

In time, she began to believe Dr. Speers. Her doubts came and went, as she transformed to Jim's accomplice in a crime. The worst crime. Murder.

One day, Dr. Speers said, "I've shown you your future if you don't repent. It doesn't have to be that way. Heaven still waits. God still loves you."

"I think it's too late for that."

"Am I to believe that you're guilty of apostasy, too?"

Seila didn't answer him. She just rolled the word apostasy around with her tongue.

Then he announced, "Good news. A woman from our congregation is being screened to come to this very prison to work with inmates on their spiritual path. She'll be helping to save your soul. Could she be Jim?"

Seila shook her head listlessly and shrugged her shoulders.

"Before she comes, I need two things. One, you tell me where you last saw your sister. Two, you admit the whole truth about yours and your sister's involvement in the Tabernacle Square bombing. Repent and save yourself and your sister." Dr. Speers added, "It's good to see you come out of denial. That's the first step. We're making progress. I think your sister would agree."

Dr. Speers called the guards to unlock her. He was taking Seila for a walk. Seila felt light and disoriented without the shackles, like she would float away.

Dr. Speers walked her slowly, because she could only hobble now, whether from physical trauma or malnourishment.

Dr. Speers opened heavy steel doors with the scan of his ID chip, the imprint of his thumb, and a trace of his iris. All this security for me, Seila thought. They shuffled to a waiting room beyond a set of glass doors, and to the left of the waiting room, to a 10x10 concrete courtyard with a couple of wooden benches. As they shuffled through the waiting room, Seila saw signs prohibiting kissing or hugging. It seemed odd and completely out of place, or from another time.

Dr. Speers took her into the courtyard and led her to a wooden bench. The sunlight was so bright, she couldn't open her eyes at first. Then she squinted. When she finally opened her eyes, they were moist, both to protect her eyes and to weep for this splendor. The almost blue sky filled the rectangular space above her and she didn't mind the cold. "Can I keep trying to walk?" she asked.

Dr. Speers nodded and remained sitting while she shuffled from one end of the courtyard to the other, panting from the exertion. It was glorious, glorious. "It's daytime."

"Yes."

"It's glorious."

"If you confess to the Tabernacle Square bombing and tell us about yours and your sister's involvement, you can be outside again. You would be a penitent working in the national parks. Your sister, too. You can still save her."

"You told me that it was too late."

"Yes, but I went outside the bounds of my office to get you a new deal. It's done."

"I don't remember anything about the Tabernacle Square bombing except for your pictures. So, when you ask about it, my mind goes blank. How do I know that it even happened at all?"

"The brain goes blank to avoid painful truths."

"But I don't know if I or Jim had anything to do with it. If I confess to these murders, I would be a liar."

"Convincing yourself that you're innocent does not absolve you of lying or murder. You're in denial, Mrs. Campbell, and that won't save you from hell. You must repent, but before you can repent, you must remember."

She felt so grateful for being outside, that she didn't want to argue with him. What if he was right?

"Hold out your hand."

Dr. Speers pulled a rose with a three-inch stem from his pocket and laid it into Mrs. Campbell's chapped and bleeding palm. It was vibrant red and velvety. It was the most beautiful thing she had ever seen, more beautiful even than the sky above them. Her eyes watered. She held the rose to her nose and finding no fragrance, she ran it alongside her cheek to feel its softness.

"Take this back to your cell and think about what I've told you. About being a penitent. It will be for life, but not such a bad life."

"Dr. Speers?"

"Yes?"

"Thank you."

"Do you really want to thank me?"

Seila looked at him with suspicion. She was hesitant. "Yes."

"Then tell me about your sister. What was she like as a child?"

Seila was relieved. This was a line of questioning she could answer. "She has no fear. Well, except for spiders and swans and chickens."

Dr. Speers guffawed. "Chickens?"

Seila smiled and said, "Yeah, she said they have sharp beaks, but when it came to other things, she was fearless. When she was a teenager, she jumped off a pier into the Ohio river. Not me. No way." Seila chuckled.

Seila continued, "She hated injustice, even as a kid. I remember her facing down a group of bullies who tormented Karen Seawell."

"Karen Seawell?"

Seila stopped smiling and said, "She was Jim's wife. She's dead now." She grew quiet thinking of Karen.

Dr. Speers asked, "And the Lord? Doesn't Jim fear the Lord?"

"She doesn't believe in the Bible. She says how can you believe something that was passed down by word of mouth over thousands of years before being written down. She used to say, 'And what did they know, so long ago? They thought women should make a sacrificial offering just for having their period.' She called the Bible tall tales from an ancient Bedouin culture. I mean, she believed people passed down the stories. She just didn't believe that God had much to do with it."

"And when did you find out that she was a homosexual?"

"When I was seventeen years old."

"And how old was she?"

"Fourteen."

Seila grew silent and regretted. How could she have forgotten where she was or who she was talking to?

"How did you feel?"

She hesitated and then said, "Confused. I thought she might be but I wasn't sure."

"There is the Cure."

"She was taken for the Cure."

"The Redeemers were clumsy back then. We have more scientific ways to handle sexual deviance now. Come. I'll show you."

Dr Speers stood up stiffly and held out his hand to help Seila walk. He took her arm in his so she could lean on him. He walked her through the corridors to a large window and operating room where a young teenage girl lay on a table with a white sheet over her and IVs attached to her hand. Only the girl's small, frightened face was outside the sheet. A nurse injected something into the IV. As they watched, her face softened and went slack. Her eyes closed.

"She's so young."

"Fourteen years old."

"Who is she?"

"A Wendell girl, Connie Mobley. It's a tragedy, really. She went the Way of Eve."

Seila was filled with dread now. "What are they doing to her?"

"Saving her."

"How are they saving her?"

"They're removing her lust. Once the operation is complete, the Devil will never again deceive her through lust.

She'll never feel the need to fornicate, except for the purpose of having babies."

A doctor stepped in front of her, and Seila could see a nurse tug the sheet from her. The doctor stood between her legs, examining her. Seila turned her head away and fainted before the doctor finished his procedure, and the red rose that Dr. Speers had given her had fallen to the floor with a small drop of blood from where Seila had gripped its thorns.

When she revived and was returned to Dr. Speers' office, he explained, "We can cure your sister. The procedure you saw can be used to treat unnatural sexual appetites, demons, such as those found in lesbians. Your sister can be saved."

"How could you?"

Dr. Speers looked puzzled. "We saved that girl and mercifully I might add. We can do the same for your sister. It's the only way we've found where we can safely release a sexual deviant back into Christian society. Don't you want her to live?"

"Please don't hurt her."

"That depends on you, on your confession. We'll honor a plea bargain."

Dr. Speers looked as if he were in a trance, looking at a distant point over Seila's head, and then he seemed to shake himself. "I wonder if Charlie would be alive today if you and he hadn't tried to find Jim?"

Seila didn't answer him.

"Where did you say Charlie was the night before he disappeared?"

"He was at the store."

"For three hours."

Seila had wondered. It was true. Where had Charlie been? She couldn't remember.

"But you must have suspected something. You must have been very angry."

"No, Charlie was a good husband."

Dr. Speers played a recording for Seila, "Alright! I imagined a violent end for my husband."

Seila looked puzzled.

"Do you remember saying this?"

"I thought I dreamed it."

"It's natural when someone has committed a violent crime to repress the memory, to imagine that they merely dreamed it."

"I wouldn't kill anyone." But Seila no longer believed that.

Dr. Speers stood up and walked over to Seila. "You've convinced yourself of your innocence, but there are lots of things that you've done, that you do, immoral things. This is enough for now, but I'll help you to remember. You'll see."

{18}

Breakdown

GEORGE'S SISTER, BETTY, finally moved in after the new year, and Janet thought that having another spy in the family couldn't happen at a worse time. However, Betty was ill and took to her bed upon arrival.

When Janet saw her pale, slight form resting on feather pillows, she was inclined to dislike her. She was inclined to dislike everybody these days. But Betty's breathing was labored, and she truly did look pitiful, sweating in that high bed.

George used to say that Betty never tired and never missed a day of church or Bible study. But on Sunday, Betty surprised everyone when she refused to go to church, saying she was too weak to go.

After George left the room, Betty took Janet's hand in a cold papery grip, stronger than it should be. Her yellowed eyes were fierce but full of tears. "We made a mistake. I think we made a mistake."

"What do you mean?"

"The world is not kind to old widows."

"What's happened, Betty?"

Betty just turned on her side. "You better go to church. You better pray that you die before George."

Janet was speechless. This was George's sister?

George and Janet went to their respective Bible study classes, and as soon as Janet was settled in the classroom, Dr. Speers began the class with the prayer. Janet was shocked to see Sister Emily in the classroom and noticed that Sister Emily was in a perpetual blush.

Dr. Speers asked Sister Mary to read from Paul chapter seven, verses two through five. She cleared her throat and read.

"Nevertheless, because of sexual immorality, let each man have his own wife, and let each woman have her own husband. Let the husband render to his wife the affection due her, and likewise also the wife to her husband. The wife does not have authority over her own body, but the husband does. And likewise the husband does not have authority over his own body, but the wife does. Do not deprive one another except with consent for a time, that you may give yourselves to fasting and prayer; and come together again so that Satan does not tempt you because of your lack of self-control. But if they cannot exercise self-control, let them marry. For it is better to marry than to burn with passion."

Janet knew that Sister Emily was thinking of her daughter and the gossip around Wendell, and was probably thinking that God was talking directly to her, not knowing that she was being manipulated by the people in this twisted church.

Dr. Speers tapped some papers against the desk to even them out. "And that brings us to little Connie Mobley."

Everyone sat a little straighter in their desks.

"Our little town has found itself embroiled in the greater war with Satan. He corrupted one of our young girls most susceptible to Satan's seductions. Though it may seem like a small struggle, it's not. This is part of a greater struggle for our communities and God's government, and Sister Emily has been called once again to make a sacrifice for God's Church."

Sister Emily's mouth worked to speak as her eyes sought out her friends and neighbors in bewilderment. Few would meet her eyes. Her white hair was no longer in a bun and was in disarray under a blue kerchief. Aunt Peggy, who sat close to her, later said that she smelled bad.

Even Janet found it difficult to meet her eyes, though she did look at her and tried with all her might to tell her with her eyes, 'I'm on your side.'

Sister Sue Ann, Aunt Peggy and Sister Sherry Hart would not look at her.

"To save her child, we attempted a procedure to exorcise the demons infecting her. But Satan, in his infinite cruelty, has so far thwarted our efforts to save her and has, in fact, stricken her with an infection of her private parts."

A sob escaped Sister Emily while a collective gasp broke out.

"We must all pray that God wins in the battle over little Connie's soul."

"When can I see her?"

"When the battle is won."

"Not before? Can't I see her before?"

"I'm afraid that's not possible. You would be in too great a risk inside the prison, and we would be faced with the awful task of treating mother and daughter both."

"I don't mind the risk."

"No, of course you don't. Women, particularly mothers, are the poorest judges of these things. That's why you have male leadership, unencumbered with dangerous sentimentality, and sufficiently armored against the Devil's seductions."

By this time, Sister Mary was wiping her eyes while indignation and rage rose in Janet.

"Would anyone else like to speak on this before we get into the lesson today?"

Sister Sue Ann coughed and then said, "I would like to ask the Lord, please Lord, please forgive Sister Emily for not attending to her child's needs and leaving her open to Satan's wiles. I ask this in Jesus' name. Amen."

Sister Emily's sobs grew louder and she wailed, "Please forgive me, Lord, for abandoning my poor Connie. It's my fault, not hers. Spare her Lord. Spare her and take me instead...because I can't...I can't..." Speech failed Sister Emily, and Sister Mary began sobbing as well.

The meeting broke down, and Dr. Speers left the room so the ladies could "compose themselves" before church. Before he left, however, he told Sister Sue Ann to join him in the hall.

Janet could see them in hushed conversation in the hallway, and from time to time, they both looked at Janet through the doorway. Janet rose and left the room, squeezing past them on her way to the Fellowship Hall. She ran into Johnny on the way. He said, "Excuse me, Ma'am."

She looked around and under her breath said, "Sonny Valdez has a conscience and might be an asset. But he needs a push."

Johnny nodded and walked past her.

Later, in the Fellowship Hall, the congregation lifted their eyes to the ceiling and with beatific expressions on their faces, sang about being washed in the blood of Jesus. When the hymn was sung and they were told to be seated, Pastor Wayne shouted from the pulpit, "Washed clean."

"By blood," was the dutiful response.

"It's all about the blood, all about the blood."

Pastor Wayne looked out at the congregation with the fierceness of a John the Baptist. Like his oldest son, Hal, Pastor Wayne had a thick neck with faint red and gray hair bristling in a crew-cut around his meaty head, and his blue-green eyes glittered under bushy gray and red eyebrows. "The Devil has been busy in Wendell." He shook his head sadly, "And I don't just mean he's been working his evil on weaker vessels in the form of our boys and girls. Oh no. No, he had bigger plans for us. The Devil knows that divided we fall. So, he's been walking up and down Main St. just as brazen as the great whore of Babylon, spreading gossip. What does James tell us about gossip! Turn to James 3, verses four through eight." He read:

> *Likewise the tongue is a small part of the body, but it makes great boasts. Consider what a great forest is set on fire by a small spark. The tongue also is a fire, a world of evil among the parts of the body. It corrupts the whole person, sets the whole course of his life on fire, and is itself set on fire by hell. All kinds of animals, birds, reptiles and creatures of the sea are being tamed and have been tamed by man, but no man can tame the tongue. It is a restless evil, full of deadly poison.*

Pastor Wayne looked around his congregation and boomed out, "A deadly poison is the unruly tongue!"

Someone said, "Amen," and Willie Chambers turned to see who it was over his long, pedigreed nose. Janet looked at Aunt Peggy who clutched her Bible to her breast and thought she saw Aunt Peggy's mouth quiver.

Pastor Wayne shook his head sadly and spoke slowly at first, then built to a rising crescendo. "No, this ain't just about my boy, Luke, and little Connie Mobley. This is a story as old as Cain and Abel. What did Cain do? He got envious and killed Abel, killed him right there in the field and his brother's blood cried out from the ground! And God heard it! God heard it! Make no mistake about that, brothers and sisters. God hears all. You better believe it, because the fires of Hell are waiting for those who don't believe that this is the literal, inerrant Word of God. Now what does James say about envy? If you turn to James 3: 14-16, you'll see what James says about envy and selfish ambition." Pastor Wayne thundered:

> *But if you harbor bitter envy and selfish ambition in your hearts, do not boast about it or deny the truth. Such "wisdom" does not come down from heaven but is earthly, unspiritual, of the Devil. For where you have envy and selfish ambition, there you find disorder and every evil practice.*

Pastor Wayne looked out over the congregation until a resounding silence had them all keyed to the pitch he wanted, and then he spoke quietly from the pulpit. "Every evil practice. He who has ears, let him hear."

When he was done, the congregation arose in various states of unease; some were alarmed that the Devil was so close, some were indignant at the Mobleys or Pastor Wayne, or the Chambers and the Camps, depending on who they sided with, and others grieved for the Mobleys and other things that they dare not name or even think about.

George turned to Janet and said, "Go home and prepare a meal. I'm bringing home some brothers and sisters for lunch. And Janet? Could you whip up some cornbread?"

Janet tried not to grimace and said, "Sure." She hurried out while Sister Sue Ann fell into step beside her. "We're holding a meeting for the prison ministry on Tuesday morning. Are you still interested?"

"Yes, of course." Janet's clenched teeth and face were so tight that she thought they might break. She imagined her hands around Sister Sue Ann's throat.

Turning her steps homeward, Janet overtook Sonny and passed him, walking just in front on the right side of the sidewalk.

He said, "Why didn't you run?"

"Why don't you?"

"My father needs money for our family. They need water and food."

When the road curved and they were out of sight of the church, Janet dropped back until they were walking side by side.

"So did you assist with Connie Mobley, too?"

"No."

Janet turned down her walkway. "I'll be seeing Seila at the prison soon. When I know the day, I'll tell you. Please. I need the audio turned off when I'm with Seila."

"I can't promise."

"I'm asking you to try and I'm asking you to think about how to get her out of that prison. You owe her that. I have the means to change our identities. And yours."

Sonny said, "You must be crazy. Speers will never let her out of his sight." Sonny increased his speed and hurried away.

~

George brought home Willie and Sue Ann Chambers, Warden Camp, and Dr. Speers whose eyes were on Janet as she laid the table with fried chicken, biscuits and cornbread, and green beans. She was glad to have made ahead the fried chicken and green beans. She only had to reheat them and bake the biscuits and cornbread before their guests arrived. But the smell and even the sight of the cornbread made her nauseous.

George thanked God for the food and asked His blessing for the meeting in Jesus' name, because they were doing God's work, always an ominous note for Janet.

Steam rose from the cornbread that Sister Sue Ann sliced, and she wiped a pat of butter on it. Janet could almost imagine blood staining the cornbread and she could almost hear Pastor Wayne saying, "it's all about the blood."

Willie Chambers wiped his long nose with his starched napkin and turned to Janet, "Me and George go back a long way."

George nodded. "Yup. Yup. A long way."

"Soldiers in Christ."

"Of course, I was the youngster." Warden Camp smiled, and light glinted off his balding head and round spectacles.

Everyone laughed except for Dr. Speers who was watching Janet and Janet who felt his eyes on her. She sat at the opposite end of the table from George and moved the green beans around on her plate, smiling when the others laughed.

"I don't believe you were ever young," George said.

"That's what my daddy said. He said I was the ugliest little cussed thing he ever saw."

"Well, I can believe that. You were the meanest Commander in God's army."

Sister Sue Ann said, "Now that can't be true. Warden Camp's always smiling like a school boy."

"Bless your heart, Sister Sue Ann. You make me feel like a school boy every time I look at you. Ain't that right?"

"You stay away from my wife, you old dog." They all chuckled again.

Then Sister Sue Ann assumed an air of innocence and seriousness. "Pastor Wayne was on fire this morning."

Warden Camp reached for the white ceramic salt shaker. "That old boy's pushing it. When we've been called to help each other live according to the good Book, Pastor Wayne shouldn't discourage folks from watching over each other. A sermon like that might be a stumbling block for folks. Instead of reporting wrongdoing, people might start keeping secrets. Evil grows in secret places."

"Temptations to sin are sure to come; but woe to him by whom they come." Dr. Speers said.

"And privacy is the Devil's tool," said Sister Sue Ann.

Janet felt like she was presiding over a feast for jackals.

Warden Camp reached over the table to grab a chicken leg. "It's a bad business in town today, a bad business. Luke Wayne won't marry the girl. Says he didn't do anything to her."

"Maybe he didn't. She say he did?" Willie Chambers asked.

"Yup." Warden Camp gnawed his chicken and held it up. "Yup."

"You think he did?"

"Yup. He's guilty as sin."

Sister Sue Ann dabbed daintily at her mouth. "The good Book says 'for if a man does not know how to rule his own house, how will he take care of the church of God?'"

"That's true." Willie Chambers said as he wiped his greasy fingers on his napkin. Pastor Wayne's not managing his house, and he doesn't manage the church funds well either. There's some who wonder where all the money's going."

Warden Camp gulped his tea and then set his glass down. "Anyone care to raise these matters in the next church business meeting?"

George and Willie looked at one another expectantly, then George threw his napkin on the table. "I'll do it."

"Good man."

"We better get the word out for folks to bring their young ones, too, in case someone calls a vote."

When the business of lunch was winding down, Dr. Speers asked, "How's your sister?"

Janet looked up from her plate and saw that he had directed his question to her. She felt chilled, but she kept her voice level. "Sorry? My brothers have passed on. I never had a sister."

"I mean your sister-in-law." He nodded to George. "Your sister. How is she?"

George said, "She's doing as well as can be expected, but she's been in bed since she got here, feeling too poorly to get up yet."

"We'll remember her in our next Bible study."

"That'd be good. She needs all of our prayers. The asthma's got her so bad, she can't leave the house for church. She's a trooper though. She'll get herself to church next week for sure."

Janet noticed a slight smile playing around Dr. Speers lips. He's trying to unsettle me, she thought. She sipped her tea and avoided his eyes.

George said, "Janet? Dr. Speers asked me today if you ever knew anyone who lived near Tabernacle Square."

"Yes, of course, George. Why?"

"Dr. Speers was looking for a suspect at Tabernacle Square and ran across your scan in that very area."

"I used to do charity work down there. I knitted items for the poor and delivered them to a clothing bank. Don't you remember me talking about that, George?"

"Was that Tabernacle Square? Well, yes it was, now that you mention it. Of course, I told my Janet not to get too caught up with the poor."

"You wouldn't catch me near them." Sister Sue Ann wiped her hands on her white napkin.

Janet looked steadily now at Dr. Speers. This man was on to her. He knew something. What if Sister Mary betrayed her? Or Seila?

{19}

Coaxing Confessions

SOME TIME PASSED before Dr. Speers called for Seila again. The silence was as unnerving as the meetings had been. Was Dr. Speers dead? Would someone take his place? Would she have to go through this again with someone else? Would they keep Dr. Speers' promise to save her and Jim? Her mind went round and round.

She called out in her empty cell, "Marco." And she imagined a splash in a swimming pool, and Jim answering, "Polo." Those were good times, weren't they?

She wished she'd been kinder to Jim when they were kids. When Seila's friends were around, she generally pushed Jim away who completely ignored all the signs taped to Seila's door, "NO TRESSPASSING, KEEP OUT, BEWARE OF SISTER," and then they would argue. If Seila could go back in time, she would welcome Jim more. She would make it up to her.

Had Dr. Speers abandoned her? Seila thought she should be relieved, but it left her with a growing sense of unease. She got up and peered through the glass window on her door, but she could only see the empty corridor, the ever-present cameras, and the guards who brought her meals. Every time they slid the tray through the door, she jumped. It was so loud.

She quit taking the pills that came with the meal, and no one forced her to. What was happening? What would happen to her now? Had they found Jim?

One night she dreamed that she was a murderer, and it had just been discovered. She had ordered the killing of those people and the realization toppled the very structures of her being. She was clammy with fear and shame, unable to take back actions that she would take back if only she could. She woke terrified and told herself it was just a dream. "I couldn't have," she said, and fell back into an uneasy sleep, picking up where she left off. In her dream, her legs were bound in chains where the police shackled her. She shook from the horror of knowing what she did. "I couldn't have. I didn't."

Evil drifts towards fear, so as Seila's horror grew, it was next to her, a monster that squatted nearby and leered, intoxicated with her terror that waxed larger.

"I couldn't have."

Then she was called back to Dr. Speers' office, as if he knew.

"Why did you do it?"

"Did I?"

"We have evidence."

"Can I see it?" Seila asked.

"It's classified," Dr. Speers said. "You know that."

"Then how can I refute it?"

"You can't because you know that you did it. In here." Dr. Speers tapped his chest lightly. "You know."

"I don't know. And if I did, how could I live with it?"

"You can repent and be saved."

"I do repent."

"Not yet. Not until you remember all of it."

"I don't want to remember." Seila felt drained, listless.

"God wants you to, so he can forgive you."

"If this is true, there can be no forgiveness for this," she whispered.

"When you unburden yourself, the Holy Spirit can come. You'll remember the rest now and make a confession. Then the Holy Spirit will come, and you can get out of here, find some kind of life doing what you like to do, but as a penitent. You'll be born again. Remember? We talked about this before."

"I don't want to get out of here. There can't be a life for me anymore."

"There can't be as long as you keep secrets. Soon you'll be lighter. You can live again."

"Why did you send me to Sodom & Gomorrah?"

"It was God's crucible. Now you know what your victim's felt when they were burnt in the explosion. It put you in crisis to help you remember."

Seila remembered Dr. Speers leaping at her with dark eyes bulging. "I thought you were just angry."

"I had to shock you. Believe me. I wouldn't have done it if it weren't necessary to bring you to awareness."

"I want to believe that, but I can't see it."

"You will. You may not realize it, but you've had a break-through, and it's taken a lot out of you. But you'll recover. With time, with confession, you'll heal."

Seila shook her head.

"Don't you trust me?" he asked.

"I don't know. No."

"Soon, you'll know it was for the greater good, for your good. You've done very well. You've come so far. Just a little way more, and you'll be free. Remember the sinner on the cross with Jesus, how Jesus forgave him and assured him his place in heaven?"

Seila nodded her head.

"Well, you're on that cross now, and Jesus is waiting for some words from you. Okay? But I'll let you sleep now and reflect."

As Seila slept, she dreamed that Dr. Speers was standing over her dressed in a white coat. "It was almost too late for this one." He reached into her gut and with a sucking sensation, he pulled her intestines out. He looked disgusted. "She's still not ready." Seila hated him and felt ashamed. "No, I love him," she assured herself because God would want her to love and not hate. But she couldn't feel it. Dr. Speers looked at her disinterested in the dream, and then he was in her face, an inch or two from her, peering into her eyes, "Whore."

She fought to pull herself from sleep, to wake up, and it seemed she had to pull herself a long way up. She shook her head.

Dr. Speers called for her after that, and when she was seated in the vinyl chair, he asked how she was feeling.

"I had a bad dream."

"Do you want to tell me about it?"

"I dreamed you said I wasn't ready."

"You're not." Dr. Speers smiled gently. "But you will be."

Inside Seila, love and hate fought for supremacy.

"Why are you being nice to me? I'm a murderer."

"Yes, but you still have a soul that needs saving, and I've never lost a patient yet. Besides, we're all sinners, but we're saved from the consequences of our sin through the blood of Jesus, by believing and following Jesus."

"But I've done that and something went wrong."

"You didn't fully believe then. It'll be different this time. Trust me."

"It's too late. Can't you see that? I have bad thoughts."

"What kind of bad thoughts."

"Sometimes I think I want to kill you."

Dr. Speers laughed out loud. "You know, I think I like the honest Seila."

"Don't be nice to me please. Don't trust me. I'm your enemy."

"And if you only love them who love you, what thank have ye? Anyone can do that. Jesus said we must love our enemies, and if someone strikes you on the cheek, turn to him the other also."

That filled Seila with an overwhelming sadness. "That's what Charlie used to say. He used to quote Buddha and asked himself before speaking: Is it kind? Is it true? Is it necessary? And he could sing so sweetly, it would melt your heart. Did you know that he sang?"

"He was in the church choir."

Seila started up, "Oh God...Oh God. How could I have killed my Charlie? It's not possible."

"Shhhh. We'll work through this. You'll see. Charlie wants you to. You have to do this, if not for me, then for Charlie. Are you ready to do this for Charlie?"

"Do what?"

"To get to the rest of the information that you've hidden from yourself."

"I don't want to know."

"It's the only way. You do want to repent, don't you?"

"Yes."

As Seila came to believe in her own guilt, she shuddered with her new memories and felt that her belief in the fundamental goodness of human beings was shattered. And why not, she asked herself, why not, when we're born into a world where survival depends on killing?

And why, why, why would she have done it? She couldn't remember why. Seila thought that there was no safe place in the world so long as people like her were alive. She looked at the ceiling listlessly and tried to pray. She stopped. They were just words now. She had changed and no longer recognized herself.

Dr. Speers came to her and hugged her, and she held tightly to him as he said, "I'm here." Then they teased more of the narrative into and out of Seila. They determined that Jim gave Seila the explosives because she wanted to make the Covenant government look bad, so people wouldn't trust it. Chaos breeds distrust. People would turn against it. Seila thought now that she agreed to help, so long as no one died, but the bomb went off too early.

And although Dr. Speers continued to pepper Seila with reasons for why any of this still mattered, she couldn't feel it. She felt an empty void where her heart was supposed to be.

In time, Seila's leg healed and the dressings were removed from her chest, leaving purple scars.

As Dr. Speers assisted Seila with 'recovering her memory' and preparing her confession, her cast was removed, and an intensive physical therapy was begun to shore up Seila's flagging strength, and to dismiss wild accusations about torture and false confessions.

Each day, Seila was led to a whirlpool bath and lowered into it. Afterwards, she exercised, although initially she did this with parallel bars, lurching forward as she clutched the bars.

As she grew stronger, she tried to walk without the bars, but she reeled off to her left, like she was intoxicated. She began to use a walker, but even with that, she couldn't walk straight. All this she did in a fugue state, automatically following orders. 'Walk,' and she shuffled forward. 'Stop,' and she stopped. Sometimes she asked, "What time is it?" but no one seemed to know.

Dr. Speers told the prison staff that until she could walk without support, her confession couldn't be televised. They didn't have to worry about the scarring of her breast and abdomen since these would be concealed by clothing.

By degrees, Seila began to regain the use of her legs. She was fed a diet of milk, beef, vegetables, and fruit. The beef made her nauseous at first, but she grew used to it and kept it down.

Meanwhile, Dr. Speers visited her daily, reminding her that he was all she had and warning her about the deluge of death threats she had received, mail he said he couldn't show her, for her sake.

"Soon, Jim will visit you."

By now, Seila had become a stranger to herself. Images, some real, some false, raced across her brain in episodic stills, Dr. Speers with a gun to his head, Seila with a canvas bag of plastic explosives in her hand, Jim showing her how to place the explosives, and prison images laced with the stench of blood, urine, feces, and sweat. These memories had become part of her and she was far from the woman she had once been, the woman who weeded her flower bed with gloved hands, or welcomed Charlie home with a warm embrace, the one who believed she was safe as long as she kept her head down and didn't complain.

She called Jesus into the cold cavity of her heart as Dr. Speers requested, and when she didn't feel the Holy Spirit, she wasn't surprised. She didn't deserve it. A million years ago, she remembered meditating with Charlie, kneeling on a big red pillow with a yellow fringe on a polished, hardwood floor. If she closed her eyes, she could remember an open window that framed the thick, hot summer night, a lamp that cast a soft, yellow light over the lacquered floor like liquid gold, and cicadas that drummed a tight percussion while they meditated together. Back then, hers and Charlie's life together kept her fears about Jim at bay. She had faith, that sensation of certainty without fact, the holy sanctuary of the child, now shattered by the barking voices clamoring for supremacy in her head, "JUST ANSWER THE FUCKING QUESTION—YES OR NO—ARE YOU A TER-RORIST, OR AREN'T YOU??!!!"

Or sometimes she could hear the dull thud of her body thrown against a wall and smell the vomit where her face hit the cold floor. It was all past, but it lived in the present.

Seila spent her final weeks before the public confession in a fog, where the world around her was muffled and dim, and only her nightmares were vivid, as well as the voices and images surfacing against the flat screen of her traumatized mind. She spent her days sleeping, and no one seemed to care anymore to disturb her. Dr. Speers was gentle, and his kindness shamed her. She asked for the death penalty, but he just shook his head.

She was completely unaware that as her confession day loomed closer, the Redeemer-controlled media planned the confession for a promotional campaign. Execution proceedings were to immediately precede and serve as inspiration for a new wave of citizen arrests under a Stop the Violence campaign.

Seila was told that the judge would read out the charges and ask, "How do you plead?" Seila rolled the word around in her mouth. Plead. She thought that if you added a gerund, you would have pleading, which is the same as begging. But without the gerund, plead and beg in this case become completely different things. The judge would never ask, "How do you beg?" or "How do you beseech?" They're all synonyms but not the same at all, not in court.

"Mrs. Campbell?" Dr Speers asked. "Are you listening?"

She nodded, but she rolled that word around, too. Listening. It has a silent t.

Dr. Speers said, "When you confess, you will point to Jim. She'll be in the courtroom. You will point to Jim and say, 'There is Ruby Lambert who was my accomplice.'"

Seila wondered if she should say 'she is my accomplice' or 'she was my accomplice.'

And then Dr. Speers reiterated, "If you point her out as your accomplice, we'll allow Jim to repent without the confessional process. We will prepare her and you for life as penitents. Your confession will be a great service to the Covenant. Remember that."

It was after one of these coaching and confession sessions, that Seila said, "I dreamed about Jim again."

"And what did you dream?

Seila said, "We were in the woods the night the Redeemers caught me there."

"In the woods?"

Seila looked up as if searching her memory and said, "And I think I was ashamed that I was holding her back."

"God comes to the shamed, Seila. God can work with them."

"Shame doesn't feel like God. I mean, shame has a bad feeling, doesn't it? Not a sacred feeling at all."

"Tell me about the woods, Seila? Why was Jim with you?"

Seila didn't seem to notice Dr. Speers staring at her with renewed intensity. "She tried to save me. She told me something." Seila looked puzzled.

"Yes?"

"She told me that Charlie had rescued her from the Redeemers, and that the Redeemers killed Charlie. She was trying to get me to a safe place in the North."

"Well, you know that can't be true."

"No, of course not."

"Tell me what else you remember about the dream."

"It was just a dream. Does it really matter?"

"Everything is important here, even dreams."

"Well." Seila reached down to touch her leg but the chain rattled and she stopped. She said, "I remember that I was in pain from all the hiking and it was dark. We were resting."

"Who was with you?"

"Jim. At first it was just Jim."

"At first?" Seila didn't notice the flush that bloomed on Dr. Speers face. "Who else? Was Sister Mary and her mother with you, too?"

"Who's Sister Mary?"

"Who else was with you and Jim?"

"It was just a dream."

A new urgency had come to Dr. Speers. "Who else was with you in the dream?"

"A woman with a teenage girl. They came later, but I didn't know them. Then the men came."

"And Jim?"

"She got away."

Dr. Speers cut the interview short and hustled Seila out.

{20}

Scaring Sister Mary

O N HIS WAY to church, Dr. Speers considered the problem of the Campbell woman and Sister Mary. Sister Mary had lied to him. How did he miss it? She was asked if anyone else was with them that night, and she said no. And he never pressed it, because he trusted in her innocence. Fool! All women were devious, weren't they?

If Janet was Jim, she must not be alone with Sister Mary, although it doesn't necessarily follow that Janet witnessed the murder of Sister Mary's mother or that she told Sister Mary. She could have been long gone by then. He thought back and tried to remember if there were instances where Mary and Janet were alone together, but he hadn't been around them all of the time. He had not paid attention to their time at the outside knitting circle, so they could have had an opportunity to talk together alone.

Dr. Speers turned his thoughts back to Seila. Dr. Speers was determined that she see Janet, both to ensure that the Jim of Seila's imagination converged with an image of Janet who might have changed physically, and to confirm to Seila that he had Jim. The risk, of course, was that Ruby, Jim, Janet, whatever her name today, would plant seeds of doubt into Seila's mind, disrupting the seamless memories, and throw the entire confession into doubt.

Even with that, it would be helpful to show Seila that he had her sister. Consequently, the visitation would have to be strictly controlled.

Dr. Speers had worked out a plan by the time he got to the church. When he entered the Bible study class, Janet was already there, and so were Sister Mary and Sister Sue Ann, punctual as ticking clocks. Sister Mary seemed to be looking at him strangely. Had Janet already poisoned her?

Sister Sue Ann was talking to Janet about giving blood for the Millennial soldiers. "I watched them take the blood from my arm. That's what got me into trouble. I can't stand the sight of blood, but if our boys at the front can sacrifice their lives for the cause, surely, I can withstand giving blood."

Aunt Peggy and Sister Sherry Hart hurried in followed by Sister Emily whose husband steered her into the classroom and placed her carefully, pushing down on her shoulders to seat her. He nodded at Dr. Speers and left the room.

Sister Emily's face was flat and her eyes were vacant.

"Washed clean," Dr. Speers said to the class.

"By blood," they intoned.

Dr. Speers bowed his head. "Thank you, Father, for giving us this opportunity to gain a better understanding of your plan for us. We want to be good Christians. Open our minds and our hearts, Father, so that we can know Your Will. Dear God, we gather together today to learn Your Word. We pray that Your Word touches and strengthens us in this time of trial, so that we might all be better Christians. I ask this in Jesus' name. Amen."

"Amen," they said.

"Sister Mary, will you read Ephesians 5:22-31?"

Sister Mary fumbled through her Bible to find the passage and then read:

Wives, submit to your own husbands, as to the Lord. For the husband is the head of the wife, as also Christ is the head of the church; and He is the Savior of the body. Therefore, just as the church is subject to Christ, so let the wives be to their own husbands in everything. Husbands, love your wives, just as Christ also loved the church and gave Himself to her, that he might sanctify and cleanse her with the washing of water by the word, that He might present her to Himself a glorious church, not have spot or wrinkle or any such thing, but that she should be holy and without blemish. So husbands ought to love their own wives as their own bodies; he who loves his wife loves himself. For no one ever hated his own flesh, but nourishes and cherishes it, just as the Lord does the church. For we are members of His body, of His flesh and of His bones. For this reason a man shall leave his father and mother and be joined to his wife, and the two shall become one flesh.

Dr. Speers looked around the room. "Now look around the class. Can any of you name an instance where someone in this room submitted to the authority of her husband? How was she rewarded?"

A glint of intelligence entered Sister Emily's eyes. She turned, looked directly at Sister Mary, and asked, "Are you and Dr. Speers getting married?"

Sister Mary blushed.

"Don't have children." Emily said.

"Sister Emily, you don't mean that."

"I do."

Janet stood up and hurried to Sister Emily, grasping her by the shoulders. "Shhhhh...hush now..." She looked to Dr. Speers. "She doesn't know what she's saying. She's exhausted."

Sister Emily's head shook back and forth violently. "I do know...I do know...ask God to close up your womb, Sister Mary...ask God for mercy..."

Sister Mary begged, "Please, Sister Emily. Please. Shhhhh...don't talk now."

Emily said, "In those latter days, blessed are the women who are barren and who never bear children."

Dr. Speers called a number on his cell phone. "We need an exorcism in classroom B."

"She's grieving and exhausted. She doesn't know."

"Don't worry, Sister Mary. We'll take good care of her. Sister Janet, take your seat."

Janet sat and covered her eyes as the Redeemers entered the classroom and pulled Sister Emily from the room.

Sister Mary looked fearfully at Dr. Speers who shook his head sadly. "She needs help. Can't you see that? The poor, suffering woman needs our help. Let's all keep her in our prayers."

Sister Mary nodded dumbly.

Janet asked, "How will you help her?"

Dr. Speers tapped his papers into a neat stack.

"Curiosity in the mind of a woman is like a gun in the hands of a child. Since the beginning of time, this has been true, since Eve first grew curious about the forbidden fruit of the Tree of Knowledge and led Adam into sin, bringing God's curse on us all. Curiosity led to temptation. Curiosity plus temptation led to mankind's curse. A plus B equal C. The Bible warns tempters, Sister Janet. Read Luke. 'Temptations to sin are sure to come; but woe to him by whom they come!'"

"I'm sorry."

"Yes. I expect you are."

The room was deathly quiet. Dr. Speers turned in his Bible and said, "Titus, Chapter 2."

Likewise, teach the older women to be reverent in the way they live, not to be slanderers or addicted to much wine, but to teach what is good. Then they can train the younger women to love their husbands and children, to be self-controlled and pure, to be busy at home, to be kind, and to be subject to their husbands, so that no one will malign the word of God.

Dr. Speers looked around the room. "Older women must teach the younger women to love their children, to be obedient to their husband, but most of all to be obedient to God who commanded that we go forth and multiply. Tell me. How does a woman find forgiveness with God for Eve's faithlessness?"

Sister Sue Ann said, "Through childbirth."

"That is correct? And what kind of childbirth?"

"A painful one. No drugs."

"That's right. That is her penance for sin. It's her path to salvation. To teach otherwise is to condemn a woman to Hell. This is what the older women should be teaching the younger women."

～

When Bible study ended, Janet rose to leave.

"By the way, Sister Janet. The paperwork for the volunteers of the prison ministry will be processed tomorrow. Perhaps we can get you into the prison soon."

Janet paused briefly. "I'll do my part." And she walked out.

Dr. Speer said softly, "Yes, you will."

Dr. Speers took Sister Mary to lunch at the diner after church where the waitress shouted orders over their heads. The waitress had the letter P sewn on to her uniform. Sister Mary picked at her salad while Dr. Speers talked and observed. "The Redeemers gave people meaning. You're too young to know what it was like. People led empty, meaning-less lives."

"Sometimes I feel empty."

"And what do you do?"

"I pray."

"And what happens?"

"After a while, I feel God's love and I feel hope."

"That's right, and that's exactly what the Redeemers gave you. Before that, people were too far from God. They had nothing. We gave them a clear vision of the world around them, helped them to see that the chaos was simply a manifestation of the Great War between God and Satan. Do you see?"

"We're afraid of what we don't know," Sister Mary said.

Dr. Speers looked at her perplexed because she had interrupted his stream of thought. He said, "Of course, the human brain fears the unknown, so when the Redeemers gave us an explanation for what was happening it the world, they gave us certainty. And more than that, they gave us a purpose. People knew they could be on God's team, could fight for something good, something greater than themselves. A man can do the work of ten men if he's first fortified with the Holy Spirit."

Sister Mary said, "I know what you mean. Sometimes I feel small. I'm a girl you know, weak, but I pray and God gives me strength."

Dr. Speers reached across the table and took her hand, saying, "And I hope that I, too, can be your strength."

Fear flickered across Sister Mary's face and was gone.

"What is it, Sister Mary?"

"I'm scared of marriage. I'm afraid I'm not good enough for you."

Dr. Speers relaxed a little. "Of course, you are." But he also knew now that Sister Mary was a liar.

Sister Mary shook her head slowly and stared into space, her eyes unfocused. "I can't marry yet."

Dr. Speers set his napkin on the table. "I believe I've lost my appetite." His ordinarily expressionless face looked sullen.

"I'm sorry," Sister Mary said softly.

"Is it that Mobley woman and the Moore woman? I fear these older women are a bad influence on you."

"No, it's you. You said you liked intelligent women, but isn't curiosity a part of intelligence?"

"Aahhh. So that's it. It was the Moore woman."

"No, I just know that I'm curious about things, too, and I don't know how to shut that off for you. I don't know how to stop being me."

"I don't want you to stop being you. I want you, Sister Mary, you with all your faults and virtues, unconditionally. You can be as curious as you want and I'll answer all your questions. Just come to me first. You must trust me. And what does the Bible tell us, Sister Mary? Since the beginning, God showed us that no human life is complete without a relationship of the greater to the lesser, as God is to Man and Man is to Woman. Yes, some women are called to be single, but it's better to marry. What does Paul say? He commands 'the young women to marry, bear children, and guide the house.' Don't fear me, Sister Mary. I will guide you, but gently and you'll guide my household. Yes?"

"Have you ever killed anyone?" Sister Mary asked.

Dr. Speers blanched. "What?" Did Mary know about her mother?

"I know it's crazy, but I had a dream that you were standing outside my house at night, and you were drunk and violent. You were coming to kill me. I woke up shaking."

"I would never hurt you. And besides, have you ever seen me drunk?"

"No."

"See there. That dream, your fear. Those are natural fears that everyone feels when they're thinking about marriage."

Dr. Speers forced a strained smile. "And you are thinking about it, aren't you?"

Sister Mary blushed.

"Before you answer that, I have an important question to ask, and you must not lie. Do you understand?"

Sister Mary nodded and trembled.

"Was there another woman in the woods the night we found you, besides Seila and your mother?"

Sister Mary reddened. She hesitated and Dr. Speers felt a rising anger, "Sister Mary?"

"I'm sorry," she said and her apology sounded like a whisper. She looked down at the table and spoke softly, "There was another woman, but I didn't know her."

"Have you seen her in Wendell?"

"No."

"No?"

Sister Mary shook her head, and he noticed the fear in her eyes. She asked, "What's going to happen to me?"

He answered sternly, "I'm going to marry you and teach you. And you will make it up to me. You'll be a good wife. Do you understand?"

"Yes."

"Of course you do. That's what I like about you, Sister Mary. You're a fast learner, and I have no doubt that you'll keep your hand to God's plow from here on out."

Sister Mary nodded, looking down as Dr. Speers held her hand in his.

Despite Mary's assertions that she didn't know the woman, he knew she was lying. But he could wait for her to come around and confess.

He had a net around Janet now and she was going nowhere. And although Warden Camp had warned him off Janet, his hands would be clean. Seila, herself, would implicate Janet. He smiled with satisfaction for his double-win. For the good of the Covenant, of course.

He said softy to Mary, "We can sign up for premarital counseling. We can learn how to speak truth to each other."

{21}

Visitation

WHEN DR. SPEERS called to ask the Moores to dinner, George had him on speaker phone. Janet waved at George and shook her head, urging him to turn down the offer. He turned his back to her and agreed to the impromptu invitation.

Janet was watching a taped television interview with Warden Camp and Dr. Speers announcing on national TV that they hoped to help the country and survivors and relatives of the Tabernacle Square bombing find closure in the confession and execution of Seila Lee Campbell, which was to be televised. Dr. Speers said he met with the families of those who died and his heart went out to them. An execution was the only appropriate response to Campbell's lack of remorse for her brutal attacks on her husband and the other bombing victims.

The execution was scheduled to take place at Wendell Prison Incorporated near the town of Wendell on February 15 in the seventh year of the Covenant government, and was to be broadcast live on both national networks who were pleased with an agreement that placed no limits on their cameras. Images of Campbell's execution could be juxtaposed with graphic images of the Tabernacle Square bombing. At the top right-hand corner would be an overlay image of God's army on the march.

Janet thought, 'Two weeks. We have less than two weeks to get Seila out.' Janet went to her room, carrying a package with new skeins of yarn that was left on her porch that afternoon. She dug her fingers into them to find the note she hoped would be there—and it was. The scrawl was Johnny's and it was simply a date, February 13. Relief swept over her. The date was cutting it close, but she would be ready. She already had new identity chips and began to prepare supplies for travel. She also had sedatives that she intended to slip into George's wine.

George tapped on the door. "Janet?"

Through an iron jaw, she said, "I'll be out in a minute."

"Are you okay?"

"I'll be out in a minute." She flushed the note in the commode, and walked out of the room under George's puzzled and concerned gaze.

There was nothing she could do but attend this dinner, and she wondered bitterly if she would be arrested before they could enact the plan. Even if they arrested her, Johnny could still go forward with the plan. Or, she could kill the monster, but on such short notice, how? She felt certain Speers knew about her. He would be on guard. Besides, she could take no action that would disrupt Johnny's plans.

~

When George and Janet entered Dr. Speers' house for dinner, Janet looked at his foyer and living room with a jaundiced eye. "This is lovely," she said dryly.

Dr. Speers smiled and Sister Mary moved items around the dining room table behind him.

"It's all confiscated property," he said.

"Really?"

"The house you bought, also confiscated." He looked at Janet with an amused expression on his face.

"You don't say? I never really thought about it." George boomed out with a laugh. "It isn't catching, is it?"

Dr. Speers tightly smiled. "I hope not. Mrs. Moore, are you alright?"

"I'm fine Dr. Speers, just a little winded from the walk." She scooted by him, and crossed the room to Sister Mary. Janet hugged Sister Mary, "So good to see you. Let me help you with the table."

Before Sister Mary could reply, Dr. Speers called Janet back, "Please come into the living room and sit down. Sister Mary will prepare the table."

Janet said, "But I'd like to help."

"No, Sister Mary will do it," Dr. Speers said, and he led the Moores to the living room. Janet sat on the edge of the leather sofa while George sprawled beside her, stretching his legs under the coffee table. Dr. Speers sat forward on the loveseat.

George turned towards Sister Mary who was setting dishes in the dining room. "So, are you and Sister Mary getting married then?"

"Yes."

George said, "You won't regret it. Marrying Janet was the best thing I ever did. We're a picture of domestic bliss, we two."

"Can I get you a glass of wine?"

"Thank you. I don't mind if I do," George said,

Janet clasped her hands in her lap, and said "No thank you." She looked around the room, making note of doors, windows and something that might be used as a weapon. Didn't Sister Mary say there was a room behind the kitchen? She wondered if Dr. Speers' dad was lurking back there or if he was away, but she didn't ask. She heard he sat in the back room spitting tobacco in a can. She met him a couple of times at church and thought he was an odious old man.

Dr. Speers returned with a bottle of wine and a single glass. He poured a little wine for George and seated himself, holding himself forward in his seat.

"You're not having any?" George asked.

"Alcohol in any form disagrees with me. I never drink." Dr. Speers looked at Janet and she wondered if he knew that she had thought of poisoning him.

George grunted.

They were silent for an uncomfortable minute, and then George shifted in his chair to pull his knees back up and to sit forward. "Hope it's good weather for the Campbell execution."

"Yes, it should be a good day to die."

"What?" George asked.

Dr. Speers smiled. "It's an old Sioux expression for when warriors went into battle. 'It's a good day to die.'"

George grunted again and sipped his wine. He said, "I hear we might get a foot of rain tonight."

Janet stood up. "I really should help Sister Mary."

Dr. Speers held up his hand. "No, Sister Mary has things under control. You're my guest. Please sit down."

Janet sat.

"Yup, the Devil never rests. Hey! I heard they're exterminating more Quakers. That true?" George sipped his wine and settled his glass on the table-top next to the coasters.

"It depends on how recalcitrant they are. We prefer rehabilitation."

"You can exterminate the whole pack of pansy-assed, tea-sipping appeasers. I don't care for them."

"We can't kill everyone we don't care for, can we?" Janet asked.

"Don't mind her. God did not give women the same degree of mental toughness as men. They just don't understand these things. A righteous man who falters before the wicked is like a murky spring and a polluted well—that's Proverbs. Too many people are still in league with Satan, and we'll never achieve the peace as long as they're alive. God didn't spare his enemies, nor should we. It's common sense." George rapped the coffee table with the knuckles of his fist.

Janet felt Dr. Speers watching her and kept quiet.

"Do not answer a fool according to his folly, lest you also be like him—also Proverbs," Dr. Speers said while he watched Janet's frozen face with ill-concealed amusement.

"What? Oh, Janet's no fool. She's just inexperienced."

She looked unwavering into Dr. Speers' eyes, and Janet held back from uttering a few proverbs of her own.

George drank the rest of his wine in one gulp, and Dr. Speers poured more wine into George's empty glass. "Speaking of the execution, let me personally welcome you to the witness box of Seila Campbell's execution."

"We'd be delighted," George said. "Maybe we could go to the diner afterwards. My treat."

Dr. Speers nodded and looked directly at Janet. "Good. I'd also like to arrange a visit between you and Mrs. Campbell."

"Me?" Janet asked.

"Mrs. Campbell will require a visit from a female member of the prison ministry. Did anyone call you?"

"No."

"It must have been an oversight. I'll pick you up tomorrow and drive you there myself."

That night Janet laid awake long into the night. She couldn't find a comfortable position, on her side or on her back, with covers, without covers. Her back hurt. Her shoulder hurt. Her neck. Why hadn't he arrested her already?

George's loud snores could not be ignored.

When Janet did finally fall asleep, she dreamed that she and Karen were back at a women's protest where stone-faced Redeemers piped in commands from surveillance helicopters, tracking them as they hurried between barricades, fences, and police on horseback. Although they hurried, they seemed to get nowhere in the crowd of protesters. Suddenly Dr. Speers was in front of them, and he knocked Karen to the asphalt. Janet heard something crack on the pavement, and jerked awake. She listened to her heartbeat thud, thud, thud in her ears.

Janet could not get back to sleep so she imagined escaping with Seila and Johnny. Maybe they can bring Sister Mary, too, and finish what Sister Mary's mother had started. Janet had the routes out of the south memorized. She'd traveled those roads many times. She would take a different route than last time since Dr. Speers would think of going back to the place where they caught Seila.

Janet slipped into another terrible dream before morning where she tried to explain to Seila what happened to Charlie, and Seila wouldn't talk to her. Instead, Seila's face was twisted in hatred. "You killed my husband. You killed Charlie," while Janet cried, "No. Seila. No." Janet woke up shaken and her eyes were wet. No, Seila. They killed him for nothing. Nothing!

～

In the morning, Dr. Speers drove Janet to the prison. To guard against terrorists during this public event, mats of steel spikes blocked the road to Wendell prison, while huge stones and chunks of concrete formed a shield around the prison fortress already protected by three deadly, high-voltage fences and razor wire.

They took a circuitous route around the barrier and entered through the first fence as it slid open. Dr. Speers acted as a tour guide. "There are three fences and sensors are everywhere. If an inmate attempts to escape and makes it past the first fence, the voltage changes from stun to lethal mode."

"I see." Janet felt like she had a flu, and sweat beaded on her forehead and under her nose. She wiped it with a handkerchief. Would Seila recognize her? If she did, would she call out and give her away? More likely, she already gave her away.

"We've been under video surveillance since we took the turn back there."

"Of course." Janet tried not to think about what they had done to Seila to make her confess to a crime she didn't commit.

Two more gateways had opened for them and now they were entering a garage. "Where are we now?" asked Janet.

"This isn't the visitor's entrance. I'm taking you to the dock where we bring in inmates. When the gate closes behind us, we'll leave the car and walk to the visitor processing area."

Janet felt lightheaded as he opened the car door for her.

Dr. Speers led her through corridors where he placed his hand on a sensor and looked into another sensor. Each time he did that, heavy steel doors popped and slid open. Would she ever get out of here or was this it? Was she done now?

They turned a corner, and Sonny and Hal walked towards them. Sonny hardly looked at her. Was he telling her something? It seemed like she had seen a slight nod of his head though. Was he telling her he got the audio off? If not, they would be recorded. Seila would recognize her and it would be recorded. Seila would say, "Jim," and they would wonder why she called her Jim.

Janet tripped, and Dr. Speers put up his hand to steady her. He told Janet to wait right there, and he walked to the end of the corridor with Sonny and Hal.

Janet turned and looked through the glass window of a steel door and saw that it was someone's cell.

She saw the toilet and a slight woman with hollow cheeks and a sunken mouth sitting on the edge of a bed. She wondered if she would be there soon, sitting on the edge of a bed in one of these cells.

When recognition finally jolted Janet, she almost cried out. Seila!

It was Seila in that cell! She looked so old!

Janet looked at the men at the end of the corridor and then back at Seila, while Dr. Speers looked at Janet and then back at the men. Janet took the only chance she might ever have. She thumped her chest once lightly with her fist, and kept her fist there over her heart, a signal they got from a movie they'd watched together when they were young, a thump of loyalty, the heart, an undying bond. One thump.

Seila just sat there and did not respond, though her pale face was turned toward Janet. Her lips seemed to form the word, "Jim."

Dr. Speers left the men and walked toward her. "We've had something come up. We'll have to cancel your meeting."

He led her out and she followed him dumbly. She knew her. Seila knew but would not give the signal. Tears rose in Janet's eyes. What had they done to her? Had Seila betrayed her? She wouldn't blame her if she had.

As Dr. Speers escorted Janet out, she walked on rubbery legs. When they got back in the car and she strapped on her seatbelt, her legs quaked and jerked, completely out of control. It was as if she were deep under dark water now and she fought to surface.

"Is something wrong?"

"That was harder than I thought."

"I'm surprised to see you shake so. I thought you were stronger than that? Judging from your forward behavior in class, I should have thought you were fearless."

"Yeah, or maybe it's the Devil making me scared."

Dr. Speers said, "Then your faith must be weak indeed. By the way, we've had a change in plans and the execution will be moved up. We have it scheduled for 6:00 P.M. tomorrow. Also, we set up a trace on your ID chip that is fed automatically by wireless to my home office, Redeemer headquarters, and the prison.

"Why have you set up a trace on me?"

"These are just formalities. We do this to protect those of us in the execution party. I have a trace set up on myself, as well, in case any Anti-Christ Subversives attempt foul play. Now I hope you and George can drive in with me tomorrow. I'll pick you and George up."

Janet's insides felt like water. Tomorrow. There's no time. "But I haven't counseled her."

"Yes, it's unfortunate. One of our guards is taking over that duty tonight. Now let me tell you what you can expect tomorrow. The television broadcast will begin before Campbell is brought before the judge. She will be asked how she pleads and will make her confession. The judge will sentence her on the spot, and judgment orders against Mrs. Campbell will be read aloud. Afterwards, she'll be led to the execution room. We felt that a hanging would be most satisfying to television viewers, so she will be led up the steps of the steel gallows where a hood will be placed over her head and the noose adjusted. A guard will press the button that drops the trap, and after the execution, Warden Camp will announce the time of death."

"Campbell has not been and will not be advised of the execution procedures, her last meal, and the disposition of her body. Furthermore, Campbell has no personal property, as it has already been auctioned off to assist in paying for the proceedings, which is neither here nor there really since she has no family left alive."

~

That night Janet laid in the dark listening to George's snoring, and something in the room beeped. She opened her eyes and waited. It beeped again. Her heart beat faster.

She looked around the room and saw the red light of the carbon monoxide detector blinking from the corner. She switched on the bedside lamp while George grumbled, and she climbed on a chair under the detector. She dismantled the dead battery and climbed down, and then she turned off the light, sunk back on the bed, and waited. She felt unclean in a way that couldn't be washed away. Did Johnny know?

She got back up, dressed, put on her winter coat and tip-toed to the front door. She needed to get to Johnny but when she peered out the front drapes, a Redeemer van was parked in front of the house. She glided through the house to the backdoor but men stood guard out back. She returned to her bed.

Against the backdrop of George's snores, Janet remembered when she came to Seila after five years of staying away from her. Janet had rapped on Seila's door, resisting the urge to look behind her to the house across the street or at any of the cameras. When Seila opened the door, she pulled Janet inside and closed the door quickly. They held each other in a tight embrace. Seila smelled like perfume, only a trace.

Seila said, "Oh Jim! I looked for you. It's been so long. Are you okay?"

"I'm fine but you have to know about Charlie."

"What about Charlie?"

Janet struggled to tell her. Finally, she said, "The Redeemers shot him in the parking garage at Tabernacle Square. He's dead, Seila."

Seila screamed and dropped to the floor. Janet bent down and helped her up, pulling her in a tight embrace.

Seila spoke faintly, "Why?"

"I'm so sorry. I'm sorry. I think...it might be my fault. The Redeemers stopped me on the street for being out past the Women's Curfew, and Charlie showed up out of nowhere and plucked me away from them and said that he was late picking me up. He saved me."

Janet remembered Charlie inside the car. He had aged terribly. Sweat rolled from his hair, and his face was shiny from moisture and red from effort as he pulled his black SUV into traffic, saying, "My God, Ruby, we thought you were dead." Headlights played across his troubled face.

"My name's not Ruby, and you shouldn't have interfered."

"How could I not? Seila has done nothing but grieve over you for the past five years, so if I could give her one thing now, it would be you."

"Yes, but would you stake her life on it?" and in the space of his silence, she said, "Don't tell Seila you saw me. You guys have to forget me now. This isn't safe!"

He slowed and stopped the car, and Janet jumped out and hurried away. She thought she heard him say, "Seila loves you."

Later, Janet struggled to tell Seila what happened. She said, "After he pulled me from the Redeemers, I was worried about him and had some friends track him. I knew his company was headquartered at Tabernacle Square, so he wasn't hard to find."

Janet pulled off her blonde wig to expose dark hair that was pinned up and damp from the wig and perspiration. She threw it on the black-lacquered coffee table and whispered to Seila, "The Redeemers were already there."

Sirens sounded in the parking lot outside, and Jim and Seila peeked through the blinds. Light streamed in where their fingers lifted a slat.

They watched a Redeemer van circle the parking lot and leave.

"My friend saw the Redeemers shout at him and saw him kneel, and when he did, they shot him in the back of the head. I think they killed him for standing up for me."

Seila stood stiffly as if in shock. "Are you sure it was Charlie?"

"Yes. It was Charlie."

"Are you sure it wasn't a stun gun?"

"I'm sure. He's dead, Seila. Now someone's blown the fucking place up. I don't know what's going on."

Janet tentatively took Seila's hand, "We've got to think straight now. We've got to get out of here." Her voice was steady, but from time to time her blue eyes skittered sideways to the window.

The power went out and they both jumped. Janet turned, and they clutched each other in the artificially darkened room. "It's just the rolling blackout. It doesn't concern us."

Seila wept then while Janet waited.

Janet groped in the dark for a candle and lit it. Her worried face flickered in the candlelight, and sulfur lingered in the air.

Janet said, "Five years ago, your jewelry got me a long way. I was able to change my identity. My name is Janet now by the way. You saved my life then, and Charlie saved my life last week. Now it's time for me to save you."

Seila and Janet heard muffled tones of people talking in the street and thought they heard someone right outside the door. Janet rose and walked softly to the door. She peered through the peephole a moment, and then returned to Seila, whispering, "It's nothing."

They rested quietly in the dark, while the candle threw light and shadow over their sober faces.

"The Redeemers said you killed someone. What did they do to you? The night you came home, I should have asked you what happened. I should never have left your side."

"Shhhh. It's in the past. I understood, and if I had stayed with you, it would have jeopardized all of us."

"You never told me what they did."

Janet's brow furrowed and said, "It's best not to know."

Seila asked, "Jim, where's Karen?"

"She died in the camp."

"Oh my God! How could I have let you go that night?"

"You didn't know, and I didn't tell you. It's in the past, and it wouldn't have made any difference. I would have gone anyway. We have to go now."

"I can't leave, Jim. The Redeemers are watching the house. They know when I come in and go out. They probably saw you come here. I don't even know how you're going to get out of here."

"I know a way out of here."

That's when they made their plan to go from Jacksonville, north to safety. But they only made it 10 miles north of Wendell and nothing went as planned.

After Seila was taken, Jim managed to get to Atlanta, and meet and marry the hapless widower, George, who was moving to Wendell where she was sure that they were sending Seila. A friend had scouted out the lonely widower for her and helped put her in his path. And Johnny applied for work at Wendell prison.

Now, months later, Janet lay awake in the dark, thinking, so here I am. And there could be no grand plan or eleventh-hour rescue. Seila would die, and Janet was convinced that she had not escaped detection either. If she tried to leave tonight, she would be followed, stopped, arrested and returned to Wendell. But even if she could escape, she wouldn't leave Seila. Not now.

What does one do when one is already dead? Try anyway?

Janet hugged an armful of the comforter to her chest as George resumed snoring. *If nothing else, I'll be there in your final moment. If nothing else, you'll see me and you'll know that someone there loves you.*

Janet did not sleep through the long night and watched dawn creep in. A leaden weight hung over her body, keeping her in the bed while the cloudless morning belied the dark deeds that would be committed this day. When George awoke, she told him she was ill and would not rise from the bed until Dr. Speers came for them. So, George went upstairs to tend to his sister, Betty, on his own.

She imagined that several miles away, Dr. Speers' father was serving up coffee and telling Dr. Speers that he had "done good" while Dr. Speers watched his computer monitor to makes sure that Janet hadn't escaped. He would be wearing a black Redeemer uniform today with the red cross shaped like a dagger over his pocket.

She imagined cutting Dr. Speers throat like she had done that other man, and the smell of pork, cornbread, and vomit washed over her again.

Maybe she could grab a guard's gun at the last minute and shoot Dr. Speers. At the very least, she would kill him.

Janet also considered that Johnny might still come through, and so that slim hope stole over her and she rose to make herself ready. She took some of George's money and her new identity chips and put them in a secret pocket in her clothing. They were in a container that blocked their transmission. She packed a medical kit for removing the ID chips from their hands, set aside some food, clothing, and water, and spiked some wine for George in case they made it back to the house.

Janet heard a light knock on the door and opened it to Sister Mary shivering on the front porch, right in front of the Redeemer van!

Sister Mary gripped Janet's hands and whispered, "Dr. Speers knows that there was another woman in the woods the night the Redeemers found us. I didn't tell him it was you, but I'm afraid about lying to him anymore. He's going to know, and I'll have to tell him that it was you."

Janet felt the blood drain from her face and the hairs stood up on the back of her neck. She looked back at the stairs to see if George had come back down yet.

Sister Mary said, "I think I trust him though. He didn't get mad at me. I think he'll take care of you if you come forward."

Janet said, "Oh Sister Mary, you don't know what he is, what he's done."

"What do you mean?"

Janet said, "Wait here." She went to the knitting bag in her downstairs closet where she hid a gold necklace and returned to Sister Mary. She looked over Sister Mary's shoulder at the Redeemer van. "Don't react. The Redeemer van is behind you. She pressed the gold cross into Sister Mary's hand.

Sister Mary said, "That's…that looks like Mama's."

"It is. I was hiding nearby when Speers was with your mother, after you and Seila were taken away. I heard your mother say his name, so I know it was him that shot her. He left her body in the woods."

"You're lying. I didn't hear a gunshot."

"He must have used a silencer. She was dead. She was shot in the head and Dr. Speers did it."

"You're lying!"

"No, Sister Mary."

Sister Mary ran out and right into the arms of one of Dr. Speers' men who told her that she had orders to spend the day at the Chambers' home.

George came down the stairs as Janet closed the door. He asked, "What's going on? What's wrong with Sister Mary?"

Janet lied, "She's worried about Sister Emily and Connie. She's going to spend the day with the Chambers." Janet closed down all feeling within her. Now was the time for complete detachment, and this time, her body didn't betray her.

Too soon, Dr. Speers sent a car around to pick up the Moores and take them to the prison. They were told that Dr. Speers had a change of plans and would not be able to accompany them.

As they drove slowly through Wendell on the way to the prison, they picked their way through throngs of people who had traveled to Wendell for the execution. How they had managed to get there on such short notice, Janet didn't know. A hired mob must have been bussed in. She noted a tall woman holding up a large poster with the caption, "The Day of Judgment Is Near," and thought there were always traitors.

{22}

Execution Day

ON THE PREVIOUS day, Seila had stared dumbly at Jim through the glass, not recognizing her, but then slowly awakening to it. "Jim?"

Something was wrong that Seila couldn't identify. She saw Jim thump her chest one time, but Seila was frozen in wonder, in puzzlement and couldn't respond. This was not the Jim who Dr. Speers helped her remember as giving Seila the explosives. And was this Jim another phantom who would vanish like other hallucinations?

And if this was Jim in the flesh, then Dr. Speers has taken her into custody.

It occurred to Seila that she felt nothing, and she was quite sure that she should feel something. When they had gone, she was not sure she had seen anything at all.

Something was wrong, but then something was always wrong in this place.

Seila lay down on her side and stared at the wall as an approaching storm intruded on her mind, a storm that lacked the proper wind like a memory that evaporates, leaving no trace.

Seila dozed and dreamed. In her dream, Charlie was behind her, holding her, and she could smell his cologne and feel his warmth.

She said, "You wouldn't love me now, Charlie, not with what I've done. We killed you."

"No, you didn't kill me and Jim didn't kill me either."

"But I remember."

"What do you remember?"

"Dr. Speers."

"Yes." And then Charlie evaporated, and Seila woke up feeling peaceful, but as she realized again where she was, she got up, went to the commode and vomited. She lay back down and turned on her side, holding her arms across her chest. It seemed that she could not catch her breath.

Maybe she didn't murder anyone, and if she didn't, then she didn't understand. Redemption kissed her so lightly that she missed it at first. It made no sense. She would have to ask Dr. Speers. He would help her clear this thing up.

Seila was unable to sleep now as she added, subtracted, multiplied and divided the mental and moral logistics of the thing, the implications. How does one get their mind around it?

Something was wrong.

If someone opened the prison door, why didn't she leave? That's the question that's always asked in a logical world where day follows night in its proper progression. So, when

Dr. Speers came to Seila's cell, she was still laying on her side looking at the wall.

He asked, "It was her?"

"Who?

"Ruby. Jim."

"You have Jim?"

"Didn't you see her?"

"I don't know."

"You don't know?"

"Perception fails. Memory fails."

"Has she changed again?"

"Again?"

"Sometimes she has red hair, sometimes dark brown, sometimes blonde."

Seila said, "It doesn't matter really. Whatever time it is now won't stay that way. It's almost tomorrow, and I'm already dead."

"Who told you that you were going to die tomorrow?"

"No one has to tell you. We're all born under a death sentence, and then time passes, and we're forgotten. Someone else comes along to weep, to thrash about, to bang on the door."

"Knock and the door will be opened, but first you must confess. Then your repentance will be genuine, and you can go through heaven's door. Seila, you're having doubts. Why?"

And then Seila didn't know why she said it. She suddenly felt slippery inside, and she lied. "But I haven't confessed everything."

"What else do you have to confess?"

"Remember when the little black Covenant flags turned up in everyone's yard after the Redeemers gained power?"

"Yes?"

"I plucked the flag from my yard, took it inside and threw it in the closet. I wondered if anyone had seen me do it. It was treason, wasn't it? Against God?"

"You were seen."

"I was."

"Yes. The Redeemers see all Seila. That's when we knew that you would betray God. No one can hide from us. Do you understand?"

Seila was afraid that she did understand. Dr. Speers was a liar. She never had taken the flag out of her yard. She made the whole story up. She felt rotten inside as uneasiness and betrayal gripped her.

"That's why you must confess, and why you must force your sister's confession. We have her now, and only you can save her soul and save her from the confessional process. Do you want her to suffer your fate?"

"No."

"Then you know what to do. Tomorrow is your personal day of atonement. Save her and save yourself."

"Tomorrow?"

"Yes, we've decided today to push the confession forwards. Tonight, we'll go over your confession again to make sure that we have it right. If you don't get it right during the proceeding, you and your sister will die. Do you understand? We will burn you both alive. It's not up to me, you know."

Seila nodded but didn't speak.

"You know what you have to do."

She nodded again, and she thought that Dr. Speers observed her with something that resembled compassion. She asked him, "Is it day or night?"

"Day."

"Thank you."

He reached down and tenderly brushed the hair from her face. "Courage."

"I never had courage."

"God will grant you courage."

After Dr. Speers left, Seila suspected that she hadn't killed anyone. Thoughts whirled. If this...then that...but. Of course, if she hoped to live and ensure Jim lived, she still had to confess to the murders whether she believed it or not. Dr. Speers had told her how they might still live. But what if he were lying about that, too?

Seila shuddered, buried her head in her hands and groaned. If she didn't confess, if she denied it all, and they killed her, people might see what these people were. No, no, no. She didn't want to be a martyr, and anyway, people wouldn't care. It would be another pointless death, two pointless deaths. She should confess to these lies and be done with it. Wash her hands of the whole thing, like Pilate. She would go along. She had always gone along.

And even if people did care, what could they do?

She remembered Dr. Speers eyes boring into her. Dense, magnetic. Evil?

But no. How could he do this to her? Surely, he meant to save her. That's what the confession was all about, to save her life.

She just didn't know, did she? Whether he was a monster or her savior. Or, maybe he was just a madman. Whatever he did to her was not because of anything special about her, good or evil, was it? It wasn't personal? She could have been anyone, couldn't she? Perhaps he believed she had done it, and maybe she did do it? She remembered doing it, but it could have been a dream. It was so hard to remember things correctly. She just didn't know for sure anymore. But he had lied, hadn't he? About the flag? She knew for a fact that she hadn't done that. And Charlie said...but that was a dream, too.

She saw Dr. Speers again put the gun to his forehead, telling her to shoot him, and she wondered if maybe that was the only honest moment there was with him. She remembered his tremor when he told her about the boy, and thought maybe there were other honest moments. Which ones? She loathed him and pitied him. She doubled over on her bed. Oh God, how did I get so sick?

Jesus. Sweet Jesus, was your suffering different from mine?

Would they be here soon? Is it morning? All her yesterday's receded in importance. Her tomorrows required no plans. There was only the ever-living present, which time could not mark.

The mounting anguish took Seila's breath away until her mind and body could sustain it no more. Her will gave way, and she ceased to think as she knelt on the concrete floor. Surrendering, without prayer and without thought, she became Anxiety itself and was Seila no more.

Then Anxiety peaked and receded as she made no mental effort to save herself. She just was. Waiting, poised, and alert in an ever-widening silence.

In the quiet of her expanding cell, she felt a rush of energy enter her, and for the first time since she came to Wendell, she felt peace. There was nothing more that she needed to do. Like the lilies of the field that toil not, she sat in perfect composure, willing nothing. Her body felt overwhelmingly light. By morning she felt something sacred in her cell with her, a gentle light that gave her peace. From this tender state, she could hear them coming, could hear chains and one man laughing.

The sounds passed through her.

Sonny and Hal came to escort Seila, and four more officers joined them. She didn't recognize Johnny.

They led her to Dr. Speers in a small courtroom, and he asked her how she was. She said she was ready, so Dr. Speers nodded and motioned to the guard who stood nearby and who she had never seen before. They removed her shackles for court, not something they typically did, but it was something that Dr. Speers insisted on. This would enable

Seila to point out her accomplice and allay any accusations of mistreatment that the Atlanta commission might raise.

He ushered Seila before the judge while cameras panned her hollowed face, revealing to the nation nothing of the splendor of her inner world.

The judge waited. Behind him was a wall of darkened glass. Behind the glass was a room where the execution was to take place. After the judgment, the glass would lighten and the room would be lit for all to see Mrs. Campbell's final paroxysms, for commentary, edification, revenge, traumatic warning, or perverse pleasure, depending on who was watching.

Dr. Speers was at her side, and behind her was an expectant crowd. Seila turned and looked out at the throng of cameras, fuzzy microphones, and people arrayed before her and felt a deep sadness for them. And for the first time since the Covenant government took over, she wasn't afraid. An expectant hush fell over the courtroom, and Seila saw Jim's stricken face in the back of the crowd.

She saw Jim and a guard at the back of the small courtroom exchange glances and saw the quick shake of the guard's bristled head. The guard looked grim. That's when Seila finally recognized Johnny. But she thought that it was too late for whatever they had planned.

Poor, poor Jim. Maybe Johnny could help get Jim out. She looked at Jim and thumped her chest one time. Janet thumped her chest in return, one time, and held her clenched fist to her chest.

~

When the hearing room settled down, the judge said, "Seila Lee Campbell, you are called here as one of those who has troubled the peace of the nation; you are known to be a woman who has promoted the corruption of youth, conspired to overthrow the Covenant government, conspired and executed terrorist plots that resulted in the deaths of three innocent people, including your own husband. You have committed murderous felony and treason. You are now charged with first degree murder in the bombing deaths of Charles Carson Campbell, Rachel Marie Burke, and John E. Sullivan III. How do you plead?"

Seila spoke softly at first into the microphone, and it was if the whole room leant forward at once to hear her. She said, "In my cell, I heard a biblical quote over the loudspeaker. 'What doth the Lord require of thee, but to do justly and to love mercy, and to walk humbly with thy God.' And I have to be just. I can't bear false witness, not even against myself." As she spoke, her voice gained strength and volume.

Janet saw Dr. Speers swivel his head as if startled, while Seila continued, "I plead Not Guilty even though you have a signed confession, got from me under torture." At that, Seila flung open her uniform to reveal her scarred and mangled chest to the cameras that broadcast from coast to coast, and beyond. "I wear the proof on my chest."

Janet shouted, "Oh my God! Oh my God!" and as the crowd surged back, she pushed forwards while the room erupted in shouts and Dr. Speers yelled, "Turn off the goddamned cameras! Turn off the goddamned cameras! Guards, get those cameras!"

Cameras were wrenched away and cameramen knocked to the ground, while Seila continued to exhort, "The Redeemers are wolves in sheep's clothing. They have exploited us!" while the judge banged the gavel.

Hal raised his rifle and a shot rang out over the courtroom as Seila fell. More rifle bursts hit her as she crumpled to the floor and her arms flopped out, opened to the heavens in a pool of blood.

Dr. Speers who had stood rigid during the attack also was struck and staggered backwards, slipping in Seila's blood. Hal stared with his eyes bulging in rage and consternation as Johnny wrested the weapon from him, knocking him to the ground. Other guards secured Hal while Johnny and Sonny moved through the crowd.

People ran from the room screaming and were trapped in the corridor from locked doors. Janet went forward and knelt by Seila, lifting her limp body, but then was pulled back by guards. Medical personnel rushed into the room, and Janet struggled against the men that held her back, unleashing a howl from deep inside her. She didn't notice that it was George, Johnny and Sonny who pushed, pulled and led her and George through the prison labyrinth until they were outside. They half dragged, half carried Janet to the prison transport and pushed her into the back. She was awash in Seila's blood." George climbed in after her while Johnny and Sonny climbed into the front seats.

In Wendell, the streets were already empty. Some Redeemers stopped Johnny's van but waved him on after checking his ID chip and asking him what had happened at the prison. Johnny said, "We're not at liberty to talk about things at Wendell prison. All I can tell you is that we're getting the visitors out now."

Rain pounded on the van as they drove through town. Power was out everywhere and the few traffic lights were dark.

George wanted to know what the hell happened in there. He held Janet and said, "Dr. Speers had no business having you in there. And you had no business making a spectacle of yourself. What was it about, Janet?"

They got to George and Janet's house in the downpour, and Janet said, "It's okay, George. I'm okay. It was just a shock. Let's get inside. I'll open you a bottle of wine, and then I think I need to lie down. Please."

Sonny said, "Johnny and I will need to get back to the prison. And George. You hang tough. We'll let you know what we find out."

~

When Johnny returned, George was slumped on the couch with his eyes closed. Johnny said, "Sonny will be in shortly. He's got a call into the hospital."

Janet noticed Johnny's questioning eyes on George, and she said, "I didn't kill him, but he'll be out for a while."

Johnny said, "We've been running all over hell's half acre, but we did find out that Speers and Seila should be arriving at the hospital in Macon soon."

"She's alive?!"

Johnny ducked his head, "Barely. They don't expect she'll make it to the hospital. She lost a lot of blood, and what with the blood shortage..." He took his black ballcap off, wiped the sweat off his forehead, and shook his head slowly. "They'll take care of Speers before they take care of her."

Janet's eyes were red and swollen, but she had washed away the blood and changed her clothing. She had a bloody bandage around her hand from where she'd already taken out her chip. She quickly sat up straight, "We've got to go Macon."

Sonny came in and stood near the doorway as if he didn't know whether to stay or go. He was looking from Johnny to Janet, like maybe it was just dawning on him that they knew each other well. He shifted uneasily and said, "I just heard she was DOA. I'm sorry."

A sob escaped Janet's lips and then she clamped it down. She said, "I still have to see her. I have to be sure."

Sonny said, "It's too risky. Speers lost a lot of blood, too, but unfortunately, he'll live and he'll be after both of us. He's slicker than owl shit and he'll set me up for this. I can't stay here and neither can you. I'm going west now, and I can take you with me."

"And why should I trust you? You were complicit!"

"And I can't make up for what I did. I know that. But me and Johnny did get you out of that prison at great cost to us. They would have taken you for sure. So, you come with me or you don't, but I'm going on."

Janet watched Sonny, and part of her loathed him for going along with Speers and part of her understood how he made the choices that he made. As she seesawed between fury and understanding, she thought, 'Why help him? Kill him or let him go.'

Except she fucking needed him.

Her face looked grim with her mouth set in a tight line and her eyes narrowed. "With Speers alive, you won't get far."

"I know, but I'm gonna try."

She asked, "And Sister Mary?"

A frown crossed his face and he looked down, "She's not at home."

She studied Sonny's glum face and finally said, "I'm going to Macon to see Seila, and if she's…" Janet stopped herself. "Doesn't matter. I'm going to Macon. It's on the way to Brunswick, where I have a friend who can help us get out. So, you go west or you come with me. Your choice. Both of you."

Johnny was watching George and pulling on his beer. Finally, he sighed and said, "In for a dime, in for a dollar, I guess, but I'm not leaving Mama. We'll need to make an extra stop."

{23}

Aftermath

WHEN SEILA OPENED her prison uniform, Sister Mary was watching from the Chambers' den. Sister Mary screamed and dropped to the floor. She knew then that Dr. Speers had killed her mama, too. She knew it and she wept. She would never see Mama again.

Others who watched the large screen TV from the Chambers' den cried "Oh dear! Oh sweet Jesus!" until the TV went white and a ribbon of words moved across the bottom of the screen, "Experiencing technical difficulties. Stay tuned."

It wasn't until later that Sister Mary heard that Seila Lee Campbell had been shot and killed, and Dr. Speers had been shot but not killed.

After guests cleared out of Willie and Sister Sue Ann's house, they drove down dark and deserted streets to Sister Mary and Aunt Peggy's home. Sister Sue Ann turned on the radio, but immediately changed her mind and turned it off. "Are you sure you want to go home, dear?"

"I don't know. Yes. You can turn on the radio if you want."

"I don't know if we should," Sister Sue Ann said.

They drove slowly through Wendell. The only people on the streets were Redeemers who wore masks over their faces and paraded up and down the streets of Wendell like bristling dogs. Signs of the late afternoon throng were still visible on the pavement, which was littered with poster board signs, "May she rot in hell," "Thou shalt not suffer a witch to live," and other signs calling for retribution.

Sister Sue Ann turned on the radio again but could only find reports about the weather and sports news, as if nothing had happened, as if they had all experienced a mass delusion, and things had returned to normal. But Sister Mary knew that things would never return to normal, not for her.

Sister Mary's thoughts circled around an image of Dr. Speers who had led her Bible study class with authority, a man she was to marry. It was as if he held out a bunch of roses and it turned into a bag of rotting bones before her eyes. How could she not know? Or maybe deep down, she did know.

At home, she barely listened to Aunt Peggy and Sister Sue Ann's conversation. She heard them say that George and Janet were not home.

She heard Aunt Peggy say, "There must be some mistake. Dr. Speers just didn't know about it. We have to give him the benefit of the doubt. How fair would it be to not hear him out? Surely, we couldn't be that wrong about someone."

Thunder rumbled and sleet rained down, splattering the porch outside. The sky was dark and cold wind whipped the house. The telephone rang. It was Dr. Speers, and he asked for Sister Mary.

She took the phone reluctantly and said, "Hello." Outside, lightning lit the whole sky and thunder boomed in quick succession, causing Mary to jump.

His voice sounded faint, and he said, "I was shot, but I'm okay. Listen, I didn't know about the burns that poor woman suffered. I didn't know. Ask the Chambers to bring you to the hospital and pray with me, and bring the Moores."

Sister Mary felt paralyzed. An image of the last time she saw her mama blended with an image of that woman's mutilated chest, causing her heart to contract and her eyes to shut.

Willie took the phone and Sister Mary heard him say that they were coming. They went by George's again, and still, no one seemed to be home. They called on George's cell phone and got no answer. Then they gave up and drove Sister Mary to the hospital in Macon.

While they drove to Macon, a radio host said that a correctional officer had opened fire in the hearing room, killing Seila Lee Campbell and attempting to kill Dr. Speers. They listened to the radio for updates and heard that the correctional officer who had opened fire was Hal Wayne, the Pastor's brother.

"I knew it had to be a Wayne involved in this," Sister Sue Ann said. "He's probably the one who did that to that poor woman."

"We don't know that," Willie said, "but one thing I do know. Dr. Speers did not do this. Why else would Hal try to kill him?"

At the hospital, Sister Mary dutifully walked with the Chambers down the dull green corridors through clusters of people huddling around patients on gurneys, families still hoping for an overworked doctor to take their case. When they got to the section of the hospital where Dr. Speers was, the hospital had less people and was more orderly. They found Dr. Speers in his bed wearing a pale blue hospital gown. His face had a high flush, and he appeared to be sleeping.

Sister Mary's face felt like a block of wood.

Sister Sue Ann rushed to his side. "What happened? What happened in there?"

Dr. Speers opened his eyes and shook his head. His typically deep voice, was faint and weak. "I don't know. With Mrs. Campbell gone, I'm not sure if we'll ever know for sure. She never told me about any abuse. Thank the good Lord you're here, Sister Mary."

"It was really Hal Wayne who shot you?" Sister Sue Ann asked.

Dr. Speers kept his eyes on Sister Mary while he answered. "I'm afraid so. He shot and killed Mrs. Campbell, and then shot me before he was taken down."

"He's dead?"'

"No, he's alive and being held at Wendell. We were like family."

Dr. Speers watched Sister Mary's face as he spoke. "I don't know why he'd try to kill me."

Willie Chambers spoke sharply, "To shut you up. That's why."

"I didn't know he'd done it. He didn't need to shut me up. As far as I knew, everything we did was by the book."

As he answered their questions, Dr. Speers continually looked to Sister Mary and past her as if expecting someone. Finally, he asked where the Moores were.

"Couldn't find them. Checked George's house."

It seemed to Sister Mary that the high flush left Dr. Speers' face and he paled.

"What is it, Dr. Speers?"

"Nothing."

Before he could say another word, reporters crowded in with their Covenant press passes, cameras and fuzzy microphones, squeezing the Chambers and Mary out of the way. They had been approved by Dr. Speers, against doctor's orders.

He faced the cameras from his hospital bed when a reporter asked him if Wendell prison was using torture on inmates. He said, "Our procedures are uncomfortable, but sleep deprivation and psychological manipulation do not involve torture. Those are procedures we use to save lives when we're faced with the possibility of an imminent terrorist attack, when we have to get the information. But this other thing, the mutilation and burns. I didn't know that was happening on my watch, and I don't know why anyone would do that? We have just discovered that one of the correctional officers took her for burn treatment in the prison hospital, and there is some talk that he may have falsified reports. We're looking for him now. About all I can tell you is that we've opened an investigation. As to the men and women who work at the prison, we may have one or two bad guards, but most of our people are professionals with a single purpose." Dr. Speers looked squarely at the camera. "To defend our women and children, our families, our values, and God's Covenant."

When the reporters filed out, Dr. Speers collapsed back on the bed, and a nurse gave him an injection of pain killer. His face grew slack.

Willie turned on the television set in the hospital room and saw other reporters interviewing Warden Camp who confirmed Dr. Speers' report. He said that he had the utmost confidence in Dr. Speers and reminded people that inmates were liars. "Furthermore, what Mrs. Campbell said in the hearing about the Redeemers being involved in the murder of her husband was utter nonsense and the hysterical babbling of a woman who had grown paranoid from the criminal abuse of a sadistic correctional officer who had acted alone to exact retribution. Be that as it may, I want the public to know that I take full responsibility and will be more vigilant in the future when screening correctional officers. It's also critical at this juncture to not let the media poison the investigation into Mrs. Campbell's case."

Hal's father, Pastor Wayne, also spoke to reporters. He said that Satan had stirred up evil rumors that circulated among certain members of his congregation who had long tried to dig up dirt on his family, and were now using the most malicious form of gossip to malign his brother. There were powerful families in his congregation, his flock, who had coveted his job as Pastor, and everyone in Wendell knew he was talking about the Chambers and the Camps. "Now I don't want to start rumors, but some folks are saying that Dr. Speers directed the entire operation, telling officers when that poor woman could have her clothes, food, sleep or physical torture, and indeed encouraged, no, forced Hal to abuse that inmate. Like I said, I don't know for sure who did what, and I don't believe any good comes from revenge, but this has devastated this town and the Covenant. I hope and pray that we can heal and find a way to put this behind us. I'm asking for your thoughts and prayers."

"How dare he?" Sister Sue Ann exclaimed.

Reporters then interviewed carefully-selected citizens for their feelings about the trial in Wendell. "When asked about the shooting of Seila Campbell, an interviewee with a black New Covenant ball cap said, "She was going to be sentenced to death anyway. That piece of crap woman deserves what she got."

The interviewee's wife stood beside him wearing a matching ball cap and nodding her head in agreement. She smiled at the camera.

Sister Sue Ann looked from the television set to Dr. Speers who seemed white with strain, so she turned off the television. Dr. Speers thanked her and said he would rest now. "You should all go home, except Sister Mary. Will you stay with me, Sister Mary?" Then Dr. Speers fell back as if asleep.

Hospitals in the Covenant states were chaotic, unsanitary, and understaffed. The plague of Wrath diseases, as well as the mass murder and imprisonment of knowledge workers, social workers and other members of the helping professions, combined to make hospitals somewhat do-it-yourself. Dr. Speers' position gave him access to the best doctors in Macon and the cleanest room, but he would still require family or friends to stay by his side and handle general tasks.

Sister Mary didn't speak, so Sister Sue Ann nudged her gently, "You stay, Sister Mary. Can you do that?"

Sister Mary nodded and eased herself into a chair. Then the Chambers turned down the lights and were gone, and she was alone with Dr. Speers who breathed unevenly in his sleep.

She watched him twitch.

Then a nurse came quietly into the dimly-lit room and shut the door. She had a syringe in her hand. Something was familiar about her.

Sister Mary whispered, "Janet?"

Janet held one finger to her lips, and then took hold of the IV tube with a gloved hand.

"Will you kill him?" Sister Mary whispered.

Dr. Speers roused as Janet pierced the IV tube with the syringe. As Janet pulled the syringe from his IV, she asked, "What does the good book say about vengeance? Turn the other cheek or vengeance is mine?"

By this time, Sister Mary was up and looking over Janet's shoulder, looking down at Dr. Speers dying, and said, "Good."

And so, Dr. Speers' accidental protégés joined him on the easy path, the path of cause and effect and consequence, the wide straight path to hell. And one day, the women of the future who would benefit most from their struggles and the struggles of the men and women who joined them, would forget them, and remember Seila! as the whispers of discontent grew to a rallying cry for all the nameless daughters of Eve.

About the Author

Wilda Hughes is a reader and writer with a deep appreciation for speculative fiction. She currently resides in the southern United States and has traveled extensively. By drawing on her lived experiences and fascination with religious cults, mass movements and history, she crafts a powerful debut novel. Her narrative speaks to the darkness of the current state of humanity in a way that makes her work hard to put down.

Note to the reader: Reviews really help indie publishers. If you like this book, feel free to leave an honest review on a review site of your choice or at www.wildahughes.com.